If Only

TENEIL JAYNE

Published by Teneil Jayne using Reach Publishers' services,
P O Box 1384, Wandsbeck, South Africa, 3631

Edited by Coraline Webb for Reach Publishers
Cover designed by Reach Publishers
Website: www.reachpublishers.org
E-mail: reach@reachpublishers.org

Tales from a

Thirty-Something-Year-Old

Single American

in Africa

By Teneil Jayne

TABLE OF CONTENTS

PROLOGUE

We danced the whole night through. I didn't even know I could dance! It was such a perfect evening. In the low light of the full moon, my white dress sparkled like a thousand tiny diamonds. To be honest, I never really saw the dress, but then again neither did he; we were steadfast in each other's gaze.

Dancing, light as a pair of feathers whirling inside a steady breeze, we spun in and out and back again. The music grew faint as our feet took us farther away from the ball, toward a large, weeping willow on the back of the imposing estate. He smiled and guided me inside the thick green curtain of the great tree. It would have been dark as pitch, but for the fireflies enchanting the hollow.

He was going to kiss me, finally. Yes. Every part of me knew this would be our last first kiss. Gently but confidently, he pulled me into his embrace. The weakness in my knees seemed to take the strength from my eyelids and they closed as I leaned into his form, perfectly entrapped by him. He leaned down and I could feel the warm whisper of my own name upon my cheek:

"Mom, look. Here is your phone."

Wait… that's not right. Lips still puckered in invitation, I cracked my eyelids open, searching for him. Instead, I found my phone with the numbers "4:32AM" glaring about two inches from my face.

"I got it for you!" My youngest foster daughter, now five years old, smiles, and I try, really, really hard to smile back.

And so, my day begins.

I'm Teneil Jayne, and I've spent the last several years alone, following God's call in Malawi, Africa. Alone, for years, in Africa, alone. . . at the ripe age of thirty-something (the details aren't really all that important right now). The key word here is, *alone*.

The more community needs that present themselves, the more foster children that come to stay with me in my little house, the more stray dogs I pick up, and the more wildlife that creeps in from the jungle surrounding our home, only makes that thorn in my side more apparent. I wasn't going to wait for a husband to serve my Lord, but that didn't mean that I ever stopped dreaming about it. . .about "him". We don't have a TV.

It hasn't been that long since I sold everything I had and bought a one-way ticket to a completely different country. I used that money to pay for anything our community of Nkhata Bay needed. Six months later, there I was, alone in a country about as far from my home as I could get, now with negative dollars in my bank account and no ticket back.

"What are you doing?" my mom asked, when we realized my account was drier than a Malawian October.

"I don't know!" I cried back. But God knew. Each day became its own miracle. (How God provided, and the rest of my incredible journey is an entirely different book.) Now, years later, with thousands of people assisted, God still continues to provide everything we want and need. Well, everything except. . .

I've been wondering if my father is the King of kings, that makes me an outright princess. So where is my prince charming?

I haven't met "him" yet. Though I've dreamed of a thousand ways we could meet, these chapters contain just a few of those stories. A good portion of these pages are based on my real-life adventures here in Malawi. Some other portions may be pure fantasy, but I'll leave it to you, dear reader, to decide what is fact or fiction.

Chapter One
IF ONLY HE WAS BOLD

Nervous? Teneil gave her reflection a forced and awkward, "Ha ha ha." Why should she be nervous? It was just a blind date. So what if she hadn't been on a date in four years? She gazed into the restaurant's bathroom mirror, looking deeply into her own artfully painted green eyes, palms resting heavily on the sink's counter. She was a vision, but that was to be expected when one primped oneself more than one did on prom night.

She had been in here for over five minutes now and was starting to feel like a coward. She was convinced that she had the worst taste in men, but truth be told, good men, like good women, were hard to find.

I'm only here tonight to get my presumptuous brother off my back, she told herself, but that was not the whole story. There was a little part of her that held out hope that maybe, just maybe, this guy would not be awful. Was that truly how bad things had gotten? She wasn't even hoping for good, just not awful.

Resolve washed over Teneil, and she stood up straight, giving herself a determined look. When it was all said and done, she had the best exit strategy: she was only in America for two more weeks before she went back to Malawi. And just like every other attempt at a relationship, she would simply blame it on distance and push away.

A long-distance relationship didn't scare her, but the idea of a mediocre relationship did. Her greatest fear was not that she would have an awful time; her greatest fear was that she would have an okay time and have no excuse to say no if he asked for another date. She had several relationships in the past that had started that way. She was terrified of settling.

"Don't be ridiculous," she muttered critically at her reflection. "You haven't even met him yet." If there was one thing Teneil had learned about life, it was that things never turned out the way she'd thought they would.

It was time, one last look in the mirror and a tooth check. Teneil gave herself a quick "this is what he's going to see" smile, then walked out of the bathroom. She got a table for two in the front of the restaurant where he would see her clearly when he came in. She was a bit early, but she couldn't sit and wait in her car anymore.

Just like any woman who dons her "lucky dress," Teneil was ready to be seen. The dark blue silk complemented her dark hair, which was uncharacteristically down, rolling in long, soft, waves past her shoulders. As confident as she felt, she still adjusted her hem repeatedly and awkwardly forced her hands from messing with her hair.

She focused on her posture and attempted to read the menu, but none of the beautifully italicized letters her eyes scanned registered as words. She noticed all the tables full of lovers and allowed her thoughts to wander through every possible outcome. She checked her phone again and saw that he was late. Almost twenty minutes late now. Feeling bereft, she was about to leave when a man slid onto the chair opposite her. She put her smile on and let her menu rest on the table.

He had a way about him that seemed intentionally not put together. His beard was cropped short in a tidy, mock five o'clock shadow. His jacket was worn but good quality, as if he wore it for his own pleasure and not for fashion. It was his eyes that caught her, dark and sparkling like polished onyx. There were all kinds of secrets gleaming there. He was handsome; at least her brother hadn't lied about that.

"Hi," Teneil said, in that practiced way that people say hi to people they think could possibly not be awful.

"He's not coming," the man said.

"I'm sorry?"

He cringed. "I'm pretty sure you got stood up."

She felt her practiced smile fade and her eyebrows raise, confused. "Wh-what are you talking about?"

"I was waiting for my business partner at a table over there, and I noticed you come in. I'm guessing the date was for 8:00pm?" He paused to check his watch. "Yeah, he's not coming."

"That's really not any of your business," her bitter pride retorted.

"Look, don't feel bad," the man assured her. "The guy clearly doesn't understand what he is missing. You are lovely to behold." His smile was wide and genuine, but the complement was lost on her.

"It's a blind date."

"Ugh, that is the saddest story I have ever heard!" he shouted louder than the dim lighting and hushed conversation warranted. She winced as many heads turned to see the trouble. "You on a blind date? How did that happen?"

She scoffed, defensively crossing her arms over the soft fabric of her dress. *How did this happen?* "What do you mean?" She tried to make her voice sound airy and unconcerned.

"You can't tell me that a gal like you has a hard time getting a date. You're a beautiful woman. Any man should feel honored to sit at your table. Heck, I myself feel honored!" He sat straight and grinned boldly at her.

"I didn't invite you." Her words were vinegar as she slouched back in her chair.

"No, you didn't." He leaned forward in a challenge. "You invited a total stranger who didn't even come."

Though his words were harsh, Teneil knew he was right. This was her first date in four years, and she had been stood up. She knew it wasn't personal, blind date and all, but it hurt just the same.

"I'm an excellent judge of character," the stranger across from her added, "and whoever this guy is, you are too good for him."

Teneil wanted to cry, but somehow, without knowing anything about this man in front of her, she knew she would not let him see her breakdown. Instead, she shifted her sadness into anger and let it burn. "You don't even know me," she snapped.

"Sure, I do," he shot back confidently. His eyes never left hers as he said, "Thirties and single, probably poured the last half decade into your work, something you are very passionate about. And looking at the color on your skin in January, I'm guessing you don't live around here. So, you are far away from friends and family. That must be lonely, even if you tell yourself that you are completely fulfilled."

Teneil blinked and lost her words. "That's-"

He held up a hand to still her. "I wasn't finished."

"Oh, good," she said sarcastically.

"You came home for a visit and someone, probably very close to you, set you up and made you promise to go. You don't want to be here, but you also don't want to be alone anymore. This guy that was supposed to be here half an hour ago is an idiot."

"Are you done?"

"Almost. You also seem like a dog person."

She had to smile at that. "You are wrong. Couldn't be more wrong."

He honestly looked shocked, and she took pleasure in that.

"I like all animals," she corrected, and he laughed. "Well, that was super fun." She rolled her eyes. "Nice to know I'm so predictable."

"That isn't what I would call you."

14

"If I'm not predictable," Teneil replied, "then you are just creepy."

"I'm an anthropologist," he shrugged. "Studying people is what I do."

"Okay." She leaned forward eagerly, elbows on the table. "Let me try."

That got another charming grin out of him. "Alright, fair's fair."

Teneil took a moment to look him over. She noticed the smile lines at the corners of his eyes, and his battered watch. He sat with an easy posture, confident, with his full attention on her.

He chuckled when she lifted the tablecloth to look at his shoes. "What are you doing?"

"Research," she said. "Let me see your palms."

"Reading my future?" he asked with a smirk.

"No, reading your callouses."

"Clever," he said with approval in his tone.

"Shh. I'm almost done." She ran her fingertips over his hands and sat up straight. "Okay, I'm ready."

"What do you got?"

She took a deep breath. "You don't stay single long, but you are fine with that. Relationships are shallow to you because you feel as if you already know everyone and there is no challenge there. You don't let anyone in deeper than skin level, because before it even begins, you know it won't last long. In that way you are narcissistic, but you hate that label because to you being better than everyone is just a fact, not a mental disorder. You are a loner; though you have many acquaintances, there are only one or two that you actually call friends, probably from childhood. You also play the guitar, but not for anyone else to hear."

She saw her words hit truth. He was taken aback. "That's-"

She held up her hand, "I'm not finished."

"By all means, continue." He gathered himself and leaned his elbows on the table, clearly and thoroughly enjoying this.

"You weren't here for a business meeting. Please. A romantic restaurant on a Friday night? You, my friend, also got stood up. But your pride wouldn't take it so you came over to my table." She took the napkin off her lap. "And you are a dog person." She tossed the napkin on the table in punctuation of her complete assessment.

"No," he replied. "You couldn't be more wrong." He took a sip from the glass of water in front of him. "I like all animals." He winked at her, and they both started laughing. "That was impressive."

"Oh, you know," she feigned indifference, "it's what I do."

"Right," he conceded. "I'm Z."

"Z?"

"My name is Boaz, but everyone calls me 'Z'."

"Boaz, as in Ruth and Boaz from the Bible?"

"That's the one."

"I thought you would be older," she teased.

"I-" he began, but he was cut off.

"Pardon the intrusion, but the lady's guest has arrived." The waiter who'd come over to their table nodded toward the entryway where a man stood looking at his phone.

Z and Teneil looked at each other and there was an entire wordless conversation that said everything but could be summed up in one word: regret. Z got up from the table and extended his hand. "This has been a pleasure."

She took his hand and was surprised when Z turned it over and bowed to kiss the back of her knuckles with complete respect and affection. And then he walked away. She watched him go back to the table opposite hers but sat with his back to her. She needed him to look back. Teneil stared after him, waiting for him to turn around, but he never did. It was like all the air had rushed out of the room.

"Hello. Sorry I was late. I lost track of time." The man who now sat across from her picked up a menu and began searching through it. "I'm starving." He hadn't even really looked at her.

Teneil glanced back and forth between the two men. "Do you like dogs?" she asked her intended date.

"No." He sniffed. "Allergies."

A loud, "I told you so" kind of chuckle barked from Z's table. Teneil looked up sharply, but her date didn't seem to notice.

"Are you from around here?" she asked just to cut the silence.

"You know," he began, his face still buried in the menu, "I can't decide between the lasagna or the scampi. Why don't you get one and I will get the other? Then we can try them both."

"Seriously?" She heard Z mutter and saw his shoulders shake with laughter. Teneil took a smaller spoon off the tablecloth and threw it at Z, hitting his shoulder. It bounced off him and hit his water glass. The glass shattered and water covered the table. Teneil looked away, solidifying her guilt, because everyone else was looking at the source of the noise. The waiter came rushing over to clean up the mess.

"Sorry, how clumsy of me," Z said in a strong voice.

Teneil laughed and tried to cover it up as a cough into her napkin.

Z stood from his table as the waiter began sopping up the water and glass pieces. Z took a step back and dropped a folded slip of paper in Teneil's lap.

With her blind date's attention still glued to the menu she'd already memorized while waiting for him, Teneil opened the paper. It read, "Do you like me?" with two small boxes. One indicated "yes", the other read "don't be ridiculous". The back of the paper said, "Outside 10 min?"

She looked up, but he was gone. Her heart began to race. "Will you excuse me?" she said, grabbing her purse.

"Need to powder your nose? Do you mind if I order? I'm really very hungry," he said, looking at the menu again.

"I'm not coming back. I'm sorry. This was a bad idea." She stood.

Now, it seemed, she finally got his attention. "What are you talking about? I just came all the way down here."

"I'm sorry I wasted your time."

Teneil walked away from the table and back into the ladies' room. She gave herself another good, long stare in the mirror. She thought about the man whom she had just walked away from, and her reaction was a sardonic laugh and shake of her head. Then she thought about Z and his kiss that still burned on the back of her knuckles. She watched herself in the glass as the blush filled her cheeks and her mouth was pulled into a sweet smile.

"Fine." She walked out of the room with purpose, excitement radiating through her steps to the front door in haste, then out into the cool night air. She saw Z there, waiting for her. "Hey," she said breathlessly.

He turned toward her, letting out a deep breath, and hung his head. "Oh, thank God." He reached for her hand, and she took it.

"He was an idiot!" she laughed.

"I told you I am an excellent judge of character." Z smiled.

"You know, I still haven't eaten." She raised her eyebrows at him. "Now is your shot. You could ask me out, if you wanted to."

"Well, there is an incredible burger and pie place just there on the corner. That's where I was headed. I would be honored if you would accompany me, overdressed as we are."

"You had me at burgers and pie." Her eyes brimmed with tears. "You had me at burgers and pie."

Chapter Two
IF ONLY HE WAS ADVENTUROUS

The trip was almost sixty hours, one that Teneil had made over a dozen times. Though she hadn't been home in almost two years, her body ached with anticipation to see her friends and family and raise much-needed awareness for her non-profit. Her journey had officially started early that morning, with a six-hour bus ride to the capital city Lilongwe, Malawi. Teneil was fond of saying that the capital was a "Li-long ways away," she was clever like that.

She always got the cheapest flights available, which meant that she had seemingly unnecessary connections and tragically long layovers. If she could save $20.00 by adding another stop or another hour to her trip, that was okay with her. She had plenty of time but very little money. She would not have planned the trip at all, but the need and hope to grow her non-profit to the degree that she would be able to finish the school before the rains started had driven her on. She checked the location of her papers and passport one last time before getting off the bus.

Teneil always stayed at the same lodge in the city. It was Korean owned and the Korean menu, a fantastic melody of spices, was a real delight compared to the salt only, five traditional dish-cuisine of her village. The lodge also had a reliable hot water reputation. Teneil was very adventurous, but when making this particular trip she preferred to start off with clean hair and delicious egg rolls.

For an extra three dollars she got a room with a private shower. She needed the chance to stand for unlimited amounts of time under a hot waterfall. This wasn't just a hot shower to her. After the last two years of bathing from a cold bucket, a hot shower was a crucial link between this world and that other world she was about to go into.

There is a kind of rift that can occur when you divide yourself between two cultures and reconciling two worlds involves something she referred to as "The Shift". It was always a lot to process, and it took a bit of reflection to do in a classy manner. Some people who spent great amounts of time in poverty-stricken countries and then returned home could mistakenly "shift" in the most auspicious places, like the cereal aisle at the grocery store.

By the time she was finished, Teneil's skin was bright cooked lobster red, her tears all poured out. Every thought, every hurt, and every request had been laid before her God in that shower. Teneil let the water flow on, while belting out the first fifteen songs on her playlist off tune. The staff gave her the room on the back of the property for just this reason. They had all watched her go through this routine on multiple occasions, but if they thought her insane, they never acted that way.

Joshua was the black sheep of his family. Everyone around him was focused on growing the family empire, an international conglomerate of every mix of businesses you could imagine. His father preferred the stalk market but also dabbled in start-up companies. His mother sat as the CEO of several design and fashion labels. Of his two brothers, one was a realty mogul, and the youngest was in law school. His family was successful by all worldly standards.

Joshua, on the other hand, saw the opulent world he was born into for what it truly was: a place of extremes. Why was his family so blessed when others suffered so greatly? He was nineteen when the truth had occurred to him: he was born with everything he needed to make a difference.

He passed the bar exam at the age of just twenty-four and set up several charitable organizations to handle the tax portion of his family earnings. You see, a person could deduct up to 50% of their AGI, and collectively, within his family alone, that was a whole lot of money that needed to go somewhere. Instead of giving it to some mega charity, like most companies did for tax breaks, Joshua's goal was to set up non-profit organizations within poverty-stricken countries based on what the community needed. He knew all too well how corruption worked, and he was going to ensure that the money went directly to the people.

He had landed in Malawi that morning and, knowing nothing about the tiny country, told the driver to take him anywhere suitable. The out-of-place Korean establishment made him laugh, having spent the last two years in South Korea. Joshua was at the front desk to inquire about any other food options within walking distance when *she* came in.

She was one of those people that made a room move around her like a stone in a brook. At the same time, she did not seem arrogant or self-important. She simply made the room hers, the way that a rose makes a bush a rose bush. The rose doesn't try to take over the identity of the bush; the innocent blooms are simply too vibrant to be ignored. This woman didn't try; she just walked in, smiled with soft, painted pink lips, and the room was hers.

She was well curved but did not flaunt it in a simple blue dress. She wore plain jewelry made of bronze, and dark, well-worn and dusty leather sandals. Her skin was smooth and brown from the sun. Her dark hair was pinned up on her head, and though it may have been a style earlier in the day, it was now loose and several pieces hung down her shoulders and back in soft curls.

She had a tattoo of a sparrow on her neck. Joshua was not fond of tattoos, but the way that this was fit to her hairline, it seemed to belong there. He realized that he was staring at her and shook his head a little, breaking the spell.

The woman called to the clerk at the front desk. "Maria!" Then they shared the kind of hug that you gave to good friends that you actually missed. "How is the family? How is your son? Are you a grandmother yet?"

Maria beamed and took out her phone to proudly swipe through many photos. The woman in the blue dress laughed and sighed and said, "What name did you give such a strong, handsome boy?"

Maria stood tall. "Sampson," she replied with all the pride and joy of a new grandmother.

"Oh, Sampson! You picked well!" Smiling at the photo, the woman repeated, "Sampson," as she fit the name to the little face.

Maria took her phone back. "I've been missing you! How is everything? How are projects in the north?"

"So good! Busy, but good. I'm about halfway done building a school, but I ran out of money. Like all the way gone, gone. Actually, I have to negotiate with the taxi tomorrow for a ride to the airport. You wouldn't happen to have any outstanding favors with any drivers, would you?" The woman in the blue dress smiled and tried to look innocent enough.

"That's no problem," Maria said a little lower. "Use the hotel taxi." Maria handed the woman a card.

Joshua stood to the side of them, completely forgotten, no more than a chair or a lamp. He thought if he stayed quiet long enough, he might overhear her name, but it was never said, or if it had been he hadn't heard it.

The woman in the blue dress got the key to her room, all the while going on and on about a hot shower and egg rolls. When she left, the lobby felt quieter. Not that the woman in the blue dress was loud; I did not say that it sounded quieter, it *felt* quieter. It was the same feeling you got after the last chord of a great song rang out and faded into stillness. Like a small death. Egg rolls suddenly sounded quite good.

"Sir, can I help you find something?" the woman at the counter asked.

"Oh, no. Thank you." He held up a pamphlet, backing out of the room. "I found it."

Joshua had gone to his room to gather his thoughts, but less than a handful of minutes later, terrified that he'd miss her if he didn't make himself available, he found himself on the patio restaurant for his dinner tryst. It was only 4:30pm.

He'd now been sitting for three hours. That wasn't accurate: he'd been at war with himself for three hours. Joshua was not sure if he was winning or losing, but there was a serious inner struggle happening. He was a fool, no; he was a romantic. She would think he was crazy, or that he was a fool. She was amazing. Yes, he was a fool, but maybe she was worth being a little foolish for.

The sky darkened and all of the tables filled with guests. He had been working on balancing a set of locked tonged forks on a saltshaker when he heard her.

Her hair was wrapped in a towel, and she was dressed in what could only be described as "comfort wear". He watched as her emerald eyes darted about, searching for a spot among the completely full tables. She began to turn, dejected and retreating from the restaurant. Was all this foolishness for nothing? He could not stomach that.

"Would you like to sit with me?" It was the boldest question he had ever made to a woman. With a sweet smile she nodded and walked toward him.

"Thank you. It seems I missed the dinner bell." A waiter brought her an ice-cold ginger beer; she hadn't had to ask for. She gave the waiter a much broader smile than she had given him. The server smiled back with great gusto and told her he had already placed her food order.

"You come here often?" Joshua asked, then, realizing what he'd said, cringed.

Her head tilted ever so slightly to one side, accentuated by the towel wrapped high on her head. She raised her eyebrows at him, and her mouth curved into a perfect and amused smirk. "Really?"

"Sorry, that's not what I-" Joshua stammered, unable to reach words.

"Nothing wrong with the classics, but as far as pick up lines go, I don't think I have ever heard that one actually used." She could see he was flustered, but he was handsome, and Teneil did not know how to flirt graciously. She was more of a "punch you on the playground" kind of flirt.

"I- yeah, I heard it as it came out. I-" He was blubbering and tried desperately to collect himself. "Trust me, I was not hitting on you."

"It's the towel, isn't it?" She scrunched up her face.

"No. I mean, you probably shouldn't wear a towel to dinner, but I don't care. Mind. I don't *mind*. I think you look beautiful- fine. You look fine." *SHUT UP*, he told himself.

She laughed at him. "No, you're probably right." She knew she looked like a mess; the lodge had way too many mirrors for her liking. She reached up and pulled the towel from her damp hair. It had seemed secure, but with a small tug the fluffy fabric slid off easily, pulling all her hair to one side and revealing the sparrow tattoo once more.

Joshua was sure it had all happened in slow motion, like a high definition shot from a movie being filmed across the table. Her movements were like liquid, not water but honey. Slow and deliberate. She reached up and ran her fingers through her wet hair, almost black in the low lighting. It fell to her lap and covered all but the edge of the sparrow's wing, like a secret. His mouth was dry.

"I'm Joshua Casset." He offered his hand; it seemed the simplest way to touch her.

"Teneil Jayne," she said with a strong handshake and dancing eyes.

"Strange name."

"Thank you." She smiled and took a drink of her ginger beer.

"No, it's beautiful, I like it, I just- I just hadn't heard it before. Is that your real name?"

"You mean. . .is Teneil my stage name?"

What was wrong with him? He had spent his whole life surrounded by super models and icons, but he had never made such a fool of himself. "No, like a name you give to men in hotels."

"Mmm." Teneil considered for a moment. "My prostitute name." She nodded and sat back in her chair, folding her arms with a curious grin on her face.

He was going to be sick.

"No," she said in a matter-of-fact tone, "I use 'Natasha' when I'm turning tricks." She winked at him.

Joshua laughed unevenly. "I'm sorry. I didn't mean-"

"I was named after a musical group that was popular in the 70s. Captain and Tennille. My dad said she was a classy babe. Though the first song I ever heard from them was called 'Muskrat love' so I don't think my dad and I agree on the definition of 'class'. However. . . I did wear this to dinner." She gestured to her outfit, if one could call it that. "With a towel on my head, so maybe Teneil *is* perfect."

"I don't know anything about the mating habits of muskrats, but I think the name suits you."

Her grin widened. "So, what's a guy like you doing in a place like this?"

He laughed again. "I run a non-profit."

Surprise and intrigue flashed across her face, and she leaned toward him. "Really? What do you do?"

"All sorts of things, really. I base it on community needs so it varies." Most organizations established themselves from their own dream and not what the people needed, and most organizations failed because of that.

His tactic was exactly what Teneil was trying to do as well and, needless to say, Joshua had her full attention.

"Tell me about yourself," he dared to say next.

"Well, there's not really much to tell," Teneil replied with a small shrug. "Small town, hardworking, God-fearing family. Decided to sell everything, bought a one-way ticket and never looked back." Without the details, it was really that simple.

The egg rolls arrived and there was hesitation at the table. She looked anxious. "I'm sorry but I can't eat these without praying. I mean I can, my head won't explode or anything, I just won't."

"Please do." Joshua was impressed.

Teneil gave him a grateful look and closed her eyes. "God in heaven, we love you so much. Well, I do; I don't know about Joshua, but at least I hope he does. Anyway, thank you for everything that you do, all the things we have seen, and all the things you have already prepared that we don't even know are coming our way. Thank you for the gift of prayer and our relationship with you. Thank you for always giving us what we need when we need it. Thank you for giving us the strength to stand, every morning and against the world. Bless this food and the hands that made it, that they would eat as well as what they serve. Amen."

"Amen," Joshua echoed. "That was nice. I especially like the bit about, 'let them eat as well as what they serve'."

"I got poisoned a couple times, so I started throwing that out there." She grabbed an egg roll, hesitated, and took a small bite. She was trying very hard not to embarrass herself by eating one roll in two bites, which was her custom. But the moment Joshua looked away, she shoved the whole thing in her mouth and closed her eyes.

"So, you are leaving the country?" he asked, looking back at her.

Teneil froze. She had way too much egg roll in her mouth. . .sorry, did I say egg roll? I meant scorching, red hot, blistering, ball of fire roll. But he was looking at her, so she barely managed, "m-hum", and nodded. He looked away and she sucked in air to try and cool the food down.

"Where are you headed?" he asked, looking at her again. Just looking, right at her, waiting for her answer.

"Amermcra." She attempted the answer but quickly broke. There was nothing more she could do. She held up a single finger on one hand and tried to cover her mouth with the other. She chewed and frantically sucked in air, squinted at the pain.

"Are you alright?"

She nodded spastically, but she was not okay. He handed her a glass of water and she took a greedy sip, sighing in relief. Finally, she swallowed. "Thank you," she choked out, her eyes rimmed with tears. Joshua called for another ice water.

"First time with an egg roll?"

"I get them once a year and now I've burned my tongue and ruined it."

She actually wanted to cry. The server brought ice water and Joshua spoke a hushed phrase in Korean (purely for the purpose of showing off). The waiter smiled and disappeared.

"You speak Korean?" Teneil asked, astounded.

He shrugged. "Only a little."

The waiter came back with a large bowl of ice cream and set it before Teneil. Her eyes grew large. "Thank you!" Then she looked to Joshua. "What about you?"

Joshua smiled. "Would be cruel to make you watch me eat all your egg rolls without compensation."

She slid her plate over to him and took a bite of the sweet cream before her.

He let her have a few bites before asking, "Why are you going back to America, if you don't mind me asking?"

"You just gave me ice cream. Now is a good time to ask anything you want." She let the coolness sit in her mouth until it melted completely. "You know how it is: ran out of money. Time to go beg for more."

"Is that what you do?"

"Not exactly. I write a blog. Take lots of photos. I talk about faith, culture, food, and share people's stories." She took another bite of ice cream. "But the money dried up for this bigger project I took on."

The school, he knew, but he merely nodded.

"I couldn't sit there doing nothing, so I used the last of my money to get the ticket. I don't even have a return ticket. I just keep moving and let God open the doors. Well, surely you of all people can understand that."

He didn't understand. Not even a little. But he said, "Yeah, I understand."

Joshua had been a baby with a literal golden spoon. He had never gone hungry, and he had never really sacrificed anything. He hadn't ever needed to; there had always been more than enough. He'd based his entire life off of his family's abundance.

He had invested in several stocks at his father's urging, and technically he was a millionaire in his own right. Joshua had never worried about money. This woman had nothing, yet she was living the life that he was hungry for. What was it like, to have nothing but faith? He would never know; his family would never allow it. He wanted to know, needed to know, more about how that worked. Something about talking to her woke all of the feelings he had when he first told his parents he was leaving. Adventure.

He watched her enjoy her ice cream. Had he ever enjoyed anything as much as she enjoyed everything? He was alive, but she *was life*. Watching her with the spring rolls had made him want one. He had eaten hundreds of them over the last couple years in South Korea, but this one, from her plate, was the first one he truly appreciated because her appreciation had raised the value of it.

From his birth Joshua had been instructed in business and he knew something was always more valuable when it was high in demand. It was not just the way she sold him the egg roll with her own gratitude. The light in her, the appreciation she held for everything, was the key. She was selling him the idea that life itself had more value. He wanted what she had and consciously or unconsciously, he'd decided that he'd do whatever it took to make that happen.

"You leave tomorrow?" he asked. "Yes. My flight leaves at 11am."

"Where are you going?"

"Colorado."

"Seriously?" he gasped, acting shocked.

"Yes, deadly serious." She laughed, then gave him a mock-serious expression with a spoon of ice cream next to her lips. "I never joke about destinations."

"That's where I'm going! I also leave tomorrow at eleven."

"Seriously?"

"Deadly serious." He smiled. "I also never joke about destinations."

"Why are you going to Colorado?"

"S-same as you: fundraising." He tried to act nonchalant.

"In Colorado, USA?" she repeated unbelievingly.

"Other people do go to Colorado, you know. You don't own Colorado."

"You don't think that's odd? That we are about as far from Colorado as we can be, and we are both headed there at the same time tomorrow?"

"I doubt we have all the same flights." Joshua said, pulling out his phone. "Let me check my schedule."

But he was not checking his schedule. The email he quickly sent to his family's travel agent read:

Gill,

I need to match a flight schedule with a colleague leaving Malawi, tomorrow morning at 11am from Lilongwe International Airport for destination Colorado USA. Match itinerary for one, Tanille Jane (check the spelling on that). One way.

J.

Then he put down his phone. "It's loading. Network here is so awful. What does your flight schedule look like?"

"I don't have it memorized; it's printed out in my room. I'll go get it!" Teneil practically jumped up and ran to her room.

In the meantime, Joshua stared intently at his phone. "Come on, come on."

One new message arrived in his inbox:

Done, sir. Here is your flight schedule with one Teneil Jayne*. Though it looks like you are in for a long trip. I could easily book you two much more direct, first-class flights and cut your travel time by more than 50%.

"Nice one, Gill." Joshua wrote back:

That won't be necessary, thank you for your prompt response as always. J.

He quickly scanned the list of layovers and mixed-matched flights on his screen and his eyes widened. A twenty-minute exchange in Ethiopia? "Can that even be done?" he murmured to himself. Then he saw a ten-hour delay in New York. "Why is she going from New York to Canada?" This was madness.

Teneil returned with a stack of folded papers.

Before she could speak, he shared, "My flights are really strange. I highly doubt that you and I are on the same ones."

"Yeah, mine too. The things we do to save a dollar, right?"

He handed her his phone so she could compare the flights, "Wow!" She hefted it in her hand. "That's a really nice phone."

"Yeah, I needed it for work," he said casually.

"I'm thinking about getting a new phone, too, but I just can't justify a thousand dollars for the latest and greatest."

Joshua's phone had been a gift from his brother, but he was fairly sure it was around $20,000. He honestly didn't even know.

Teneil froze when she scrolled through the itinerary before her. "We are exactly matched up." She didn't look excited: she looked confused. "That can't be right!" She kept flipping through papers. "You're sitting next to me in every seat."

Gill was the best, but even still. "No. That's not-" He grabbed the papers from her. "What?!" He didn't have to act much because he was actually surprised. He would need to thank Gill personally next time he was in New York. Well, not the very next time, obviously, but the time after that. "I don't know what to say."

"That's bizarre." She was not smiling. Teneil was looking very directly at him. "Can I be really honest with you?"

"Yes, sure. Of course."

"Since I met you, this whole thing has felt planned."

Joshua suddenly felt nauseous. There was no possible way she was that clever. Had she figured him out? What a creep he must seem to her. He did not know how to get out of the fabrication he had concocted with direct honesty, so instead he just repeated, "Planned?"

"Yeah, like it was all sort of organized. . .predestined." And while Teneil was experiencing a spiritual awakening, the knot in Joshua's stomach finally gave way.

"Totally, yes. Exactly," he agreed in earnest and took a big drink of water. "I suppose that we should probably share a taxi, too?" He remembered that she had bargained for one at the front desk and added, "I prepaid mine earlier, if you want to just go with me."

"That would be great!" The serendipity of their meeting had put her in one of those rare moments. She felt like she was exactly where she was meant to be. It was like being centered perfectly on a ball on which she'd been trying to balance her entire life. "I guess this is good night, then." She took out what she needed for egg rolls and put it on the table.

"No, please. Let me get it."

"You get the ice cream, but I ordered my own dinner."

"I insist."

"I insist," Teneil said swiftly, "and if you argue with me this will be the longest next few days of your life."

"Alright then." He smiled and put his hands up in resignation.

"See you tomorrow," she said.

"Good night."

"Good night."

It was not until later in his room when Joshua was away from her intoxicating presence that he truly thought about what he'd done. Intoxicating, yes, because surely if he had been sober, he would not have done what he did: lie and manipulate a kind and beautiful woman. What was wrong with him? To top it off, he'd completely neglected his work. What was this reckless idea going to cost his organization? He had one week to figure out the location for his next site in Malawi and now he was suddenly leaving? He knew nothing about the tiny country. Thousands of people were counting on him.

Even if he took a direct flight back from Colorado, he would only have one day to map out the entire project. This was the most idiotic thing he'd ever done. But the smile on his face only grew. He lay in bed filled to bursting with guilt, excitement, anxiety, but what really filled him was her. Most of all, he just thought about her.

That morning he woke early and looked closer at the flight schedule. The first flight was also the first backward move: three and a half hours down to South Africa and a two-hour layover. Next was five and a half hours to Ethiopia with that quick twenty-minute plane switch. Then, seventeen hours to Ireland where they would wait two hours on the plane for fuel and flight checks. Ireland to New York was eight hours, and next was the part he was dreading the most: a ten-hour layover at JFK. What followed was the next backward step of one and a half hours to Ontario, Canada. Only a one-hour layover there and finally, six hours more, to Denver.

This was crazy. A total of barely under sixty hours. He had just arrived from South Korea less than twenty-four hours ago. No. This was an awful idea.

90% convincing himself that he was going to tell her he had malaria and was going to miss the flight. The other 10% of him wanted to tell the truth and buy her one first-class round-trip ticket. But when he saw her at the breakfast bar drinking coffee and reading a book, he was 100% going with her.

"Good morning, stranger," Joshua said, pulling out a chair. And he meant it; he hardly recognized her in this deep blue dress that contrasted perfectly with her eyes. She was beautiful with her hair pinned up, makeup done but not overdone, and delicate, long earrings. He was not sure which he liked more: last night's Teneil or this woman. But then she smiled and brought the two visions together.

"Hi!" She put her book down and gave him her full attention.

"You look nice," was all he could manage.

"World travel was made for rock stars, not yoga pants." She winked. "Don't worry. In sixty hours, I'm sure I'll be back to my old self."

They didn't say much but slid into an easy routine.

Not until they were on the first flight to South Africa, did she say, "Have you ever been through the Jo'burg, South Africa, airport? It's the most beautiful airport I've seen."

"I honestly don't remember. Aren't all airports the same?"

"I think you would remember this one. It's beautiful, you'll see." She was excited. Excited to go back to America for a visit, and excited to be on this adventure with Joshua.

"I guess I will." He smiled. This was a good idea. And when they arrived, he did see the beauty, though not right away. The floors were marble, and the shops artfully decorated. Zebra pelts and diamonds were everywhere, signatures of "South Africa".

"What is beautiful about this to you?" he asked, trying to understand her mind.

She looked at him like he wanted her to explain why things fall down. "It's so sparkly!" she said in wonder, gazing at the diamond displays. "You know, I spend most of the year in one of the poorest countries in the world. There you're lucky to find an unbroken pane of glass, and if you do, it's covered by burglar bars. Even the floor sparkles here." Whatever they had used throughout the airport was flecked with bright blue illuminations, like stars in the ground. "It's like walking on diamonds."

"I suppose you are right." Joshua had to admit it was beautiful, but he would have never seen it on his own. He thought about how she would react if he took her to some of his favorite places. If she could find beauty in an airport, what would she do if he showed her the sunrise on Mount Bromo, in Indonesia? Or to swim in the blue Verdon Gorge, in France?

"Beautiful, right?" She looked knowingly at him.

He met her bright eyes. "Beautiful."

She blushed, then something caught her attention and she gasped. Teneil hurried over to a window display of a gorgeous crown, along with jewelry fit for a queen and dozens of loose stones.

"I'm not surprised you like diamonds." He laughed. "If you love the floor so much."

She scowled at him and whispered to the diamonds, "Someday." Teneil tapped on the glass like there were puppies behind it instead of rocks.

"We better get to the gate." Joshua practically dragged her away.

The next flight was five and a half hours North to Addas Abba, Ethiopia. It was by far the smallest airplane he had ever been on and because it was packed with children, Joshua decided that somehow Teneil had booked a child's flight. As the plane took off, the pressure in the cabin changed. Children and babies began screaming all around him. This would be the longest five and a half hours of his life.

Teneil nudged him. "Can I get by?"

Without hesitation, she climbed over him. She had on a perfume that he caught only briefly. The scent was not like candy, not like flowers, and not like musk. . .something different. She was reaching up, getting into her carry-on bag, and he was looking directly at her navel. He did try to look out the window.

Teneil pulled out a large bag of suckers, then walked up and down the entire plane offering them to all the children. The crying instantly stopped, and Joshua sat back in awe. She was a genius. The bag now almost empty, she gave several to the attendants and sat back down with one for each of them remaining. "Saved the best flavor for you."

"I don't eat sweets."

It was like he had insulted her mother. Her face completely changed. "I don't understand."

"I don't eat sweets," he repeated, as if that explained it.

"Like. . .What exactly do you mean?"

"I mean, I don't eat candy."

"Like. . .ever?"

"Never."

"When was the last time you had a sucker?"

"I don't remember."

"I don't understand."

"My family never gave us candy as children. I went to a boarding school by the time I was nine, and there was no sugar allowed there."

"Well, it's no wonder you are so. . .you."

"Me?"

"Just try this." She unwrapped the banana-flavored lolly. "I'm fine, thank you."

"In my family you always graciously accept a gift, even if you don't want it." She held out the lolly for a long while, looking between him and the confection.

Finally, he sighed and stuck the sweet in his mouth. At first, he tasted nothing but sugar. It was so sweet, but then the sugar faded away and a smooth, caramel banana flavor emerged.

"Nice, right?" She grinned around the sucker stick in her own mouth.

"Sweet," he grumbled.

She laughed a little.

"What flavor do you have?" he finally asked.

"Same: banana."

Joshua had the feeling not entirely unlike sharing a pair of headphones. "It's not bad," he admitted.

"Not bad? It's travel size bananas foster. It's amazing! Don't worry, you don't have to say it. I can see you agree by the way you haven't taken it out of your mouth." She smiled but closed her eyes and rested her head back.

He did the same, following her silent instruction. He closed his eyes, rested his head back, and savored the candy and the hum of the airplane engine. He had almost completely surrendered himself to the mental holiday when Teneil crunched through the second half of the sweet. Surely, she had to have broken a tooth. Eyes wide, he stared at her. "What?" she asked innocently.

When the plane started its descent, she disobeyed the instruction of the captain and immediately began moving about the cabin. "What are you doing?" he whispered.

"Making our exit strategy. Remember, we have only twenty minutes to get to our next gate. They know we're on this flight and they'll hold the gate for us, but in my experience, that'll last only about ten minutes."

The flight attendant waved at Teneil. "Let's go."

Joshua quickly got up and followed her. Curious gazes of many children and their parents followed him down the narrow plane's aisle. "I'm with her."

Teneil gave the flight attendant one of her "I don't know you at all but my love for you is absolute" hugs. He sat on a chair next to the exit and watched their exchange. He could not hear them over the sound of the engine so close to the door. They spoke for only a moment before both women were crying. They laughed and hugged again. Then Teneil came back and sat with him.

"What's wrong?"

Teneil looked confused, "Wrong? Nothing. You okay?"

"Why are you crying?"

"My eyes just do that sometimes."

"And her?" He pointed to the attendant who was still drying her eyes.

"She is a lovely woman," stated, as if that cleared everything up.

They boarded the next flight and were indeed the last to arrive. It was their longest flight, or as Teneil would say, "the fattest leg." Seventeen hours to Ireland. Their seats were at the very back of the plane. Joshua had been on countless fights, but if he was being honest, he had no idea planes were so big. He had never gone past first class on a flight this large.

"I don't know why, but they always put me in the very back of the plane." Teneil took her seat next to the window and Joshua sat next to her. "The best part about these big flights? All the free movies! This is where I usually get all caught up on the new releases!" She tapped the screen in front of her, but nothing happened. She tried several different things, but it never came on. She reached over and tapped his, and it lit up right away. "Figures. Oh well."

She looked out of the window as the plane took off, but after they were in the sky for a while the flight reached its ultimate high altitude. She nudged him and said, "I picked the left side of the plane, window seat, for just this reason. Switch me seats." Again, she was not asking and left no room for argument: she climbed over him, and he gladly slid under her.

"Why?"

"You'll see."

He thought maybe it was the working screen on his side that she wanted, but she never touched it. Because the flight was moving northwest, the sunset was delayed. What should only take ten minutes of heavenly colors took over thirty. Joshua watched the suspended sun, red orange, in all of its glory, until his neck hurt.

When was the last time he watched the sun set? Had he been "too busy" for things like this his whole life? It was like making up for lost time, this perfect sunset viewed from on top of the clouds. When it was finally over, Joshua turned to tell Teneil "Thank you" but she was asleep.

Her face was so soft and perfect. He watched her eyelashes dance, and when the flight attendant came by for drink orders, he asked for an extra pillow instead. He very gently encouraged her closer to him and rested her head on the pillow that he positioned on his shoulder. She woke up just for a moment, slid her arm through his, sighed, and burrowed her face deep into the pillow. Joshua had never been so happy in his life.

She woke a few hours later, feeling completely rested but she knew she would crash at least once more before the trip was over. She was awake but she refused to move. Her head was resting on a sleeping Joshua's shoulder. Her arm locked with his, his hand resting over hers. Teneil knew there was much more to this man than he let on.

Why was he so shy? She loved him like she loved all people. She did not care what people did; she cared who they were, and she could tell Joshua was a good man. She was happy just to be next to him, but she wondered why he was so guarded with her when destiny had clearly brought them together. She didn't push, but that should not suggest that she did not want to push. In his own time, he would tell her everything.

Joshua woke up in a dark cabin while Teneil was watching the latest superhero movie. He hated movies. They were a "waste of life", his father had always said, but he wished he had an extra headset so he could be in the movie with her. Watching her watch a movie felt like he was far away from her. He decided to go for the subtle, over-exaggerated "stretch and moan".

Teneil popped off her headset and smiled broadly at him. "Good afternoon!" She had been waiting hours for him to wake up.

"Afternoon?" He pulled up the blinder on the window and was blasted with sunshine and several moans of protest from the cabin. Teneil reached over him and snapped the blinder back down.

"They don't let you open them," she explained. "Let the other passengers sleep. Easier transition for the time change, I guess? Easier to watch movies? I don't know." She shrugged. "Coffee?" Teneil climbed over the sleeping aisle seat passenger and disappeared in the back of the cabin. Several moments later she came back with two large cups and a small metal tin. Joshua took the haul while she soundlessly climbed over the seat again.

"Took a while, sorry. Got us a fresh pot." She winked and opened the container to some kind of pancake dish. "You missed breakfast, so I had them keep this in the warmer for you."

It should be noted that Joshua was not a morning person. No, that wasn't entirely true; he loved mornings, just not the first five minutes of the morning when dream and reality blurred together. Her "bounce" was a lot.

"You make friends everywhere you go." His tone turned the sentence into an insult somehow. In his cranky wakefulness, it occurred to him that he was just another cast member in "Teneil's life" and he hated her for it.

"Lucky thing I make friends easily. That's how I got you." She winked at him.

He grunted and took a sip of the brew. The bitter coffee edged the bitterness from his mind. He had to admit, she hadn't tricked him into being here; in fact, he had tricked her. He had been willing to follow her to the other side of the world after sharing one meal with her, so of course the attendants had made her a fresh pot of coffee. And then, like a memory from long ago, she had winked at him.

"Thanks for the coffee." He sat up a little and straightened his hair.

"We got to watch out for each other, right?"

"Yeah, that's right," he agreed, but to himself he was screaming, *tell her the truth, you fool!*

"So, tell me something about you," she pushed, just a little.

"Like what?"

"Something, anything. I don't know."

That was the opening he needed. He thought about saying, *"if you liquidated the assets, my family, collectively, is worth just over one billion dollars. Oh, me? No, I'm nothing like them. I only have 18.6 million."* He settled on saying, "Oh, I don't know. Um, I love to cook?"

"Really?" She was delighted. "But that doesn't mean that you're any good. I love to sing. Doesn't mean that anyone wants to hear it."

He smiled, because he had heard it, at the Korean lodge when he had wandered past her room hoping to run into her. It was awful. "I'm a good cook."

"What kind of food do you like to make?"

"Lots of things. I like to cook from scratch." Then he added, "And you? Tell me something about you?"

40

"I'm an open book." She put her palms face up to emphasize that she wasn't hiding anything. "What would you like to know?"

"Tell me about the tattoo."

"The bird?"

"A sparrow, right?"

Without thinking about it she lifted a hand and cupped the bird. "After my first year in Africa, I. . ." She hesitated, tears welling in her eyes. "I realized that I could never be enough. There were too many empty stomachs, too many bare bodies, too many sleeping in the dirt. So, I raged at God, 'Why would you show me all this suffering that you know I can do nothing about, knowing that it would break me?'"

She took a moment, shaking her head and wiping away heavy tears. "But God answered me back, 'It is not your Glory to feed and clothe and house all of my children. I know every sparrow that falls.' And I remembered reading, 'do not worry about your life, what you will eat, or what you will wear. Is life not more than food and clothing? Look to the birds of the air, they neither sow nor reap nor store up food in barns, their father feeds them, are you not more valuable than they?'

"It was like the weight of the world fell off my shoulders. I was not God, and though I only had a little, I could do what I could do, and that was all I was asked to do. God didn't break me: he freed me. The sparrow reminds me that there are things far out of my control, and that's good. Otherwise, I wouldn't need God."

Joshua had no words. He had gone to bed night after night, year after year, with the weight of the world on his shoulders, too. But suddenly it was gone from him after hearing her words. He wanted to thank her, but he didn't know how. *Tell her the truth.* "Teneil I-" he began, but the captain cut him off with news of their descent.

She rolled her eyes. "Nothing worse than the two-hour re-fueling wait. You can't get off the plane but you're not going anywhere either."

He made a mental note that idleness was her kryptonite.

The second half of the flight to New York was better. There was familiarity and comfort between them, and a couple hours into the flight Teneil very consciously put her head on Joshua's shoulder. "Is this okay?" she asked, working her head into the right spot.

"Yeah," he whispered, trying to force casualness. "That's okay."

"It's just that. . ." she sighed, "you have such soft shoulders."

"Soft shoulders?"

"Yup," she said sleepily.

"That's not a compliment."

"Mmmm." She nuzzled him one more time before drifting off.

They both slept most of the flight, but about an hour before descent, Teneil got up and took a small bag to the bathroom. She came out a completely different person. While everyone else looked like they had melted, Teneil had changed clothes, from the dress into blue jeans and a white t-shirt. She freshened up her makeup, even changing her earrings and shoes. But the biggest difference was that her hair was down. The bun she had worn for the entire trip had curled her hair and it fell in shiny waves.

"I don't think that's fair," Joshua observed.

"What?" she said, pulling out a tube of coral lip gloss. "I told you, world travel is for rock stars."

Joshua knew rock stars, plenty of them, and they still looked like trash after almost forty hours on a plane.

After making their way through customs, they rechecked their bags. Joshua's suitcase had nothing but a smaller suitcase inside, since he left all his things in his room at the lodge in Malawi. Picking up the empty case was the hardest reminder that he was lying to her. What happened when they got to Colorado? How was he going to tell her the truth? When *was* the right time?

They made it to the next gate after walking around for hours to stretch their legs, eating at an airport cafe, killing time by perusing each shop, and buying several types of familiar American candy. Finally, Teneil sat on the hard ground.

"What are you doing?" There was a distinct note of panic in his voice. Joshua was wrestling with the idea that he truly loved this woman, but there was no way he was going to get on the floor at JFK.

"The hard ground feels good, and my feet are swollen like an old maid's." She pointed and he saw the truth. It was the most unattractive thing he had ever seen, her sausage feet.

"Do they hurt?"

She laughed at the face he made. "No, it doesn't hurt. I just need to put them up."

He stood there for a long moment, debating what to do. "I'm sorry," he finally said flatly. "I can't."

"Can't what?"

"I can't sit on the floor with you."

"Why not?"

"Because. . ."

"What?"

"That's gross. It's too much, I'm sorry."

She laughed and got off the floor. She reached in her bag and pulled out a large square of fabric. Teneil laid it down before sitting on one half and patting the ground invitingly next to her. "Just like a picnic."

Joshua couldn't help but notice that directly opposite them was an elite club. He could easily buy her a massage for her disgusting, plump feet and they could even lay in a real bed. Those ideas alone were enough to push him further toward telling her the truth. But he stumbled. He thought about the club beds. There was no way she would take one bed with him. As comfortable as they were together, that wouldn't be right, but if he stayed here, he could actually lay down with her. Only it would be the floor of the airport! He took a small step toward her.

"Not the shoes," she warned.

That was too much. Did she really want him to take his shoes off and lay down on the airport floor like some kind of vagrant?

He shook his head. "Teneil, I-"

"Joshua?" He heard a familiar male voice, and his stomach sank. "I thought that was you!"

Joshua turned and found Gill standing right behind him. "Gill. Nice to see you." Joshua automatically extended his hand toward the man. At the same time, he also turned his back to the clearly homeless, shoe-less, girl on the floor of the airport.

And that's when Gill ruined everything: "Booking all of those flights was so last moment. I wasn't sure you would arrive well. I only live around the corner, you see. I thought it would be best to just come round and make sure you got in okay before continuing on to Denver."

Joshua did glance at Teneil then; he couldn't help himself. No one had ever made such a sad, confused expression look so beautiful, and he hated himself for being the reason. She nodded as if everything was made clear and did not look up again. Joshua thanked Gill, who always went above and beyond for his family, and walked with him back out of the gate. When Joshua looked back, Teneil was gone.

The gate for their flight had been moved, and he quickly ran after her. Catching her in the boarding line, he shouted, "Teneil!"

"Go away Joshua."

"Teneil. . ."

"No." Teneil gave her ticket to the attendant.

Joshua scrambled to find his ticket and followed after her. Finally getting through the travelers storing their overhead treasures, he sat in the seat next to her. "Teneil, please let me explain."

"You lied to me. This whole thing has been a lie." She was not concerned with who overheard such loud, heartbreaking words in a small space.

Joshua sighed, regretting not taking every chance he had to come clean. "I thought that if you knew I was rich, you wouldn't care to get to know me. That you wouldn't think that we were the same. I-" He was pleading with her now. "I wasn't ready to let you go."

"Because you have money? That's why you think I'm mad?" Her eyes were rimmed with tears. "Am I so shallow?"

"Okay, if you don't care about the money, then what is it?"

"You made me feel like an idiot." Her tears finally fell. "I thought this whole thing was God's perfect plan." She gave a sad chuckle. "But it was just *you*. I actually used the word 'serendipity'! Ugh! I hate that word! You manipulated me into loving you. You used me, my faith and my kindness, because you had to know more about me? You wanted and you took. Money or not, you are a selfish, spoiled brat. And I'm a fool."

". . .you love me?"

"Get away from me, Joshua."

"Teneil." He reached toward her.

"If you touch me, I will scream." Her eyes were hard, and he knew she was serious. "Go back to wherever it is you're supposed to be."

She was right: he was selfish, spoiled, too, but he could not let her go. He buckled his belt.

Teneil glared at him. "Get off the plane, Joshua."

"What if it's both?" Joshua tried next. "What if I'm a jerk and it is also a God thing?"

"I don't want anything to do with you."

"That's not true," he insisted. "You love me, you just said so."

Teneil hit the call button for a flight attendant in the same way contestants hit the answer button on a game show and was overjoyed when one immediately came to assist.

"Can I help you?"

"This man touched me inappropriately," Teneil declared, drawing even more stares from the surrounding passengers. "I need a new seat please."

The attendant stuttered, and Joshua said, "Teneil, be serious."

Finally, the attendant spoke up: "You know him, Miss?"

Teneil appraised Joshua for a moment. "No, I don't."

"You can have my seat." An extremely large man in jeans and a leather vest that boasted of various biker gangs said from the aisle seat a few rows ahead.

"Oh, bless you!" Teneil quickly gathered her things and pushed past Joshua, who sat speechless. Teneil hugged the large stranger, actually hugged him, and he genuinely hugged her back. "Don't you worry about a thing, darlin'." He wiped her tears and she let him. "I'll handle this."

Joshua rolled his eyes.

Despite every flight he'd already taken that day, *that* was the longest journey of Joshua's life. The worst part was when they debarked, Joshua called to Teneil, but she never looked back. Teneil's guardian had put his arm around Joshua and wouldn't let him leave until Teneil was long gone. The next flight was a quick connection to Denver and Joshua ran. He just needed to talk to her.

But he missed the flight. Joshua watched her plane take off and he felt the tie between them stretch and snap. He thought long and hard about going to Denver; there were other flights. He knew he could find her and make her--

He stopped. She really was right: he was selfish and spoiled. He didn't deserve her, no matter how badly he wanted her. He watched as her plane turned into a speck on the horizon. Then he made his way to the counter and got his ticket all the way back to Malawi.

Teneil got to her parents' house drained in every way. She slept for two days but still had trouble getting out of bed. Her mother finally asked what was really wrong and Teneil burst into tears. She told her mother all about Joshua and their trip. Afterward, Teneil's mother said, "And you let him go?"

"No! I threw him away!" Teneil began crying again and burrowed her face in her pillow.

It was on the flight to Colorado that Teneil realized a piece of her was missing. She spent the entire journey looking at the empty seat next to her. She had six hours to let her temper cool, and when it did all that was left was love. She did love him. She wanted him. And she had thrown him out.

Her mother's advice was the best: "Let go and let God." Let God do what He does best. So, she let go. For the next seven weeks she spoke at churches and Bible studies. She loved her friends and family. She gained ten pounds off nothing but Mexican food, and before she knew it, she was back on a plane to Malawi.

She watched movies, read in her books, and did all she could not to hate the stranger sitting next to her on each flight. The five-hour taxi back into the bush didn't get her in until after dark. She left her bags packed, loved her dogs, and crawled into bed.

Several days later, her friend Grace came to check on her. "Hey, girl! How was your trip? You okay? Are you sick?"

"No," Teneil replied. "I'm not sick, just tired."

Grace was bursting with energy. "Well? Did you call him?"

"Who?"

"That's all anyone is talking about!" Grace had a bright smile.

"What are you talking about?"

"You haven't seen it?" her friend nearly shouted.

Teneil winced. "Grace, it's too early."

"Put your shoes on. We have to go!"

Teneil protested at first, but a walk did sound nice. It was a few miles to the other side of town and Teneil thought about going back to bed the whole time. "What are we doing, Grace?"

Grace stopped and turned around at a particular spot. Teneil admitted the view was nice: you could see the whole town from this one entry road.

"Not that!" Grace grabbed Teneil's chin and adjusted her focus from town to the old cooking oil billboard. But it was not advertising cooking oil anymore.

COMING SOON

A second chance?

Teneil, if you want this billboard taken down,

Please call Joshua

Teneil stared at the Malawian phone number at the bottom of the board. Did that mean he was still here? In Malawi? He was in her town? Could he be that close? Her eyes welled with tears. A thousand times she had cut herself open with the knowledge that she would never see Joshua again.

Wordless, Teneil reached for the empty pocket where her phone should have been. Panic filled her eyes and she looked at Grace. "My phone! I left it at the house!"

Grace laughed and handed Teneil her own phone. Teneil's hands were shaking, and tears ran down her face in a torrent.

"Hello?" Joshua answered on the first ring.

"Joshua?"

Chapter Three
IF ONLY HE WAS A FAMILY MAN

Here's a story of a lovely lady who was bringing up three very lovely girls.

The oldest, Gift, now seventeen, was also the first to arrive. She was an orphan from an early age, raised by her grandmother, who was raising six other grandchildren. Agogo, grandmother, was a no-nonsense kind of woman for obvious reasons. Gift was twelve when the police pulled her off the street as a runaway. She eventually ended up with Teneil, who was not intimidated by her hard exterior and 24/7 bad attitude. Teneil had loved her through her rage, and Gift had blossomed into a beautiful, strong, and witty young woman. Gift's 24/7 bad attitude was greatly improved to 21/7. *And they said it couldn't be done.*

Tapiwa was the youngest at five years old. She had a mother and a father, both bouncing around in the prison system for various charges that ranged from theft to assault of a police officer. She had lived with Teneil from her infancy. Tapiwa was fearless, friendly, and quick as a whip.

Being thirteen made Regina the middle child, but she was the newest to arrive at Teneil's house. She spoke no English and had no education. She was dropped on Teneil's doorstep less than a year ago. Starved to bones and covered with deeply infected wounds, Regina's family had refused to allow her in the house, a fear of whatever she had, leprosy, they thought, spreading to them.

After months of heavy calorie intake and medical care, Regina's cheeks had filled in, her eyes cleared, and she became a sweet, shy girl, with bright almond eyes and a voice like a nightingale.

They lived in a little cottage next to the beautiful lake. They were a mismatched family, full of stories and love. Life was good and simple.

From her experience, Teneil knew there was such a thing as "universal languages". There were human truths that all people across the globe had in common. Most commonly known was the universal language of love. Less talked about was the ubiquitous presence of incorrigible old men, town gossips, and hormonal teenagers.

Gift was home from her boarding school on a three-week break. She instantly did what instincts and hormones (the bondage of all teenagers) told her to do: migrate toward water. The large beach, only a five-minute walk from their home, stretched in the form of a large crescent moon, and was full of all kinds of teenagers who felt the same indescribable pull to gather in small groups at the water's edge.

Gift was never a swimmer nor was she into beach sports. She did not wander around and she did not dance. She preferred to sit, watch, and listen. Her aloof nature made her mysterious and her listening ear made her a good friend. It did not hurt that her skin was flawless, her smile perfect, her hair thick, her lips full, and to top that off she was indifferent to most subjects. Gift was in a perpetual state of 50% indifference, 48% irritation, and 2% encompassing the remaining spectrum of human emotion.

What is it about beautiful, indifferent teens that makes them so popular? Anyway. . .

From her position, Gift could see the entire beach. The usual people went about in their usual dance. Boyfriends and girlfriends were breaking up, only to get back together. Troublemakers were sneaking alcohol.

Preteens, who hadn't understood that the pull to the beach had nothing to do with playing in the water, splashed around and dove into the waves. Gift's group consisted of three or four friends that switched out regularly. The order of the switch was always based on who was dating who and who was mad at who.

There was no way Gift's mother would allow her to bounce between boys like the other girls did. Her mother had always said, "If he is good enough for you, he is good enough to come to the house and have dinner with the family." That embarrassment was enough to keep Gift out of the dating pool. Gift would never admit it to her mother, but she was glad for it; she already would have made several mistakes with who she would have chosen.

A bright white Frisbee fell at Gift's feet in the sand. She stared at it like a fly on her cake. It was not hers and it was not her responsibility.

"Could you throw that back?" a boy called from down the beach.

Gift rolled her eyes and turned back to her friends, refusing to touch the disk. The boy was forced to fetch his own toy.

He jogged up to her. "Hey?" he prompted, but Gift ignored him. The boy sat down so hard in the sand next to Gift that she was forced to acknowledge his presence.

"What?" She spat a rhetorical question, but when she looked in his direction, Gift saw the most handsome boy she had ever seen.

He was lean and dark. His face beamed out from under long, black curls. His smile was playful and wicked. He let her drink in the look of him. For a moment Gift thought she was falling, but only a moment. Then she remembered that she didn't like liking things and looked away again. Her friends were another story; several openly gasped.

"Just because you are beautiful?" he asked. "That's why you think you can be mean to strangers?"

His words did not flatter the chronically underwhelmed Gift. She simply rolled her eyes.

Mark had never had trouble with girls. And he was positive that no girl had ever rolled her eyes at him. His teenage, narcissistic self took a massive blow. He didn't see her friends falling over each other; he only saw her, the one who refused to even look at him. Challenge accepted.

Inside of Gift there was a mass of emotions that never surfaced. She did feel things, of course; she felt things deeply, like the butterflies in the pit of her stomach, which were making her nauseous right now. She felt the smallest of smiles pull on the corners of her lips and quickly fought it back down. Her mother always teased her about how much work Gift had to put in, in order to contain her smiles, but this one had slipped. Gift had hoped he didn't see, but he did.

Mark had witnessed girls breaking up with their boyfriends because he'd talked to them, girls who changed schools to be closer to him, and girls simply offering themselves to him with no strings attached. Because of this, Mark was not easily flattered, but that tiny, quick, upward flick in this girl's perfect mouth was the most alluring thing he had ever seen. She was not falling over herself to impress him. She was not a foolish girl like these others who were batting their eyes so much he thought to ask if maybe it was a sand issue.

"I saw that," he said quietly.

Gift shot a look at him like he had invaded her private thoughts. "What?"

"Your mouth wants to smile but you forced it back into its frowning cage." He laughed.

She did smile then, caught off guard by such a description. She was quickly irritated with herself. She rolled her eyes, scoffed, and stood up to walk away.

"Wait!" He jumped to follow, but she kept walking. He fell in step with her as the beach's sand gave way under his desperate feet. "I'm Mark."

Gift continued without saying a word.

"Can't you talk?"

She stopped and gave him an impatient glare. Of course, she *could* talk. Was he stupid? She rolled her eyes again and when she continued on her way, she gave her mouth permission to say, "Yes."

"Wow!" Mark laughed. "A whole 'yes'?"

Gift was quickly approaching her boiling point, which was not far from any other of her points.

"Can I know your name?" Mark pried at her defenses.

Without stopping, she said, "Gift."

"Gift." He tasted the name slowly. "Gift, would you like to make a bet?"

She stopped in her tracks, putting a hand up to shield her eyes from the sun when she looked back at him. There was really only one thing that Gift enjoyed, and that was a challenge. She turned in the sand to see him a few paces behind her, smiling. *Ugh.* She rolled her eyes again. "What?"

"If I can make you smile again, you have to play Frisbee with me."

"I don't *play* Frisbee." She folded her arms.

"It's easy," Mark insisted smoothly. "I can teach you."

That sounded like the worst possible idea, but it was easily avoided. "And when I don't smile?"

"I will give you. . ." He looked around for an easy answer but found none. "That's not even worth discussing. You'll smile."

"Fine. When I don't smile, you leave me alone." To be honest, that was the last thing that she wanted, but like many teenagers, she did not know how to turn off disdain.

"Deal."

"Fine, let's get this over with."

"It's a riddle you have to answer."

She only stared at him, so he took that as the okay to continue: "Two elephants only have one small umbrella but neither gets wet. How is that possible?"

Gift thought and thought, but finally settled on a shrug. "Fine, how?"

Conspiratorially, Mark answered, "It wasn't raining."

The stupidity of it all and the way that he said it made a quick flash of a smile cross her face. But it was gone just as fast. "That is so dumb." She rolled her eyes and continued walking. The thing Gift hated more than everything else she hated, which is a big list, was losing.

"Whoa, whoa. Where do you think you are going?" He chased after her. "Dumb or no, we had a deal!"

Joy was suddenly fighting irritation and indifference within her, so she settled on her favorite word: "Fine."

She stood unmoved while he retrieved the Frisbee from his two little brothers. The youngest, John, threatened to cry, but Mark explained that it was for a pretty girl. Luke, the middle child, made air kisses and teased his brother. Mark cuffed him on the back of the head and Luke stopped. . . stopped with the noises but continued the movements.

Mark began by instructing Gift on how to throw the disk. It was impossible to tell how many times Gift rolled her eyes, but she was beginning to have a headache. He ran some way down the beach and assumed a position that indicated he was ready for anything she could throw.

Gift fully let herself smile now. Mark had taught her about what she was playing with, and it was time she taught him about *who* he was playing with. She purposefully threw the disk at the halfway point between them so he would have to fetch it. He brought it back to her and instructed her on "more power." She did exactly the same halfway throw again. And again. And again. Finally, seeing his utter frustration, she burst into laughter.

His head shot up at the sound and he realized she had been teasing him. She likely knew how to throw a Frisbee. He was such an idiot. She was probably a pro and he had just assumed she was ignorant. "Fine." He called out to her, "Why don't you catch it for once?" He picked up the disk and cocked it to throw. Never before and never again would he make such a perfect pass. With flawless form, he aimed at his target and released the disk.

But Gift was not a pro. She had only ever thrown a disk once before this, and when she'd realized she had no natural talent for it, she'd given up. The bright white object came barreling directly at her and she was neither prepared nor qualified to stop it. It hit her perfectly between her eyes and she fell flat on her back.

The story about that moment would travel far and wide. More than one hundred eyes watched the event, and each had their own perspective. In later weeks, the truth would get misconstrued to several elaborate, dramatic versions. The closest version to actual events, though still almost complete fabrication, was that Gift broke up with that new guy Mark and he'd hit her in the face, or he hit her and so she broke it off. It should come as no surprise to know that "the rumor mill" among young adults was also a universal language.

Gift lay flat on her back. The sand was hot, and the blood running down her throat was gagging her. She rolled over and blood poured from her face. Several people rushed to her side, and she allowed them to help her up. Her eyes were watering too badly to see clearly. Arms slid under hers and began walking her home. There was a hum of low murmurs in the crowd. Mark was there with his brothers arguing.

Luke was saying that it was the pass of a lifetime. The throw was perfect! Could not have been better! Horrified, Mark was threatening to knock him out if he didn't stop. Mark gave Gift his shirt to hold to her bleeding nose but even still, by the time they arrived at her house there was significant damage done to Gift's clothes.

They entered the gate and made their way to a back patio. Gift said nothing, assuming her mother would have enough to say for the both of them. Gift's mother, Teneil, always did have the lion's share of any conversation.

Tapiwa ran to the gate to greet the group, but when she saw Gift and all the blood, she pivoted to tell her mom. It was not out of concern for her sister that she ran; Tapiwa just loved having such an event to relay. She was a vicious nark. "Mom! Gift is outside and it's all the blood!"

"What?" Teneil had been clearing cobwebs from under the couches and beds, and now stood covered in the dusty strings. She walked outside to assess the situation. Quickly, she grabbed all that she needed for the little that could be done for a nosebleed. Holding a wrapped ice pack to the girl's face, Teneil finally asked the group what had happened.

"That was my fault, ma'am," said a very handsome young man.

Gift looked at her mom and Teneil could see the plea in her eyes that said, *"Please, for the love of all creation, do not embarrass me!"*

In Gift's defense, her mother was fond of singing to her in public places and yelling things like "make mommy proud!" whenever Gift left the house. She even went so far as to fake crying hysterically every morning when Gift left for school, reaching through the gate like prison bars, shouting about how much she would miss her while she was gone. "Please come back! Don't leave me here alone! I will be good, I promise! Don't leave me!" Her mom did this especially when Gift had friends around. To Gift it was the worst thing about her mother, but to Teneil it was good parenting.

"And who are you?" Teneil asked not unkindly to the young man.

"I'm Mark. This is my brother Luke and our youngest brother John."

"I don't think I have seen you around before." Teneil could feel Gift's fingernails digging into her leg, but Teneil only smiled at the confirmation of Gift's affection toward this young man.

"No, ma'am. We just moved in down the street."

Regina came outside to see what all the trouble was about. Her bright almond eyes took in the whole scene. She was a shy girl, but she was very compassionate and without being asked grabbed a pitcher of clean water and more clean cloth.

Teneil loved all three of her girls, but because they were hers, she knew that they were not without their own issues. She could clearly see Mark's concern. He seemed like such a nice boy. Teneil knew that Gift was stubborn to a fault and was probably miserable to this young man. Teneil would need to interfere on his behalf. Gift would either thank her or kill her.

"Mark? Can you come hold this ice for me while I wash my hands?"

Mark jumped up at the request, eager to help. Gift reached for the ice herself, but Teneil shooed her hand away with a wink. Regina used the pitcher of water to pour over Teneil's hands, and when she was finished, Teneil stood. "I'm just going to check on something."

Then she went inside, lay on her bed, and opened a book. She left Gift in the capable hands of the handsome Mark. There was little that could physically be done for Gift. Maybe this would give them a moment to fix any nonphysical damage that may have occurred.

As five-year-olds do, Tapiwa and John were instant best friends and pulled every toy in the house out for inspection. Luke hadn't said much after Regina came out. He just sat awkwardly next to her in a rigid posture as twelve-year-old boys do around pretty girls they have no idea why they like yet.

She spent almost half an hour reading before Teneil heard the gate open and close. She put her book down and sat, waiting for Gift to come and reprimand her. But she never did. Gift quietly slunk to her room to lay down. A few moments later, Teneil was there with fresh ice. "How ya doin'?"

True to the nature of Gift, she said nothing.

"That boy's mighty handsome." Teneil attempted to coax a reaction out of her daughter, but Gift merely removed the bag of cold water, glared at her mother, and put the new ice pack on her face. "How about I make you some fresh cinnamon buns?" That was Gift's only weakness and Teneil only exploited it on rare occasions. Slowly the ice bag lifted, and Gift looked at her mom with hurt eyes. "Oh, baby. I'm sorry. I know you are hurting."

Gift had taken a serious hit and dark rings were forming around both of her eyes. But mom's cinnamon rolls could fix it. "Fine," she said, knowing her mother would require her to speak or worse.

"Not good enough," Teneil insisted. "You know what I need."

Gift tried to roll her eyes, but it hurt. She pulled her lips up in a fake smile.

"No, not that one. I want a real one."

Gift glared.

"Hey, you want cinnamon rolls from scratch? That takes time. All I'm asking in return is for a few teeth."

Gift bared all her teeth in the way a rabid dog smiles.

"Not that one either."

Gift laughed a little.

"There it is! That's the smile I'm looking for." Teneil left the room to make the cure-all.

Teneil was as she was every time she baked: covered in flour and surrounded by a pile of dishes marred by doughy fingerprints. There was a knock at the back gate. "Coming!" Teneil called out, and told her ever-present, tiny shadow, "Go see who is at the gate."

Tapiwa took off like a shot. "Who are you?" She said in the rude way that only small children could get away with.

"You know Mark, Luke, and John? I'm their daddy." He smiled at the little girl.

Tapiwa gave a nod of understanding and yelled, "Mommy! Daddy's here!" and opened the gate to let the stranger in.

Confused, Teneil took off her apron and almost ran into the man on her patio. "Oh!" she cried in surprise.

"I'm so sorry, this little princess let me in," said a classically handsome man. His smile was enchanting, his posture strong and commanding. His eyes were dark and sparkling with humor and compassion. Tapiwa beamed from the man's princess remark and went inside, suddenly remembering she had a crown in her toy box that needed to be worn.

"I'm sorry," Teneil said. She was a little breathless from the startle and a little breathless from the thief before her who had taken it away. "How can I help you?" *Know you, be close to you*, echoed in her mind.

"I'm Mathew." He shook her hand. "Mark, Luke, and John's father."

"I'm Teneil." It was an autopilot response, because her mind was empty.

"It is a pleasure to meet you." He gave her a slight bow, *like a real prince charming*. "Though I wish it was under different circumstances."

"Different circumstances?" Teneil was unable to think of anything past his chiseled jaw and full lips. She was a blank slate, ready for him to paint her like Leo did for Rose on the Titanic.

"I came to check on your daughter. Mark told me he may have hurt her?"

Teneil's mind was confused. *Daughter? Hurt daughter?* She stared blankly at him.

"Gift?" he encouraged her.

"Oh! Gift! Yes! No! Yeah, she's fine."

He let out a deep breath. "Oh, that's good to hear. Mark made it seem like a pretty substantial injury. I'm glad to hear that she's alright."

Irony chose that moment to bring Gift to the door asking for more ibuprofen. The start of some very dark rings and swelling around both of her eyes were visible, as well as the red-white plugs in each nostril.

"Lord above," Matthew whispered to himself, eyes wide in horror. "Is that what Mark did?"

"Just an accident." Teneil turned to Gift. "Baby, go lay back down. I will be right there." Gift sluggishly disappeared into her room again.

"That looks awful!" Matthew said in a hushed but serious tone.

"She'll be fine," Teneil repeated with a reassuring smile. "So what brings you to the neighborhood?"

"I, um. . .work. I-I came for- Are you sure she's okay? Should we get her to a hospital or something?"

She had thought this man could not be more handsome until Teneil saw the concern he held for her girls. Swooning, she said, "No, really, she's fine." Teneil couldn't help batting her eyes and playing with her hair, which was a bad idea considering her fingers were still covered in dough.

Matthew chuckled at her awkwardness and added, "I feel really awful about this. We would like to make it up to you." Then, as an afterthought, he added, "I mean Gift."

Teneil smiled and tried to lean casually against the doorway. She misjudged the distance and stumbled but still tried to play it smooth. "That's not necessary."

"Yes, it is!" Gift shouted from her bedroom, but Teneil ignored her.

Matthew chuckled. "My son broke your daughter."

"I have two more." She waved her hand in dismissal.

He laughed in earnest. "Even so, I think it would reflect badly on our family in our new community if we did not at least try. I insist."

"If you insist." Her voice was dreamy and far away.

"How about dinner? Let us cook for you?"

In about three octaves lower than her regular voice, she said, "Okay. Yeah, no, yeah, that would be nice."

"Tomorrow night?"

"Yeah. Perfect."

"Seven o'clock, okay? It's early but I like to get my youngest into bed by 8:30."

"I love you."

"Excuse me?"

"We'd love to. Do. That. Thang." She was beyond awkward.

"Did you just say 'thang'?"

"Yes, I did. Yeah, and it will haunt me for the rest of my life."

He laughed again. "Alright, then. We will see you tomorrow night."

Chapter Four
IF ONLY HE WAS HANDY

Mrs. Jayne shook her head. "This is a horrible idea!" she told her husband of almost forty years.

"What?" Mr. Jayne was not at all slow-minded, but his love of hunting had left him mostly deaf, especially to the particular tone of his wife's voice.

"She's not going to like this," Mrs. Jayne said a bit more forcefully.

"Who?" Mr. Jayne asked absently, sitting in his recliner and looking through a stack of papers.

"Your daughter!" Mrs. Jayne shouted in frustration.

Mr. Jayne scowled through his ever thickening "reading" glasses. "What about her?!" He could barely hear, but he also did not appreciate being shouted at by his wife. The irony was overwhelming.

Mrs. Jayne, who was also not slow of mind, knew exactly what her husband and son were doing. She rolled her eyes and decided to leave the room. The house was small and over a hundred years old, so Mrs. Jayne finally decided to start the laundry in the basement to drown out the sounds of their plotting.

Mr. Jayne looked across the stack of papers strewn across the coffee table to where his son sat helping him and winked. Talon Jayne, first-born of only two children, laughed and continued inspecting the photos with a critical eye.

"I think it's a great plan," Talon naturally spoke a little loudly, for he shared his father's love of hunting and therefore his range of hearing as well.

"Of course, it is!" Mr. Jayne smiled a wicked smile. Mr. Jayne's goal was to find the perfect husband for his daughter. Teneil had refused any male attention for years, but her living alone in Africa had not been easy on her family. And so, Mr. Jayne had come up with a brilliant plan (or asinine plan, depending on which Jayne you asked).

The plan went roughly like this: Teneil was about to finish a big project in Malawi and had recently complained to them about the difficulty of the work. Each member of the Jayne family would choose a champion to send to Teneil for four days. Teneil would know nothing about this, because no doubt she would spoil it by saying something like "no" or "absolutely not." Mr. Jayne had found an international tour guide company to organize the trip for the men from the Malawian end, so as to not add any untoward burden on his green-eyed sweetie pie. Teneil would have no reason to complain.

None. None whatsoever.

"Okay," Talon said, slamming a photo onto the table. "I have my pick."

Teneil's brother had chosen his champion purely for the reason that the profile had said "ARMY". Talon had joined the ARMY himself at seventeen, forging his mother's signature, and had very recently retired after a fruitful military career. It was not out of duty to his sister that he chose this particular hero, but out of duty to his country. Talon's pick, Ash Redman, AKA "Red", had a neck thicker than his head. With his military service completed, Red ran a chain of fitness stores in . . .

But that was where Talon stopped reading. *Good,* he thought. *My sister needs a strong man.*

Mr. Jayne had picked his man before he ever brought up this brilliant idea to anyone else. He had met his champion in a gas station parking lot last week. His name was, aahh. . . Mr. Jayne thought for a short moment before concluding that names were not important. The man drove a jacked up pickup truck that pulled a trailer of snowmobiles. It was the fresh set of elk antlers that caught Mr. Jayne's eye.

They quickly became engrossed in hunting conversation, which then evolved into sports, which devolved back into hunting. In Mr. Jayne's eyes, his champion was perfect. Mr. Jayne had wasted no time in showing him a photo of his daughter and asking if the man had ever been to Africa. It turned out he had, twice, to South Africa for guided hunts. What more did Teneil need?

Mrs. Jayne refused to pick from the countless photos her husband and son pushed on her. This was ridiculous. Her daughter was, "never going to speak to us again if we carry on this way." She stood, mumbling her way through a basket of clean clothes. "What did Teneil ever do to deserve this?"

She was struck with a memory from last April Fool's Day, when Teneil had paid the local Malawian police to put her in handcuffs. Teneil had posted a story on social media that she had been arrested on charges of a stolen car, which about gave Mrs. Jayne (along with everyone else) a heart attack. The Jayne family was known for elaborate jokes, but that was definitely the worst joke ever (or the best, depending on which Jayne you asked). As she folded the last pair of socks, Mrs. Jayne couldn't help the grin that broke her brooding. Suddenly she knew exactly who she was going to send as her champion.

Teneil needed many things. She needed 200,000 bricks, she needed sixteen tons of cobblestone, she needed five trucks of cement, and she needed the dang electricity hooked up by the guy who promised to be at the new school she was building two weeks ago. When she saw the truck coming down the dry, dusty road she thought she may have reason to celebrate.

Shading her eyes, she stood at the end of the drive and waited for them. The day was hot and her second-hand, black leather, military boots felt like foot prison. The sun was a lot for her pale skin, so she had learned to wear long, loose fitting, lightweight cargo pants with a long sleeve, button up, linen shirt. An old, brown leather hat that reminded her a bit of Indiana Jones, with a pair of brown aviators protecting her eyes from the sun and dirt.

Her old hat cocked to one side and her face twisted in confusion when she saw the side of the truck read "Guided Africa, Tanzania" with a koala bear winking and giving a thumbs up. Three men, clearly foreigners, stepped out and walked toward her. Teneil flashed each of them a smile. "You boys lost?"

"No, ma'am. We are here to help," said the man who was a walking, talking, brickhouse.

Her head cocked to the other side, like a dog trying to sort out a new sound. "Are you here for the electric, then?" She could reason nothing else. They all responded at the same time, and she couldn't quite understand any of their explanations. "Hold on," she cut in. "I'm confused. What are you doing here?"

"We're here for you, darlin." The one in a cowboy hat and tank top winked at her, then backed it up with a greasy smile that promised he was in fact here for her. . .all of her.

Her nose wrinkled in the same way it did when she contemplated stepping on a cockroach, but then remembered that she would have to clean up the mess if she did.

"Hello, Teneil." She looked at the boy, using the term "boy" because surely, he was not a man fully grown? Then a shock of recognition hit her.

"Hubert?!" she gasped.

"Nice to see you again!" His smile was full of teeth that seemed to be too large for his face. Actually, everything seemed to be a little too large for him: his mouth, his nose, and his big watery eyes. She figured that was mostly because of his Coke bottle lenses; all of his features seemed as if they matured faster than his bone structure. Teneil knew Hubert had to be about twenty-five now, so she didn't expect him to fill in much more than this.

This boy had been in love with Teneil since she had babysat him during the summer of her junior year. He had been eight at the time and she thought it was strange that he needed a babysitter at all until she saw how many medications he was on. Allergic to everything on God's green earth, she had given him an epinephrine shot once because he had fallen into a patch of grass.

"What in the world are you doing here, Hubert?" Genuine concern and confusion wove in her voice. She hadn't ever noticed how much grass was in Africa until she saw Hubert standing here. Teneil looked around, now seeing the green blades like knives that made up the six-foot-tall patches of grass, their flowering stocks in full deadly bloom.

"Your mom invited me!" He smiled his Hubert smile. As large as his teeth were, his gums still seemed to dominate his face.

"My mom?" Confusion replaced panic.

The brick house spoke up: "We are just a group of guys who knew that you needed help and we have come here to do it. I can do just about anything, so tell me where you need me." He clapped his monstrous hands and the sound was deafening.

"You came here from America to help me?" Teneil was fully staffed with the workers she had used for years, but she was not ever going to turn down free help. "Um, okay then!" She was still a little uneasy, but not ungrateful. "That's great!" She motioned for the three newcomers to follow her to the storage room to outfit them with shovels and direct them to jobs.

She glanced back at the tour guide truck in the driveway and noticed another man who remained in the driver's seat. "He's not coming?"

"He's just the driver, sugar," the cowboy explained and winked at her.

Teneil squinted in the sun and watched as the man in the truck adjusted his seat, put his feet on the dash, and covered his face with his hat. If the cowboy's comment had upset him, he hadn't let it show.

Teneil was bouncing between one roof being set, several walls being painted, and bricks being laid. The almost-school that sat before her was the biggest project she had done yet, and she was almost finished. That meant there were very few materials remaining and nothing was ever where it was supposed to be. The three men were not so much help as they were extra side projects she now had to manage.

The "brick house" she found out was ironically named "Red." When he'd properly introduced himself, the perfect name, Red Brick House, made her snort-laugh. Then she had to cover her uncouth snort with a mock sneeze and an awkward declaration that, "A fly flew in my nose." As soon as the words came out, she realized they sounded more believable in her head.

But instead of letting it go, Teneil backed herself up with a light outward blow through her nose, just for effect. Only she had been breathing dirt all day, and a massive brown booger came out instead. Slightly mortified, she turned away from Red and blew her nose into her handkerchief. When she glanced back, she saw a very green brick house watching in perplexed disgust.

"I got it," she assured him, then more awkwardly walked away.

Cowboy turned out to be named Tex that fitted him perfectly. Every time she went by him, he attempted to grab her attention, but she was truly too busy managing the hectic goings on of her worksite. More than anything, on top of the deadlines and the deliveries, she had to make sure that poor little Hubert didn't die.

Several times Hubert had gone into the bush with her crew to haul more bricks, and each time he had come back out, Teneil started breathing again. With one brick in each hand, he was sweating through his slacks and polo. Teneil had to hand it to the kid as the grueling hours went by; he was really holding on in this heat. "Hey, Hubert!" she called as soon as she had a moment. "Come here, would ya?"

Hubert dropped his bricks and ran. He ran how one of those sticky hands that you get out of a $.50 machine would run, if it could run. Teneil was not fond of the saying but, "Bless his little heart" escaped her lips. In the ten meters that he ran to the storage room he was wheezing.

"Hi, Teneil! It's so nice to see you."

"Yeah!" she replied, trying to match his enthusiasm. "I was thinking that too! 'Nice'! Totally nice! I just, um, you know, wanted to catch up. . .see how things are with you and home?"

"Oh yeah! Great!"

"You mentioned my mom earlier. How is she?" Teneil smiled, but her mind was too busy to make the happy gesture authentic. Her mom was involved in this? Had she missed something? She talked to her family at least once a week, or at the very least every two weeks. . .at the very, very least once a month. Actually, *when was the last time they talked?*

"So good! They were all so nice to put this together!" He produced a small envelope from his pocket. "Your mom told me I should give this to you right away. Sorry, I was a little overwhelmed when I got here."

"No problem, Hubert. I'm just so happy you could come. How long are ya here?"

"Just four days, but I'm so excited! This is great!"

Seeing his bright, pink gums light up his overly pale face reminded Teneil of something. "Have you put any sunblock on? Here, take mine."

She pulled out a tube of lotion from one of her bags. "Don't forget your ears and neck."

"Yeah, yeah, I will!" Hubert tinted himself even whiter with a far more than generous amount of the thick, white, SPF paint that had only diluted a little in his sweaty palms.

Opening the note, Teneil noticed her mother's handwriting. It read: "**Bill,**" Her mother's nickname for her:

> "**Bet you are just as mixed up as a rooster in a rabbit hutch right now. Frankly, I was against this whole thing. But you know your father and brother. We were all supposed to pick someone to send, so I will let you figure out who is who. Have fun with Hubert. Enjoy the chocolate that I put in his bag for you.**
>
> **I love you, Mom**
>
> **PS: Next time you go to jail it better be for real.**"

You have got to be kidding. Still, she was impressed. Truly. How much more loving could a family be? "Hey Hubert?" Teneil began, tucking the letter away. "Could you do me a massive favor? Could you get water for everyone on the site? But start with you first."

He took off at a sprint. Water boy was a great job for him. Maybe she could keep him alive for four days.

"That boy runs like a jello tower in an earthquake," came a man's voice behind her.

Teneil laughed and turned her attention to the man lounging in his truck. "You're American?" she asked, noticing his accent.

"Yeah. Why not?"

"Well, you are in Malawi, in a Tanzanian truck, with an Australian logo?" He quietly waited for her to go on. "That makes sense to you?" she finally pushed.

"No, I could see your confusion." He leaned back and covered his face with his hat.

Well, at least we cleared that up. She asked, "My parents, did they send you, too?"

He raised his hat just enough to say, "Your dad's a real nice guy."

"Mm, yeah. . ." That wasn't exactly the word she would have used today. "He's great. Crazy and highly inappropriate, but good people."

She stood for an awkward amount of time, unsure of how to respond to the man who seemingly fell asleep during his very curious introduction. Finally, she awkwardly turned back to the job at hand.

Red was turning cement with a shovel better than a truck could. Tex was setting bricks. She had her bricklayers go in behind him to fix all of his work, but she figured it wouldn't cost too much in overtime.

"How are you doing, Tex?" She felt bad that he'd chosen the only job in the sun.

Tex didn't feel bad; in fact, he seemed ready. As if he had been waiting all day for his cue, he turned to face her fully. "It's warm out here," he said, putting his trowel down and pulling his shirt off in one fluid movement. He was not in bad shape, but next to the Red Brick House, everyone looked lazy.

"You probably want to keep your shirt on," Teneil suggested, holding back a laugh. Even the Malawians wore long sleeves to protect themselves from the sun. "Hubert? Bring Tex some water, would ya, buddy?"

"You worried about me, darlin'?" Tex leaned his forearms on the half-built wall, a prime flexing position that had the added bonus of putting himself just a little bit closer to her. "I'll be alright." He sucked air through his front teeth.

He wouldn't, though; Teneil knew that. The crew did too, and they had a running bet on how long it would take before Tex broke beneath the unforgiving lashes of the African sun. Within about thirty minutes, Tex's skin was itching. He continued pouring water on himself, which kept Hubert busy, but made the burning worse.

Pride, that was what had kept him topless until the day's end. He was shivering by the time they called it a day and he got back into the truck. No one had won the bet; the closest had been off by several hours.

"Sure you are okay, darlin'?" Teneil asked, not entirely unkind.

Tex said nothing but whimpered as the other two climbed in around him.

"Thanks a lot for your help today, guys. Why don't you all take the day off tomorrow and get yourselves settled? I know it's a long journey."

Even Red was visibly beat. "You run a mean crew! That was the best workout I have had in years. Mind if I come back tomorrow?"

"Um, yeah, sure!" She couldn't deny that he, at least, had been a massive help.

Hubert agreed that he would also come, once he found out Teneil would be there. Their driver tipped his hat. "See you tomorrow."

By seven the next morning, she'd managed the short distance across town to the lodge the men had been put in. It was by far the grandest in the area. The lodge was known for its extensive gardens and views of the bay. That was all well and good, but Teneil also knew they made a nice breakfast plate. This was a good excuse for waffles, real coffee, sausages, and more waffles. Also, to greet her American visitors properly.

She had been feeling badly about her reaction to them the day before. They had come far to help her, regardless of their motivations, and she could at least be grateful, no matter how inconveniencing it may be. She found them already at breakfast. . .well, not all of them. "Where is Tex?"

"Last time I saw, he was lying face down while Hubert over there rubbed aloe onto his lobster red hide." Red laughed through his answer. "Serves him right."

Teneil grabbed a waffle off a tray on the table and sat down to eat. Today was going to be a good day. Full and good. She had gotten confirmation that morning that the electricity would finally be installed today, and really, she couldn't wait anymore. Currently, she'd been using one of the local business's generators and it was costing a fortune for her to rent. Also, she got a message that the carpenters had dropped off a set of door frames, which meant the walls could go up on the last schoolhouse building.

They arrived on the site just after 8:00am, and most of the crew was already there. Red started stretching, which made many of the Malawian workers laugh, but Teneil knew they all respected him after yesterday. Hubert filled water jugs and, at Teneil's request, helped Grandmother Abi, who was responsible for preparing the lunch for the workers.

The request was not so much for Hubert as it was for the hard as nails Abi. The grandmother that looked scornful, even when laughing, could be sixty or three hundred years old, depending on who you asked. But she was spry enough to feed Teneil's small army of workers every day.

Grandmother Abi prepared the food on charcoal, in pots large enough to bathe a small child in. Several times Teneil had offered to hire another person to help, but Abi flat-refused. It wasn't pride; she just hated folks in her way. In fact, Teneil had to pay an extra day's wages to her upon making the request that Hubert join her. But once Abi had the money in hand, she lit up like a Christmas tree, delighted in the lanky man's presence.

Teneil barely had a chance to turn around and begin to manage the next task when her foreman tracked her down. "Teneil, we have a problem."

He led her over to where the carpenters had delivered the door frames. Her jaw fell open and the words that got started in her throat rolled over and died on her tongue. The wooden frames were massive, she guessed at least double the size they ordered. Teneil laughed at the monstrous frames. "What?" she finally managed.

Things like this always happened here. Simple misunderstandings were a part of life she could handle, but this? She had worked with this same carpenter for years and she couldn't wait to ask him what had happened. There was only one problem: these would never fit in her hatchback. If only she had a truck. Her legs were already moving toward the upbeat koala parked in the shade on the corner of the property.

"Good morning!" she said cheerfully to the driver. The man was in his usual spot with his feet on the dash, hat over his face. No response. Hesitantly, she reached through the window. Unsure of where to touch him, she finally tapped his shoulder. "Excuse me?" Still nothing. Again, "Excuse me?" Why hadn't she asked his name yesterday? She finally, slowly, tipped his hat off his face. He looked so peaceful sleeping.

"That's so rude," he said abruptly, which made her jump and hit her head on the door frame that she had been leaning into. "And you deserved that."

"Can you help me?" she hissed, rubbing the top of her head.

"What do you want?"

"I need to get these frames back to the carpenter's shop and get new ones made. I'll pay for your gas," she explained, finally giving up on massaging the goose egg that was forming.

"No," he said flatly.

"No?"

"No."

She just stood there, speechless for a while. "W-why not?" She was trying not to be mad but honestly, how lazy could this man be? He'd sat here all day yesterday waiting for the others to finish their work, and it certainly seemed like he was planning on doing the same thing today. If there was one thing Teneil hated, it was a perfectly capable lazy man. She was just about to give him a lecture on that very thing when he said:

"Because you didn't say please."

She folded her arms and took a long breath, trying not to smile. "Please?"

"Too late now. Maybe next time."

He put his hat back on his head and feigned sleeping.

She stared at him, perplexed, before walking away. He used one finger to raise the corner of his hat and watched her go. When she turned around abruptly and walked back, he lowered his hat as quickly as he could.

Teneil stopped next to his truck again. "Kind sir." She put on a proper and dramatic voice this time. "Master of sleep and king of the koala." That part made him laugh under his hat. "Bestow your generosity on my incongruous request."

"'Incongruous.' Good word," he said under his hat.

"Shut up," she snapped. "I'm groveling here."

"Sorry, carry on." He waved a hand in her direction, allowing the royal pardon to continue.

"Please, M'Lord, grace me with the assistance of your 500-steed powered buggy."

He laughed in earnest. "That will work, but I want gas and a cold drink."

"Done!" she agreed, and he went out to help her load and tie down the massive wooden frames in the truck's bed.

Once the truck was started back up, he rolled up the windows and turned on the AC. "M'Lord is gracious indeed," Teneil said, closing her eyes and feeling the cool breeze.

"Ma'name is Gideon." He laughed at her.

"Gideon, like the Bible story?"

"You know it?" he asked.

"It's one of my favorites. Gideon, a *nobody*, really," she looked pointedly at him, "who took on a massive army with a handful of men."

"My parents are missionaries in Tanzania," he pronounced the name Tan-zan-ya, the traditional African way. "I was born there. I still live up that way." The border to Tanzania was only a few hours from where she lived in Malawi.

"So, you never left?"

"No, I went to school in America, but I just couldn't make it fit. The culture there, it's just so. . ." He faded off and struggled with the right word.

"Fast?" she offered.

"Yeah." He looked at her briefly. "Fast and cruel." His attention went back to the road again. There was a moment of silence. "And you? How did you end up here?"

"It's a long story."

"We got a long journey," he said.

And so, she told him. Teneil began at the beginning, explaining how she'd sold everything she had and only meant to be in Malawi for two months. She told him about how God had tricked her into the desire of her heart: a life where she lived to love.

Finally, they arrived at the carpenter's shop. Teneil laughed until she had tears in her eyes when they went inside and spoke to the shop owner. The paper the carpenter had written his notes on ended with "x2". Teneil and the carpenter knew "x2" meant "two frames", but the apprentice he had subbed the job out to had doubled the size of all the measurements instead.

The carpenter apologized profusely and offered to do the job right then, having the frames finished within the hour. Teneil agreed, still red faced from laughing.

"Come on, let's go get your cold drink," she said to Gideon.

"Do you ever get mad?" he asked. "I mean, just in the last two days, I have watched you laugh your way through some stuff that would make most folks lose their minds. You aren't going to snap at some point, are you?"

She gave that some serious thought. In the past, she definitely had let things bottle up inside, causing a complete meltdown. But nowadays, particularly today, she felt happy, with no explosions looming. "I don't think so." She took a long drink off her ice-cold ginger beer.

"You sure?"

"Things like this happen all the time. I've learned to roll with it."

"And the three men your father sent? That a frequent complication, too?" He laughed.

Teneil rolled her eyes. "No, thank God. But I don't expect much trouble from Tex. It should take him the remaining couple days he has here to heal enough just to go home. I like Red. He's a nice guy, but he seems more interested in turning concrete than wooing me."

"And Hubert?"

"Oh." She gave Gideon a wink. "Hubert's a sure thing." Gideon laughed so hard that orange Fanta came out of his nose.

On the way back to the site, normal frames in tow, she asked, "So you just drive people around?"

He looked at her sideways. "No," he amended. "Not usually. I do all kinds of different things. I lead safaris, for bird enthusiasts mostly. Some scientists and researchers. Even anthropologists and archaeologists from around the globe. They know all about Africa from books, but they don't know anything about really living in the bush. I just keep men smarter than myself alive long enough to publish their brilliance."

Teneil thought about Lewis and Clark, who were often credited with discovering the "new world", though they wouldn't have lasted a day without their true American tour guide.

"So, you are basically Sacagawea?" she teased.

"Something like that," he smiled.

"Can I ask you a serious question?" She didn't wait for a reply. "What's with the koala bear?"

"You don't like koala bears?"

"Well, they aren't exactly native to Africa."

"What kinda sick person doesn't like koala bears?"

"I didn't say that."

"So, you do like them."

"Of course, who doesn't like koala bears?"

"Exactly."

"That's. . ." She rolled her eyes but laughed, too.

He said nothing else, only focused on the road.

Back at the school, the frames were quickly unloaded and set in place. Teneil headed straight for the back side of the finished building and began shouting in a language that Gideon did not understand. Just for safe measure, he walked around the corner to see what the problem was.

There was an empty green electrical box hanging on the wall with a few disconnected wires sticking out. Teneil held a phone on speaker as it rang, and she was not smiling.

"Bho bho," a man answered her call.

Teneil let loose a torrent of language that made the Malawian men around her take a step back, but several broke out in laughter. "It's an empty box!" she shouted in English. "What do I do with an empty box?!" She hung up the phone and sat down. The men around her went back about their business, but Teneil sat, staring angrily at the green box.

"So, this is you mad?" Gideon guessed.

She glanced up at him and let out a deep breath. "He was supposed to be here two weeks ago. We've needed the electricity hooked up. I'm renting that generator over there by the month. Tomorrow is the first and I can't afford another month, but if I don't pay for it, we can't keep working. If I do pay for it, I can't pay the workers." She managed another deep breath. "Any ideas?"

He examined the side of the building and noticed that the only thing left to hook up were the circuit breakers. The electrical boxes themselves were nowhere to be seen. "I can finish it for you," he offered.

"Can you do this? Really?!" Teneil was on her feet and her smile was back.

He loved how quickly her smile resurfaced. "Be right back," he said and hopped in his truck to get to the hardware store before they closed for the day. But he did not return even after the sun started to set.

The crew had left by then, and Teneil waited with Red and Hubert for a long while more before loading them in her small car and driving them back to the lodge herself. There was no way for her to get a hold of Gideon to make sure he was okay or ask why he'd just disappeared.

She was admittedly worried and a little irritated, but there was nothing she could do, so she stopped by to see Tex, who was absolutely no better than the previous day. But he was, in fact, quite a bit drunker. "How ya feeling, buddy?" she asked, kneeling before the bed where he laid face down.

"Hey, darlin," he said with a slow, painful slur. This time it did not bother her.

"Hey, cowboy," she said as if she was coxing an injured dog. "How you feeling?"

"Good, good," he murmured. "Just hurts to be alive is all."

She laughed a bit, but the blisters on his back were no joke. She truly felt bad for the guy. "Can I get you anything?"

"Whiskey," he replied. "Big one."

"You got it." She chuckled and headed to the lodge's bar. No one was there and the lights were out. That was odd, considering the time of evening, "Are you guys closed?" she asked a server who was sitting at one of the dining tables, looking bored out of her mind.

"Yeah," she replied lazily. "Someone stole all of our breakers for the kitchen so we can't make anything."

"You're joking." It seemed that Teneil was talking to the girl in front of her, but she was actually focused on the image that had formed in her mind of Gideon breaking into the electrical box of the lodge and stealing their breakers.

She tried to disapprove but crawled into bed that night with a smile on her face. The next morning, she found Gideon at the breakfast table with the others.

"We missed you at dinner last night, Gideon." Teneil took a bite of her waffle and looked knowingly at him.

"I ate in town," he shared with a smooth smile.

Red looked between them and laughed to himself. "We leave tomorrow."

"So soon?" Teneil asked, looking between them all. All but Tex, who was still in his

room.

"Four days, and today is day three. Our flight leaves tomorrow afternoon. Should probably head out early just in case the roads. . ." Red let the thought trail off, feeling the tension at the table.

"Well, that's a shame. It's a long trip to come for such a short time." Teneil refused to look at the end of the table where Gideon had stopped eating.

Power was on at the school, and even the workers rejoiced when she flipped on the switch that lit up the first two buildings. That day, Grandma Abi refused to take more money for keeping Hubert busy. The boy was so eager to work that Abi had gotten over her prejudice and now looked at him like a son; not one she would brag about, but a son, nonetheless. Hubert never changed.

Red worked tirelessly all day. Teneil had never seen such a hard worker. "I think we'll miss you here, Red."

"Actually. . ." Red stood, sweat pouring from him. "I had a thought, if you're interested. I teach a high intensity training class and I would love to bring them here for an intensity retreat."

She thought of how much work an entire team of Reds could accomplish and heartily welcomed them.

Gideon had left earlier that morning to buy replacement parts from the hardware store that had closed early the night before. He left them in a bag at the front desk of the lodge with a note that just said, "Thank you." When he got back to the job site, Teneil was there waiting.

"I can't believe you did that," she hissed with more awe than disapproval in her voice.

"Did what?" He winked at her.

"Seriously, I don't know how to thank you." She had left the door wide open for him, in case he was interested in her thanking him any sort of way. . .like, perhaps, dinner? But he refused to walk through it.

"No need." He tipped his hat to her, and she noticed his blackened nails.

"Nice polish." She lifted an eyebrow, picturing him taking a shock last night that was strong enough to make that kind of damage.

He curled his hand into a fist. "Was born with it," he said while putting his feet up on the dash of his truck. "If you will excuse me," he added as he tipped his hat over his face, "it's time for my nap."

She smiled at him but walked away.

The next morning, she came early to say goodbye. Red picked her up and kissed her on the cheek. "Your brother is right to be so proud of you. You did not disappoint." He squeezed her tight enough to make her cry out, then dropped her. Red threw his bag in the back of the truck and got in the front seat.

Tex limped over to her. "I'm sorry," he said.

"For what?"

"Tell your dad he can still hunt on my land." He attempted to hug her, but he had a hard time raising his arms. Instead, he patted her on the shoulder and got in the truck.

Hubert, sweet, darling Hubert, was next. His eyes full of tears, he wrapped his arms around her.

"Oh, Hubert. I'm so proud of you." Teneil smiled at him. "I tell you what: if I was ten years younger. . ." She winked.

He blinked rapidly at her. "What?"

"It- it's an expression!" She sighed. "It means that if I was your age, we would be perfect for each other."

His eyes went wide now. "You know I always thought that too?"

"Really?!"

"Yes! Even ask my mom. I have said that so many times!"

She grinned. "Someday, Hubert, you are going to make a woman very happy." She kissed him on the cheek and watched the bright red creep all the way around his neck as he got in the truck.

"Well," Teneil said, looking at Gideon.

"Well." Gideon held her gaze for a long moment, studying her features in the hope he could draw her in his mind later, like he had since the moment he first saw her. Then he turned and got in his truck. The airport was five hours away, and he knew better than to drive recklessly on these roads.

Teneil was cleaning the cement off the shovels at the day's end, having sent everyone home already. She had pushed them all so hard this last week and they had really come through for her. That, and she just wasn't ready for this day to be finished. Once she fell asleep, her time with Gideon would officially be over. So, she was doing her best to stretch the evening's hours out as much as possible. Dusk brought the call of frogs and crickets when she finally closed the lock on the storage room and made to leave.

She let out a scream when she saw a man standing right behind her in the darkness. She fell back against the door before recognizing the laugh of Gideon. "What are you doing?" she demanded. Teneil laughed at herself but mostly because he was laughing so hysterically. The laughter died a bit and she asked again, "Gideon, what are you doing here?"

He took a couple deep breaths and smiled at her. "I thought," he said between breaths, "maybe you needed me."

EPILOGUE

Mrs. Jayne sat for almost three hours listening to Hubert's cliff notes from his trip. Most of them were about a sour-faced woman named Abi and pumping water at a well. Mrs. Jayne accepted this as her punishment for sending Hubert in the first place. Just as he was about to leave, Hubert burst out, "Oh! I was supposed to give this to you right away, but I was so excited I forgot!" He produced a folded envelope from his pocket.

Mrs. Jayne thanked him and saw him out door. The note read:

> **"Mommy dearest, well played. Bravo to the whole family. Tell father I have secured him the land he was coveting for next year's hunt. I'm taking some time off to go to Tanzania for a hunt of my own. There's something I need up that way. Wish me luck! I love you, Bill."**

Chapter Five
IF ONLY HE WAS SUPERHUMAN

To read this story properly, you will need to step into my head for a moment. Please, allow me to set the stage. To begin, create an image of a city in your mind, one that feels like Dick Tracy and Batman got married and had a baby. Paint that lovechild in black and white. Got it? Give the dark alleyways a touch of rain. Yeah, nice. Now add a bluesy saxophone and a whole lot of steam.

This was a city married to crime with corruption as its mistress. It was hard, but its people were harder. Nkhata Bay, the Gotham of Malawi. Steam rose alongside the music of the busy city streets. She crouched alone on top of the city *(cue saxophone solo here)*. Her city *(another saxophone solo)*. Or rather, it would be her city, when she took it back from the evil that threatened to overwhelm it. She would, too. Teneil didn't know how to lose *(saxophone crescendo)*.

She leapt from the building, the only sound was her cape whipping through the wind. She was right on time. She had been scouting this dock for weeks; she knew it was the hub for the new synthetic drug "Blue". Blue was an artificial heroin, cheaper and with more kick. She had heard of several people already overdosing on the drug that had only been on the street for merely months.

"You boys come here often?" she asked the men loading the trucks.

She was greeted with shouts of, "It's her!" and, "Get her!" A few tried to run away, but she wasn't worried about them; she had already used her super strength to warp the metal on the gates. No one was going anywhere tonight, except maybe prison.

Using her super speed was like fighting in slow motion. These boys never stood a chance. There where ten of them, and in as many moves, Teneil had them all incapacitated. It was all thanks to a mix of every martial art in the world that she learned from an extensive ten-minute montage almost four years ago. She had promised her Kung Fu master on his deathbed that she would protect the innocent, and because of that promise she had never stopped fighting. These men went down easy. . .too easy. Something wasn't right.

The next move was to check the truck and then call in the authorities with an anonymous tip, of course. They would know it was her. The last dozen busts had been, but she liked to remain annoyingly aloof. Teneil picked up the first shipment box and knew right away that it was wrong; this was too light. . .it was empty, and so was the next, and next.

She'd been set up. Her blood boiled and she couldn't contain her frustration. "*Ahhh!*" She let her battle cry ring out into the rain. And then she saw the red light of the camera, high in the upper corner of the warehouse. Someone had set her up, and they were watching her. She felt violated, manipulated, but most of all angry. How could she have let this happen? Teneil palmed a throwing knife and in one perfect swing, she clove the camera in two and flew away. . .because she could also fly.

Not until she entered her own house did she feel the sting. The cut that now screamed across her back had been her one misstep tonight. She had thought it was a lead pipe when it struck her, but by the looks of it, it had actually been a machete. The suit she wore was lined on the back and torso with a thick leather hide, it did nothing for her figure except keep it in one piece.

She peeled back the torn material with a hiss when she saw the damage beneath. Even in the small round mirror that hung on her wall she could easily tell that the wound was deep, and it needed stitches. She knew the face of the man who had struck her, and her mouth curved into a twisted smile. The goon was no doubt the hero of his crew today, but tomorrow she would pay him a much more personal visit. The simple act of turning her head was agony; she couldn't help the curse that made it past her lips. There was no way she could stitch her own back. "Shower first," she told herself.

The water was cold, and she let it wash over her for a good long while before ruining a towel by wrapping it around her freshly bleeding back. She took four ibuprofen and grabbed the bottle of 100% proof alcohol she'd kept for just this reason. Knowing she would likely black out from the pain or blood loss, Teneil sat down in the center of her bare apartment.

She bit down on a stick of soft wood and, with trembling hands but without hesitation, poured the liquid fire down her back. The pain was excruciating, and she swayed, but did not go out fully. Shame. She was hoping she would black out and make the pain stop for even a moment, but no; she felt everything. She finally spit the stick out, drool and a little blood from her bit lip pooling on the floor as she sat, unable to move.

Teneil felt him. Someone had entered her apartment. Every part of her tensed, replacing her pain with adrenaline. She was a creature of pure instinct, always ready for a fight. In the middle of the bare floor, naked except for the blood-stained towel, she had no weapon, but she'd never needed a weapon. She sprung in a fluid spinning kick and connected with him. It wasn't his face like she had hoped for; he was faster than her and caught her leg. Before she could counter, she went down, flat on her back.

She sucked in her breath, but she didn't feel the pain fully. She got back up quickly and attacked again. Whoever this guy was, he was fast and strong. Somehow, he'd anticipated her every move. On and on, every punch, every kick, was blocked but never countered. The harder she tried, the quicker she failed, and the more damage her apartment took. She was wasting precious energy and soon she swayed and fell against the door frame. "Who- who are you?" she managed to gasp.

"A friend," the man said coolly.

"A friend?" she repeated with a laugh. Her adrenaline was wearing off and she struggled to keep the blackness from swallowing her vision. "Why are you attacking me?"

"I didn't; you attacked me."

"You broke into my house," she bit back.

"I should have knocked, that's true. But I saw the blood and I was worried."

At his words, strength left her knees and Teneil sank to the floor. He rushed to her side, but when he put his arm around her shoulders she gasped in pain. His arm came back slick with blood. The copper tang of the blood trail he had followed to her now overwhelmed him. Touching her, like everyone else, meant he felt exactly what she felt. He shared her pain, and he had a hard time keeping his words from shaking.

"You just don't know when to quit, do you?" There was a touch of admiration in his voice. She had seemed so strong but now he could feel that it had all been bravado. There was nothing left in her; she was weak. Her utter defenselessness called him on a primal level. "You need stitches."

She said nothing, unable to argue. He found her medical kit in the bathroom easily enough and carefully laid her face down on the bare floor. She didn't make a sound while he stitched her up, starting on her shoulder blade and working his way down, slowly, respectfully, adjusting the towel to her opposite hip. She hated that she needed help, but she was grateful this "friend" had come when he had. Those two emotions were so strong and conflicting she was left with nothing to say.

"My name is Michael," the man said at last. "I came a long way to find you. I have heard about your abilities."

"Hope I didn't disappoint," she said, pretentious even while laying half-naked and helpless on the floor.

"Not at all. You've lost a lot of blood, otherwise I think you may have presented a challenge to me."

He was cocky and arrogant, but after seeing his skills, she supposed that was his right. From the time her Kung Fu master died, she had never once lost a fight, fair or otherwise. With Michael, she hadn't landed a single blow. She wanted to hit him as much as she wanted his autograph. And again, her two conflicting emotions left her speechless.

"One more stitch and we are done," he said from above her. The sound of the surgical scissors cutting the line punctuated his sentence.

"Clearly you have done this before."

"Stitches? Yes," he laughed.

Stubborn, she refused his hand and sat herself up so she could face him. "Are you stalking me?" she asked seriously.

"Yes."

She narrowed her eyebrows, doing her best not to let any surprise or pain show from the tension in her back muscles. "Why? If you wanted me dead, you could have killed me a dozen times."

"I don't want you dead."

"Clearly," she snapped impatiently. "So, what is it, then?"

"I just have a few questions."

"In exchange for the stitches, I will give you three."

"Where did you get your abilities?"

"God."

He smiled, and maybe it was the blood loss or the pale light of the moon's glow, but she found that smile charming, you know, for a stalker. "How interesting. . ." he mused. "What exactly can you do?"

"Anything."

"Anything?" He raised his eyebrows.

"With God, all things are possible." She gave him a sassy grin, but there was blood on her teeth.

He chuckled, and the sound echoed pleasantly around the empty room. "All things, except beating me."

Teneil's face fell and her body coiled, ready for another round.

"Don't," he spoke as if she was a wounded feral beast, not commanding but pleading. She liked that. "I was only joking. You will break open your stitches."

"You were not joking," she said coldly.

"Maybe that's because you are not supposed to fight me."

"Doubtful." Her smile worked its way back onto her face. "That's two questions. One more and we are done here."

"We should work together."

"Sorry, that's not a question."

"Can't you feel it?"

"Is that your question. . .? Can I *feel* it?" Her voice dripped with sarcasm.

"We are the same, you and I." He looked at her, the scars and bruises only making her more beautiful for the sacrifices she made to protect others. He had spent his entire life doing exactly the same, having had his montage at the tender age of seven. He was already thinking of all they could accomplish together. "When I first saw you, I knew."

"You knew?" She was acting cool, but she had felt it, too. There was a sort of intended feel about him, but due to the pain and humiliation of the night, there was no way she would agree with him on anything right now. "What exactly do you 'know'?"

"I have searched the world over," he explained, serious lines showing up around his eyes and mouth told her the truth of what was a long, arduous, journey. "I have been to the farthest corners looking for you." Longing, joy, pain, gratitude, rest, and excitement, all sparked in the depths of his eyes.

Teneil swallowed, her throat suddenly dry. "For me?" she asked. "What did I do?"

"Do? It is not what you can do, it is who you are."

"And who do you think I am?"

"You are bone of my bone and flesh of my flesh."

Right. She concluded, then, that he was insane. "First off," she began, "not a fan of the word 'flesh' being used in everyday conversation. Who talks like that?" She mocked his deep voice: "Bone of my bone?" Her laughter pulled on her stitches, but she couldn't stop.

He sat, unmoved, and let her chortle. Finally, he rolled his eyes. "Would it help if I told you that I know who set you up tonight."

Her laughter died in her throat, and anger burned bright in her chest at the prospect of catching whoever had made her life hell tonight.

"We can get him. I know where he is and what his next move is. Just say yes. Say yes, stand by my side, and we can end this once and for all."

"How do I know that they didn't send you?"

"They didn't."

"Well, I guess that settles it," she scoffed, not trying to hide her skepticism.

"There is only one way that you are going to know for sure." He moved to sit directly across from her. "I know you."

"You don't know anything about me."

"I don't need to know anything *about* you," he replied smoothly. "I know what you stand for. I know the God you serve, and I know the trail of gratitude and healing that you leave everywhere you go. I may not know what you like to eat or what kind of perfume you prefer but make no mistake: I know you."

"But I don't know anything about you."

"I'm just the same as you. What more do you need to know?"

"If you were the same as me, you would know the answer to that question."

He gave her a knowing nod. "I understand that you have been betrayed before. I'm not them."

"Such pretty words from such pretty lips. Unfortunately, your spell has no effect on me."

"I'm not trying to trick you. I'm serious."

"So am I. You have all the passion of a teenage vampire angst romance novel. It's a little over the top."

He put his hand to his chest. "Team Jacob."

She gave a proper snort-laugh. "You're absurd."

"I want to show you something." He attempted to put his hand on her back, but she jerked away from him like an abused pup. "Please. Trust me just this one time."

The cautious expression never left her face, but Teneil stopped retreating. It was true that if he wanted her dead, he would have easily killed her. His hand was slightly cool, and it did not hurt where it touched her tender wound. In fact, there was no pain at all. His hand grew colder, and she felt a terrible itch but also the perfect scratch. She could not help the moan that escaped her lips.

Then the coolness grew to warmth. It started on her back and slowly wrapped around her whole body. She hadn't even known that she was cold until he showed her warmth. She felt the cool kisses of the cuts and bruises mending across her body, but there was more. The warmth rushed through her, and along with it came a knowledge of who Michael was. It was his memory; not in pictures but feeling.

Teneil suddenly knew him the way that people only know one another after a lifetime. He was kind and generous. He loved fully. He was courageous and he was stronger than her, but not just physically. He was stronger than her in every way. But she also felt what she was to him. It was clear that no matter how she refused him, he would never stop. With him, she was truly trapped. She had been from the moment he'd found her.

She was so full that the breath she had been holding onto left her to make room for the extra presence in her body. As she exhaled, the vision was ripped away from her. Dunked into a cold dullness, she opened her eyes and found that she was in her room on her bed. Her body was new, completely healed. "What was that?" she said, a tremor in her voice.

"What was it to you?" he asked from where he sat at the foot of her bed. She raised her arms and felt no ache in her back.

"Did you heal me?"

"Yes."

"Well. . .why the heck didn't you do that in the first place?!"

"I-"

"You made me sit through stitches?" she cut in disbelievingly.

"You would have just attacked me again and I needed you to listen."

Teneil glared at him, trying to find fault in his assessment, but there was none.

"What else did you experience when I healed you?"

"It itched." She folded her arms and continued to glare.

"I know you felt it. I showed you everything, all that I am. Why are you being so difficult?"

"Frankly, I think the stitches thing was rude and I'm still a little irritated about it."

"That's fair," he conceded. "I apologize."

"And call me old fashioned, but I kinda like the romantic idea of a first date. I feel like I was cheated."

"I hadn't thought about that. I just wanted you to see me the same way that I see you."

She sat, obstinately turning her attention to the window, her chin held a little too high.

He chuckled at her behavior. "Now who's being dramatic?"

She hmmphed and unfolded her arms. "Okay, what now?"

"Now, you go to bed. You need rest."

"Agreed. I'm fairly sure you know where the door is, since you let yourself in. Mind letting yourself out?" She climbed under the blankets on her bed, suddenly more exhausted than imaginable.

He didn't bat an eye at her tone. He knew her beyond what she said, or her mood. Besides, for all of her outward anger, he could feel the joy and excitement boiling within her. If she was only tired, and she had a right to be, he could not fault her for that.

"May I still have that last question?"

She thought for a moment and a small smile pulled at the corners of her mouth. "I suppose."

"Would you do me the honor of accompanying me on a date tomorrow morning for coffee?"

Her face turned a deep crimson, and she buried it in the blanket to hide her smile. Then, putting her attitude back on, she pulled the blanket back down and repeated, "I suppose."

"I saw your smile."

"Shut up." Joy and irritation fought for control of her expressions.

"You're still blushing."

"Get out!"

Chapter Six
IF ONLY HE NEEDED ME

Teneil was being pulled through the night on a strong current of black water. The ancient boat moaned in protest, the old wood snapping and popping under her feet. Her dress, like the sails on the ship, almost glowed in contrast to the black of the night. Excitement was beating drums inside her. She'd dreamed of this moment her whole life, but she'd never been strong enough and the current had never favored her like this. She was gaining speed. She was not afraid; there was no reason to fear. There were dangers, but she slid by them with ease.

Faster! the boat cried out to her, and she dug her nails into the decks railing to hold on.

Faster. She planted her feet. *Faster* and *faster* and–

Pounding on the door broke through to her. Teneil sat up, still mostly asleep. She was not sure why she was sitting up, drenched in sweat. Her bedroom was too quiet without the hum of the fan. Apparently, the electricity had gone off at some point.

She let out a deep breath and sank back on her pillow. Again, the banging came on the back door. Her pounding heart echoed in her stomach. People did not go out this late unless there was trouble. On occasion some kinds of trouble found their way to her home, either drunk or insane. Sometimes both the drunk and insane came to bother her late at night, but no one ever went beyond her gate, for fear of her dogs.

They were right to be afraid, especially after dark. But, for some reason, her dogs were not disturbed by this particular intruder, who had made it all the way to the back door of her house. Even in the pitch black her hand fell exactly upon the box of matches, and by the third knock she had lit the candle, donned her robe, and was reaching for the latch. One look through the small window and she was quickly opening the door.

Several teenage boys she had known since before they were teenage boys stood with a body gathered limply in their arms.

"What happened?"

Each of them looked as if they would drop from fatigue. She took the tablecloth off the table and laid it on the rug in the center of the floor. The rug that was typically exclusive to the three dogs and one cat would have to do. A chair, a small table, and a bed were the only furnishings in the small house by the lake. There was no way she was putting this sopping wet stranger in her bed; selfishly, she was already dreaming about crawling back into it.

"What happened?" she asked again. This time, she used a firm voice in the tribe's language as she made her way to the emergency kit.

The words poured from the youths in a torrent. Though she had been here for years, the language was complicated. What she could gather was that this man had gone out with the fishermen, but they had trouble when they pulled a crocodile up in the net. The kids were on the beach when the small canoe ran aground, and the boys took him to the only place that they could think to go: the same place where they went when their toes were busted from playing football barefoot.

Someone had wrapped the injured man in fabric, but it was blood soaked. What skin she could see in the low, dim glow of the one candle was ash white or slick with black blood. She sent one of the boys to a clinic about two miles away. It would be closed, but the doctor and his wife lived in the apartment above it, and he owed her a favor.

Teneil quickly told the other boys to start the charcoal and fill all her basins with clean water. Who knew when the electricity would come back on? Without the help of the electric water pump, the village water storage supply would soon be gone. She stripped the sheet off her bed and cut it into several different sized bandages. Then she pulled out every lantern and candle stick in the house, rolling up her sleeves and gathering her hair up in a tight knot. She cut the fabric around the man's body and exposed his wounds.

Several of the friends that had brought the man to her had crowded around to see more clearly. Candles were knocked over and voices got loud. . . and she decided it was a good time for them to go. She shut the door behind them and went back to work.

Her breath caught in her throat. Part of her was frightened that this was a lost cause already; maybe he had lost too much blood. The skin she could see was pale, but his pulse and breathing were strong. So, she continued.

His face was completely covered in gore, his sand-colored hair a matted mess. Firstly, she examined his head, but the only damage she could find was a serious black eye, and that his ear had a rather large slice through it. It was bleeding quite a bit, but she spent no time on it. Her attention instead was drawn to his upper shoulder, which was a mess.

As gently as Teneil could, she washed away the dried blood. Deep puncture wounds decorated his skin and were badly swollen. Some greater rings of discoloration were already starting around the site. Though they had all clotted nicely and there was little fresh bleeding, crocodiles had incredible pressure in their bite, about three times the strength of a tiger. If his bones were not broken it would be a miracle.

The man only woke once, when she ran her fingers along the length of his collarbone. He hissed in pain and his eyes shot open. He looked deeply into her, not through her like people often did when they were in great amounts of pain. The fire in his eyes had burned into her mind. There was no fear there; it was a great, blazing fight. He was in the middle of a war, and she would not let him fight it alone. She hoped he spoke English. "It's alright. I'm here. I'm going to take care of you." His eyes glossed over, and he was gone again.

She sat back on her heels, allowing him to fall down into the void of unconsciousness before she finished.

It took almost an hour to clean and bind all of his wounds. The doctor from the clinic came by and did his own quick assessment. Flatly, the man declared that there was little that could be done. He left her with the knowledge that he would be back in the morning with stronger pain medication and antibiotics.

Teneil felt frustration at his words. She glanced down at the unconscious man on her rug. The gravity of responsibility and the reality of her situation made her want to crumble. She had promised that she would fight for this man, but she just didn't know how. She thought the doctor would have more answers, but ultimately, he was right. Little could be done about a broken collarbone. There was no scanning available for internal injuries. It was a wait and see situation. She sighed, hoping that this stranger would make it through the night.

It was almost 3am when she finished washing and hanging the soiled linen outside. Several times she had thought about leaving the job for the morning, but she knew that he would need fresh bandages the next day and these rags were all she had.

She took the mosquito net from the bedroom and hung it from the ceiling over the man. She blew out all but one candle. If he woke up, she did not want it to be in total darkness. She debated crawling in her bed, but she knew she would never sleep. As tired as she was, her adrenaline was high and her concern higher. She'd helped treat minor wounds from children and adults in the past, but this man seemed to be dancing dangerously between life and death.

So, Teneil brought her pillow out and laid down on the ground next to the stranger. She spent the next hour listening to his breathing for signs of any wheezing or gurgling, but his breathing was clear and strong. She listened anyway to the steady rhythm, and thanked God that he wasn't in worse shape.

She knew nothing about this man except that he was clearly not from around here. She knew everyone in this area, and she would have remembered him. He was handsome, in the dim candlelight, wrapped up in strips of her bedding. Several times she told herself that she was watching his chest rise and fall because that was a medical thing and she wanted to make sure that he was breathing steadily.

As the dead hours of the night went by, Teneil felt her mind wandering. She was content with her life alone in Africa, but she did often think about falling asleep next to someone. However, in all her dreams, she never fantasized about being on the cold concrete of her living room floor without a mosquito net. And it was safe to say the man of her dreams was never half dead to begin with. At some point, she finally pulled a blanket over her head and drifted off into dreamless sleep.

A mere two hours later, her dogs woke her. When Teneil sat up, she was aware of every bony process in her spine. It had been a long time since she slept directly on concrete, and everything hurt. All of her complaints died when she saw the man lying on the floor next to her.

The room and all the horror of the night before seemed strange in the light of day. He was mostly covered, but she noticed all the changes that had taken place in the two hours she had taken her eyes off of him. She noticed the change in the color leaking out from inside the bandages, and the swelling in his face. Without knowing a thing about this injured stranger, she knew today would be one of the most physically painful of his life.

In the light of dawn, she could see him more clearly. She hadn't realized how large he was last night; looking at him now, there was no way that she, by herself, would be able to move him. She needed to get him off the floor. She had no problem giving him the bed now, but how would she get him there? Maybe she could drag him on a blanket? That's when she had a brilliant idea:

Coffee.

Without another thought, she let the dogs outside and started a hot kettle of water to boil. Thank God, the electricity was back on. She brewed a large pot of coffee, knowing that this was bound to be a long day after an extra-long night. She took a few moments in her bathing room to clean out under her eyes and appreciate that it did nothing to help her. She tried to fix her hair from the messy knot in which she had slept to another more intentional messy knot for the day, but the difference between the two styles was indistinguishable.

She brushed her teeth, the only positive change, then put on jeans and her favorite "Wonder Woman" t-shirt. She didn't know what today would look like, but she knew it would be better in blue jeans. She appraised the dark rings under her eyes and surmised that if the coffee was ready, who cared how she looked? Her only guest was unconscious, and above all, coffee was ready.

She moved silently out to the patio where she needed five minutes of time alone with the thick, black, magic liquid and a quiet mind. Then she could save the world, or at least figure out what to do with the stranger on her floor. She couldn't keep referring to him as, "*the stranger*". She played through a list of names and settled on Mr. Doe. Mr. John J. Doe. Then she made a mental joke about asking him what the J. stood for, then chastised herself for a joke in such poor taste.

He was locked in a dream of pain. Pain and darkness. He searched for something, desperate for anything other than the void and agony. He was hanging on the edge of some great mountain. His arms were aching. His fingers were slipping. The mountain was on fire, he was alone, and he was going to die. He thought about the value of life and weighed it against his suffering. He was tired, and he wanted to let go. He tried to open his hands and fall into the desperation he felt, but his hands would not open. They had melted to the cliff's edge. He cried out in frustration and anguish.

"I'm here." A voice like cold water ran over his scorching face.

He looked up and saw her. He could only make out a hazy outline, but he knew her. She was holding him, keeping him from falling.

"Let me go!" he begged her, but the words were burned to ashes before they reached her.

"I promise, I won't leave you." Again the coolness drifted on her words. She pulled him up and up. He stood on the top of the mountain, still dark, but his arms were wide open, allowing the gentle wind of her presence to wash over him.

He knew that this was a dream, but he also knew this was not a dream. Not a dream, but also not reality. For example, he knew that he was far away, but he also knew that she was there. He had heard her promise not to leave him, and she hadn't, she wouldn't, and he was clinging to that. He knew nothing about her, but he knew that. He needed to know that, for it to be the truth. Without her, he would have burned alive.

Or was that part a dream? The fire? Was it fire? Then the pain came again. He remembered nothing. Darkness, like a cloud of ink poured into water, settled on his mind and he cried out in panic and frustration. Again, she was there. She was speaking but he couldn't understand her words. Instead, he made them up: "You are okay. I'm with you." Her presence was like an icy brook on his aching muscles. He focused on her voice and the sound of her wrapped around him as she sang him back to sleep.

The doctor came and went daily, giving "John" antibiotics in an injection. After three days, he had only woken up that one time when they first brought him. The first forty-eight hours were horrible; a fever had taken hold of John. His body burned and he moaned so weakly that it broke Teneil's heart. When the fever finally broke on the second day, Teneil, at long last, slept.

The doctor told her that the fever was the worst of it and John was on the mend. He assured her that he would wake up soon. The women from the village came daily, bringing new bandages, clean clothing for the man, and food. Teneil never left. She changed his bandages frequently and adjusted his posture throughout the day. She read books to him, talked enough for the both of them, and kept candles burning throughout the night.

He would not call it sleep; he was vaguely aware of a certain passage of time. He had moments of lucidity, but he could not open his eyes, and he had no control over the darkness that pulled him back under at its own will. It was better that way. When he was unconscious, he couldn't feel the pain, and the confusion of being awake was driving him mad.

He knew he was not alone. There was a girl. She was always there, always talking, but he could never make sense of her words. Was she the reason? Did she do this to him? He could hear her now, in another room, brushing her teeth. That was a good sign; psychos didn't brush their teeth, did they? His eyes still refused to open, but he could smell coffee. That was another good sign. Psycho killers didn't drink coffee, did they? Blackness overcame him again and he welcomed it.

Teneil was sleep deprived to say the least. She had barely tended to her own needs beyond a little food that the mothers of the village forced on her. They had also taken to bathing John, for which she was grateful. She used that time to bathe herself. But before the towel was off her head, she was back at his side. According to the clinic's doctor, at any moment he would wake up and she needed to be there. She had given him her word when she thought that he was dying. That was the kind of promise a person should take seriously.

But she had reached her limit. She had been fitfully sleeping on the ground next to her bed where John had lain for the last two nights. Mosquitoes weren't the only thing that a mosquito net protected a person from. There were all sorts of nocturnal creatures that roamed the floors of her home each night. Every time she would drift off something would scurry, bite, or walk over her.

Finally, tired beyond words, she gave up. Reasoning that it was, in fact, her bed, Teneil climbed into the net next to John. "Now, don't get fresh, Johnny." She laughed and then scolded herself at the inappropriate nature of flirting with a comatose man. When her head hit the pillow, she slept like. . .well, like John.

It was early morning when she woke, her body tucked cozily into John's side. She sighed, still mostly asleep, and nuzzled his arm with her nose. Her lazy smile ebbed away, and her eyes grew wide when she'd realized what she had done. She retreated as if she had been bitten by a snake.

"Honestly, Teneil!" she scolded herself and buried her beet-red face in her hands. She glanced at him, horrified. What if he had woken up to find her playing the role of "little spoon"? *Thank God he's still in a coma.*

"Thank God he's still in a coma?!" she hissed out loud, burying her face back in her hands. Taking one last look over her shoulder at him, she pushed her side of the net out from under the mattress and climbed out.

"Coffee, you nut job." She turned on the kettle, rolling her eyes again and repeated in a mocking tone, "Don't get fresh Johnny."

Ugh. Her face remained in the palm of her hand until her coffee had cooled enough to drink. With her belly full of high-octane fuel, she forced herself back into the bedroom and began pulling the net up. John was supposed to wake up today. It was stupid, she knew, but she was wearing her blue dress. Today *had to be* the day, right?

She sat in her usual place with her usual books, after, of course, straightening up the side of the bed she had slept in, or rather, the middle of the bed. It was a weird thing what she had done last night, but she thought it would be even weirder if, upon waking, she had to explain why the bed was all messed up. *"Oh, yeah, about that. . .I cuddled with your unconscious body last night."* Better just to make it seem as though she had never been there.

Without awareness that he was even awake, he opened his eyes. The room came into focus little by little. The trill of birdsong came from behind thin, colorful curtains that let the light shine through them like liquid stained glass. In blew a breeze that made the fan at the foot of the bed nothing greater than white noise. It had been a dream. . .until he attempted to sit up. Pain shot through him. He sucked in a deep breath, which also sent sharp pain through his shoulder and neck. He held still, forcing himself to breathe slowly.

He discovered that he was not flat on his back but propped up on an excessive number of pillows. He slowly began to focus on the room. It was simple, with a good-sized desk that was currently covered in bandages. Next to the fan was a tall, slender cabinet. Two walls had windows and the breeze running through the room smelled like fresh rain sweetened with perfumes.

There was not much to the space, with the exception of the books. A bookcase at the foot of the bed was overflowing to stacks on top of the cabinet. He could pick out more books pushed to the back corners of the desk, camouflaged by gauze. This was not a hospital room, or a guest bedroom, for that matter. He heard soft wind chimes in the distance, and his eyes followed the sound to rest on her. Her bottom half was seated on a low stool and her upper half lay stretched out on the bed. Her face was away from him.

Under her head, her arm was reached out toward him, the other hand tucked tightly to her chest. He watched her sleeping form for a long moment. Her dark brown hair was falling out of her chaotic bird nest of a bun, and two books lay open in front of her. Clearly, this was her room.

He had no idea who she was or how he had come to be in her bed. He watched her shoulders rise and fall and prayed thanks to God that whatever he had just gone through, somehow, he was alive. He thanked God also for this woman. An appreciation for life grew in him to a level that only people who tasted death knew. It was an appreciation of sanity after what felt like a lifetime adrift in confusion and darkness. He was alive.

He looked at her outstretched hand and remembered flashes of her in his dreams reaching for him, grabbing onto his hands, and pulling him up. He painfully moved, closing the few inches of space between them and took her hand, grounding the nightmares at last. Tears rolled down his face. *Alive.* The sleep that came then was blessedly dreamless, no longer a void but true rest.

Late in the morning of the fourth day, Teneil woke to find that John was holding her hand. He had woken up after all! But had he needed her, and she was asleep? She kicked herself. He was awake, which brought her to the second knowledge that he would leave soon. That was good, she told herself; whoever this man was, he had a life that was surely missing him. People must be worried sick about him.

She was making chicken broth in her tiny kitchen, knowing that John would definitely want to eat the next time he opened his eyes. The dogs laying steadfast at her feet suddenly jumped up and ran to the bedroom, wagging their tails fiercely. She wiped off her hands and walked around the corner to find John standing in a pair of ill-fitting shorts. Standing!

Teneil rushed to him just before he wavered and fell against her. Even after days without food, he was too heavy for her, and she bit back a groan. "Whatcha doin', big boy?" she laughed. She was overjoyed to see him on his feet, but also worried about how she would safely get him back down.

"Privy," was all he said.

"Privy?" She was confused for a moment before embarrassment hit her. "Oh! Yes, of course. Through here." She helped him to the small room and stood more awkwardly than she had ever stood before, waiting to help him back to bed. How would he react when he realized that she had been his nurse for the last week? And, because of that, he no longer had any secrets from her? She blushed brighter than a tomato.

He opened the door, and, without looking at her, he reached where he needed her to be. He leaned on her heavily, then wordlessly headed back to the bedroom. She adjusted his pillows, leaning over him to grab the thin blanket she kept on him for modesty's sake.

John breathed in deeply, inhaling her. That was the perfume constantly woven into the background of his mind. "You smell amazing," he murmured.

She blushed and backed away quickly. "Would you like some broth? I'm making lunch." But he was already sleeping again.

Hesitantly but eventually, she went back to the kitchen where the broth was beginning to boil. She took the pot off the coals, and, rolling her eyes, she pulled the front of her shirt to her own nose and took a deep breath. Not kicking herself for once, she had put her perfume on that morning. She blushed again, then scoffed at herself and finished tending to the soup.

He dreamed of a field of flowers. The colors and the smells all encompassed her. She was there, but he could not see her. She was always there, but he could never see her. He lay in the grass next to her, chewing on a honeysuckle stem while she read him her books. The breeze carried a soft music. The sky was dappled with puffy white clouds, the kind that always looked too perfect in paintings. For the first time in as long as he could remember, he was not concerned with where he was. There was a sense of rightness here. Things were good here and that was enough.

He woke to the smell of broth, and his stomach lurched with need. She was there, in her usual seat next to the bed, reading a book he didn't recognize. He could not see her face, buried in the pages, but he could see her hands holding the book open. They looked soft and delicate, but he had felt the strength of them when he had almost fallen on her earlier. He wanted to say a thousand things, but there was a hesitation. Part of him felt that if he spoke to her, she would vanish as she did in his dreams each time he tried to grab onto her. So, he laid there, watching her.

Teneil couldn't focus. She had reread this chapter a dozen times and she still couldn't tell what it was about. She had started with the book flat on the bed, as she always had. But her eyes drifted off the pages and over to John's resting form, where they attempted to continue the story. There were no words written on him, but she could guess countless answers, each one more intriguing than the last.

Where did he come from? Why was he here? What was his name?

"You smell amazing," he had said. Not, "good" or "nice". He'd said *amazing*. And the way he had reached for her? She played the vision of him standing in the doorway over and over. The blush ran up her neck and flooded her face. Finally, feeling silly, she propped the book up in such a way that she could no longer see him. Still only feet away, she stared at one word on the page for several moments before finally giving up in frustration.

"Oh, this is stupid!" she hissed, slamming the book closed only to find him awake on the other side of the small barrier she'd built between them. "OH!"

"I'm sorry," he croaked out of a parched throat. With a half-smile, he added, "I don't think this has been very convenient for either of us."

He looked at her for the first time. She was beautiful in a way he hadn't expected. He had never considered that she would be. He had no reason to think anything about her except that she was the kindest person he had ever met, so he had assumed her older, more of a mother figure. She was nothing like any mother he had ever seen.

Her eyes were bright and alarmingly green. Her hair was all he knew about her, dark brown and always kept up in a knot on her head. Her embarrassed smile was wide and perfect. Her full lips and cheeks flushed bright pink. Freckles dotted the bridge of her nose and cheekbones. Was he still dreaming?

"Not you, no. You're not stupid. It's this book, this- it's- I'm. . ." She was flustered. "Soup?"

"Water?" His eyes never left her as she crossed over to the desk and poured a small glass of water. She adjusted the pillows and gave him small sips from the glass. Then, without asking, she portioned out a serving of the soup.

"It's not much, just chicken broth. I thought you should start light." Without thinking, she took a sip and winced at the heat, then took another spoonful and blew on it for a good while before putting the spoon to his lips and allowing him to drink. For a time, they carried on in silence until she said, "My name is Teneil."

He didn't really catch her name, but he didn't want to look like a fool, so he just said,

"Levi."

"Levi?" She tried the name out. "I was way off."

"How long have I been here?"

"Four days, unless you count the first night, then it's been five. The doctor has been by every day. You had a pretty bad fever a few days back." She continued to spoon the broth into his mouth. He wanted to pick up the bowl and gulp down the golden liquid, but he knew she was right. He didn't want to make himself sick, and he didn't want to think about what kind of pain retching would cause, so he sipped, and he listened. Her voice was so beautiful that he found himself craving the sound. In the darkness, it was always her voice that kept his attention, like a lifeline.

"Do you remember anything?" she asked.

He did but trying to form it into words was like holding onto water. Frankly, at that moment, he didn't much care to think about it. This woman. . .where had she come from? What was she doing here? How exactly was it that he came to be in her bed? Nothing else mattered. He would have suffered whatever horror it had been again and again, if he could only hear her voice. But now, to see her face?

The only thing that stood out from the blackness and pain were her words that she would not leave him. She hadn't and he was alive because of it. He watched her blow on the broth, the way a soft blush never left her cheeks, how she constantly pushed the dark strands back out of her face. The concern on her brow as she told him of the last four days. Her smile. Had there ever been more beauty contained in one person? What good fortune had he fallen into bloody and broken to have the blush of a woman like this?

She had reassured him that she would not leave him, that she would take care of him. And, if it was at all possible, if she could allow it, he would offer her the same promise in return.

Chapter Seven
IF ONLY HE WAS GENEROUS

Teneil woke up that hot African morning bursting with energy. Today was going to be a good day. She let classic American rock set the beat of her morning routine, dancing and singing. Though neither was done skillfully, there was great passion. She showered and dawned her favorite blue dress. There was no occasion for the garment. The calendar said "Tuesday", but Teneil knew ways around the mundane.

She reasoned that it was a big world and there was bound to be at least one country celebrating a holiday. So, today was a holiday, and she could be fancy if she wanted to be. She added a layer of mascara and sparkling earrings. Still, she wore her hair piled high on her head, too hot to do otherwise.

She only had one errand to manage today. In town there were several small bottles of paint tint and a new hand drill that she had ordered from the hardware store in a neighboring village. She strolled easily along the two-mile road down the mountain to town. She loved walking to town by herself. There was never any rush in this part of the world.

The first year she had lived in Malawi many had laughed at her American quick step. These days when she saw tourists speed-walking, she laughed a little, too. She took her time greeting old friends, enjoying the sun on her skin and the easy path downhill.

The town of Nkhata Bay was small and uneventful. Neither of her orders had come, but she was given the traditional promise of, "Any time from now." That phrase always made her laugh. Her work would be delayed another day, but she was grateful for the mostly empty bag when she began the hike back up. All she had in her bag was more empty bags and a little bottle of water to weigh her down. Well, that and the excess ten. . .okay maybe twenty pounds she naturally carried, mostly on her hips.

Teneil heard the ruckus before she saw the kids. The road split halfway up the mountain where a large mango tree provided shade from the hot sun. It was a common resting point, especially now that the mangoes were ripe and begging to be enjoyed. She made her way toward the guffaws and saw mangoes raining down. Kids, the most she knew, laughed with their shirts stretched into makeshift baskets, overfull with fruit. She took out her unused bags and offered them up to the common purpose.

Only a few older kids were brave enough to climb the large tree, notorious for several broken arms and even more bruised egos. She looked up in the branches and tried to see who was responsible for this harvest, but she couldn't see anything through the dense green.

"Be careful!" she shouted, and the branches froze for just a moment before resuming the erratic shaking and mango raining. She helped the children fill the bags but palmed two of the best-looking mangoes for herself and the kid high up in the precarious branches doing all the work. Moments later the bags were full, and she yelled as much to the treetop. The children all quickly departed with their sweet treasure, little ones falling over from the added weight.

Teneil was a bit surprised to see them all leave while their brave friend was still stuck in the tree. Craning her neck up into the tangle of thick branches, trying to catch a glimpse of the courageous mango-philanthropist, she sighed. She'd have to wait for the boy to make his way down safely before she continued on.

She took a seat on a large, well-worn root and leaned against the trunk of the great tree. She could hear the effort being made by the boy to get down, but she would not shame him by offering advice, so she focused on rinsing the fruit with the bottle of water from her bag, saving just enough water to clean herself up when she was done.

After living here for years, she still did not know how to eat a mango without looking like she needed a highchair and a bib. She tried, as she always did, to keep the ripe fruit from running down her chin and arms, but her efforts were in vain. Teneil eventually gave up, as she always did, in her attempt to eat the large mango with any decorum. Instead, she gave herself over to the pleasure of a hot, sun-ripened fruit. It was a repugnant routine.

He had woken that morning with energy and enthusiasm. He had a feeling that today was going to be special. He had jumped in the lake at sunrise and swam until he thought his arms would fall off, but still he was full of restless energy. He'd walked to town and back while the sun rose, and the pathways became spotted with other people. The mountain was steep, and his legs ached, but still a burning inner excitement would not allow him rest. He was irritatingly jumping out of his skin, like a person with too much caffeine in their system.

The sun had come high in the sky and coupled with the uphill climb, he was drenched in his own sweat. His shirt clung wet to his skin, a sensation that he hated. Crossing his arms in front of his body, not wanting to stretch the fabric out, because he was a man who took care of what he had, he slowly took off his wet shirt. The sun beat down on his hard, exposed chest, but the slight breeze connected with his sweat and had him sighing deeply with his face toward heaven.

(Writer's note: that was a little graphic. Sorry, Mom.)

In his pause, he noticed some kids trying to knock down mangoes with stones. He didn't hesitate to climb into the big tree to help. He liked climbing trees and thought it would be a good reason to give his legs a break from the mountain. Quite a bit of time passed as he cradled himself skillfully in the branches, knocking down countless fruits to the happily squealing children below. The work was fun, and the children were laughing and cheering him on. Every time he looked down, there were more children than the time before. First, he spotted three, then five, and now there were about a dozen, so he just kept on.

He saw her through the branches, on her hands and knees, picking up the fruits and putting them in a bag. At first, he thought to say something like, "Hey, lady! I didn't climb up here for you! These mangoes are for the kids!"

But he bit his tongue. He must have knocked down close to a hundred by now; was it really a problem if some tourist woman took a few? From his perch in the treetop, he could see the large, well-worn ferry boat docked in the bay. The water was a brilliant cerulean blue, reflecting the cloudless sky. He had climbed high enough to see the town with its lunchtime cookfire, smoke and endless rivers of people. *What a glorious day.*

He heard the woman below yell that they had enough and saw the kids running down the hill struggling under the burden of the bags' weight. "You're welcome," he laughed to himself. No matter: he had climbed the tree as much for his own pleasure as for the kids'.

Now the children were gone, but the woman remained under the tree, no doubt to make sure he did not break his neck. It was a good thing, too, for at that exact moment his overwhelming energy was gone completely. His arms and legs were numb and heavy.

His descent was sloppy, but when he expected her criticism to echo up toward him, he only heard the sound of slurping, sloppy, mango eating and the moans of delight that a perfectly sun-ripened mango would invoke. Good, he didn't need to know who she was to know that she was a woman. He didn't want to look weak in front of *any* woman, even a lazy tourist woman.

It was a man thing.

His feet hit the ground on the opposite side of the tree from her, and he wobbled unsteadily like a newborn calf. He needed to sit down for a moment. He slid down the tree next to the woman, who never looked up from her mango. Glancing over, he cringed. What had she done to that poor fruit? It looked like a firework had exploded in her hand.

"I saved the best one for you." She gestured with a hand, covered in thick, sticky, yellow/orange juice, to a mango resting on top of her bag. "I washed it."

"Thanks," he said, with true appreciation.

Her entire body stiffened. Her eyes, which had been looking at nothing in particular on the ground, went wide. That was not a boy's voice. She lifted her head and found a handsome, shirtless man sitting beside her. His sun-kissed body glistened with beads of sweat and flecks of the tree's bark, chest heaving with exertion. His head resting against the tree was exaggerating the pulse hammering in his corded neck.

(*Sorry, Mom-ma.)

Eyes closed, elbows on his knees, his large hands deftly, expertly, peeled the fruit she had saved for him before half of the golden treasure disappeared cleanly into his perfect mouth with little more than a light slurp.

He rolled his head and looked at her. The first thing he noticed was that she was beautiful. Her wide eyes were rimmed with long black lashes. She had dark hair and flushed skin. He was suddenly grateful that he hadn't yelled at her from the treetops. It took a moment to realize the entire bottom half of her face was covered in mango.

He was reminded of the time his friends gave their one-year-old baby a bowl of spaghetti with red sauce. It was such a hard contrast to the beautiful face before him now that a burst of laughter forced its way out through his sinuses in a snorting, donkey-like bray.

She knew exactly what he saw. This was why she ate mangoes at home, alone, usually at night, when no one was likely to come visit. But there was nothing she could do about it now.

"Did you get any in your mouth?" he finally choked out.

Perhaps it was because she loved the sound of his resounding laughter or because she was raised by wolves, but she shrugged and pulled her lips into a wide, toothy smile, revealing a bed of frightening orange moss, all of the mango fibers that had been strung between her teeth.

Chapter Eight
IF ONLY HE WAS A TOTAL NERD

Living alone in her particular community forced Teneil to recognize some wisdom in having a personal curfew. Resort towns were the same kind of trouble across the globe. Here it was tropically beautiful, and people came from all over the world to stay at one of the lodges in the bay where they could enjoy all kinds of activities, like diving and snorkeling in the crystal-clear waters of the massive lake. Full of little monkeys and stunning birds, there was plenty to enjoy even if you didn't want to get your toes wet.

Because of this, Nkhata Bay had more jobs than other smaller villages, and being one of the poorest countries in the world meant that people from all different tribes came for the possibility of employment. Gatherings of tourists on holiday also brought many criminals to the area looking for easy targets.

The crime rate was very high in the bay, but it was not limited to foreigners. The police were mostly for hire and scarce after dark. Anyone walking alone late was likely to be jumped and robbed. Teneil had patched up many people who were caught unaware. Folks usually walked in groups of three or more, but that was not always possible.

Teneil decided, after attending to a dozen split lips and blackened eyes, that there was nothing that she really needed after dark. For her safety and the safety of the children that stayed with her, she did not even entertain visitors to her house after dark, unless of course, if it was an emergency.

Teneil tucked the children in bed and retired to her own room on the other side of her small house. She sat at her desk and began the routine task of plaiting her waist length hair in a thick braid for sleeping. She hadn't gotten to her laundry for the last few days and settled on sleeping in a soft pink dress. It was not really a "sleeping gown" but the fabric was light enough for the hot night. *Besides*, she thought, *storybook princesses always sleep in beautiful dresses.*

Her head had barely touched the pillow when there was a shout at her back gate. Teneil's heart sank. It was never anything good when it was after dark. Either some troublemaker was drunk from the beach and looking to make a new friend, or someone was hurt. She grabbed her "bat", a hardwood cane she kept by the back door for just this reason. Teneil was surprised to find an older couple, trembling and begging her for help.

"Please, our oldest son was attacked on his way home."

The woman's frail voice and desperation broke Teneil's defenses. "I'm very sorry to hear that, but I'm not sure what you want from me. Did you go to the police?"

"Yes." The man's voice was curt. "They have stated that after we take him to the hospital, he should go to the police station to make a report." They looked nervously at each other and at her.

Teneil tried to hide her frustration with the local authorities; she knew they had their hands full. "I'm sorry, I'm still not sure how I can help you . . ."

"We can't get him to the hospital!" The woman began to cry.

"Do you need transportation money for a taxi?" Teneil let out a breath of relief. Money for transportation was something she could do easily.

The man held a pained expression and shook his head. "No one will go there. We tried already. Our son is on the far side of Chizowa. They all say it is too much mud from the rains."

Teneil could feel the color drain from her face. Chizowa was the hub of trouble; it was not the promise of mud that would keep an experienced driver away. The village of Chizowa was a seemingly postcard beautiful fishing village on the outside, but inside it was little more than a local brewery. A type of moonshine was brewed there in old steel barrels that were originally used to transport motor oil. The "spirit", as they called it, was brutal on the system. Teneil had to wonder just how much of the trouble in Nkhata Bay was blamed on "spirit" alcohol.

The woman begged, "Please." Tears streamed down a face that had seen too much for her years. She gripped Teneil's arm with desperation. "Please."

Teneil broke. She had a hatchback. *100% not a minivan*, she had told herself over and over, because minivans didn't have four-wheel drive, and she did. See? *Not a minivan.*

She quickly put her black leather work boots on, not bothering to change from her pale pink dress. She told the oldest girl in the house where she was going and when she expected she would be back. She was about to drive into the heart of the problem, at the worst time of day, with who knew what kind of roads. She needed someone to know, just in case she didn't make it back out.

As she got closer to the village, tension filled the cab of her hatchback. This time of night, the street was full of stumbling, slurring, or passed out, drunks. Teneil was forced to stop on the outskirts of the town center, so they could move a sleeping body out from the middle of the muddy road.

Teneil was counting the minutes until she could leave. Silently praying and nervously humming, she slowly navigated the washed out and overgrown path that led deeper into the belly of the beast.

The way narrowed down to more of a suggestion than a real road. She slowed even more, reflexively looking in her rearview mirror, where she saw something that turned her blood to ice. Several people had noticed her car struggling in the slick mud. With a foreigner driving, the potential for easy income must have been too tempting to pass up and they followed, slowly.

The slick roads were not easy on foot either, but they had determination and when Teneil got hung up in a deceivingly deep puddle, they swarmed around the vehicle. Angry, they beat on the windows demanding money from her, no doubt for more of the drink. They rocked her car and shouted.

The couple in the back seat cried out, the woman in fear, the man in frustration. Teneil had no comfort to offer them; the best she could do would be to get them out. She let the car reverse out of the hole and then gingerly tapped the gas. The car crunched loudly as the frame connected with the ground and got more angry shouts from the people who were forced to move. Others who had gotten splashed by the muddy water yelled even louder, but they were moving again and putting a little distance between the car and the mob.

Teneil let out a nervous laugh when they turned the last corner and found the end of the road. Ahead of them lay the body of the battered son, and the people who had dragged him up to the roadside. She quickly got out and opened the hatch, and they all helped to slide the body of the broken young man into the open space at the back of the car. He moaned and Teneil thought, *At least he's conscious.* They had indeed beaten him mercilessly, and she knew he would likely be in the hospital for a week or more.

"I think we should take the back road to get out," Teneil said as she got back behind the wheel, tucking the hem of her dress out of the way of the muddy door jam.

"It is quite wet from the storm yesterday," the boy's father warned.

"If we stay on the road, it should be alright." Teneil was a little worried, but the rain- washed back road was worth the risk to her: she wasn't sure she would make it back through the heart of town again without worse trouble.

The back roads in Malawi reminded Teneil of the back roads where she grew up in Colorado. You really needed to know where you were going, or you could easily get lost. Teneil had worked in this village for years and she knew several routes to get to the hospital. Calming her racing heart, she renewed her grip on the wheel, picked a route that she thought would be the most passable, and drove on slowly. Some moans emerged from the back when the car was jostled, but otherwise the road was dark and quiet.

Her taillights disappeared through the dense trees, but that did not dissuade the several inebriated stragglers who followed the sound of her engine. Like mindless zombies, they had nothing more to do than to chase the possibility of good fortune. Teneil knew that they were not going to give up so easily, but there was not much to be done about it. If she got stuck, it would be trouble, but as long as they kept moving it should be alright.

The road was narrow, but on the dryer spots Teneil was able to speed up a little to put some distance between her and the walking dead. She was almost to the end of the muddy path and back onto a more traveled road.

"Don't worry," she said, projecting her voice to the parents in her backseat. "The hospital isn't far now."

In the blackness of the back roads, she suddenly glimpsed an alarming beacon of light through the trees. "What in the world?" Teneil muttered to herself.

It looked like the kind of spotlights that clubs in major cities used to attract patrons, and they were headed straight for it. As they got closer, Teneil could see a large vehicle in the middle of the clearing. The field before them was a notorious sinkhole. It was the flattest place around and so naturally, it had been made into a football pitch, only used on dryer days. The small valley often pooled into a shallow pond during most of the rainy season.

Teneil learned about this place the hard way the first year she had lived here. It had taken her and two others over an hour to push her small car out. That was also how she found out about this small back road. Teneil slowed her car, trying to mentally sort out what her eyes were telling her. Someone was clearly caught in the bog.

Creeping closer, she could see the large, all-terrain vehicle was built like a tank. Locked provision boxes filled the rack on top and fuel reserve cans sat on the sides. The huge 4x4 even came equipped with a roll cage and a snorkel, just in case the driver needed to. . .cross a river, she supposed?

Teneil had seen these utility vehicles often. Tour guide companies, usually based in South Africa, offered them for rent, under popular taglines like: "For the adventurous spirit who wants to camp across Africa". It was the rich man's backpacking. The top, she knew, folded out into a "safely sleep and view game in the built-in roof tent!"

She always smiled when she saw them parked at lodges and driving down the paved roads. She smiled now, too, seeing the "Go anywhere!" mobile that couldn't make it across the soggy, flat soccer green. She stopped smiling when she remembered the mob following just behind her. Whoever these people were, Teneil had just put them in a whole mess of trouble.

She spit out a few inaudible words, then spoke to the family in the back seat. "We have to take them with us, too." No one argued. They knew better than she did that the explorers dream- stuck in the mud screamed money and opportunity. Whoever was there was no better off than sitting ducks in season.

Teneil got out of the car but left the engine running. She ran as silently as she could toward the light, not wanting to alert those following her by shouting out. When she finally reached the truck, she was out of breath. "Hey!"

Peter had stood up when he heard the soft footfalls coming toward him. To be honest, his first thought upon seeing Teneil was, *ghost*. Her pale skin and light, flowing dress running through the blue haze of the full moon was a vision. He was frozen in shock and frankly a little horror. She stopped at the edge of the grasses and breathlessly said, "Hey!"

Do ghosts say "hey"? He didn't think so. *Not a ghost, then.* He shined his powerful flashlight at her in reflex. She had on some kind of black work boots and her long dark hair was in a thick braid. The dress was a pale pink and she was clearly out of breath. Was he dreaming? She was the most beautiful woman he had ever seen. *She's an angel, maybe?*

Teneil was not an angel. She was, however, tired and irritated. "Please get that light out of my eyes!" she snapped. Though she'd shielded her eyes with her hands, the 6000-lumen beacon had done its damage and she could see nothing. Well, that's not entirely true; she could see the scar of brilliance the light had burned into her eyeballs.

"Oh, sorry!" He moved the light away. "Who are you?"

"We need to go, now," she insisted. "You're not safe here."

"Are you a terminator or something?"

He was being 100% honest. He had dreamed about this his whole life. . .well, at least from the time he was seven and his older brother let him watch "The Terminator". But that was not unusual; he also frequently tried to focus his Jedi mind powers and strongly felt that "The Matrix" was closer to reality than most people cared to believe.

Teneil laughed. "Yes." Then she did a horrible Schwarzenegger impression: "Come with me, if you want to live."

Peter's dad had told him on multiple occasions about the moment when he had met Peter's mother. "Lightning" was what he'd always described. And Peter had just been struck.

She was bent over, catching her breath and blinking her eyes furiously. Switching back to her regular voice, she added, "But, no. Really. We need to go now. Seriously. There are some troublesome folks headed this way and when they find you here with this car . . .? They won't hesitate to hurt you, maybe even just for sport. So, whoever else is here with you, lock up the gear and let's go now."

His mind was racing. He had a million questions. What was her favorite flower? Was she a morning person? He bet she smelled like honey. Did she ever play "Call of Duty"? She seemed more like a board game person, but that was okay; he liked board games, too. She was probably smart. Not smarter than him, but that was also okay. She had more than just intelligence, she was-

"Are you moving?" Teneil prompted, breaking apart Peter's inner ramblings. "I can't tell if you're moving or not, but you need to be moving."

Go? Yes! Go with her? *Absolutely! Wait. . .* "What about the truck?" he asked.

"I will take care of it. Just lock it tight and let's go." She turned to leave, and he quickly followed. She stumbled in her blindness, and he reached out for her. She pulled her arm back quickly, unwilling to rely on a stranger. "You blinded me with your light," she snapped in vindication of her clumsy feet.

"Sorry about that. You caught me off-guard."

She could hear men shouting in the distance and knew their time was running out. "We need to run." She grabbed his shirt and pulled him behind her, but it was only a few steps before he was practically carrying her over the brush and secret rocks that dotted the treacherous track.

They both tripped multiple times but made it to the car moments before the gang of men descended on the vehicle.

Teneil hit the lock on the doors and the men outside beat on the windows in protest. Rocking the car brought painful moans from the back and sent fresh chills down Peter's spine. His first thought was, *ghost*. He spun around in the front passenger seat and cried out in fright at the entire group of people in the back of the car, staring back at him wide-eyed.

"I can't drive!" Teneil shouted. "I still can't see!"

Without another word she grabbed Peter's shirt and pulled him toward her, then lifted herself up to switch their seats in the tight space. He was not a small man. He had been, all of his life, the smallest in his class. But that all caught up with him a couple years after college, when his metabolism finally slowed down.

These days Peter often mined for weeks straight to get the core samples he searched for. The work was backbreaking, but it had done much for a man that would never set foot in a traditional gym, naturally turning his once bone-thin and sickly pale form into something sculpted and bronzed by the African sun.

He hadn't ever noticed how large he had become, until that moment when he traded seats with a beautiful woman in the small, Japanese import that boasted economy over all else. He said a silent prayer of thanksgiving as she slid her body over his, until her black work boot caught him in the jaw.

"Sorry!"

"That's alright," he said, and meant it.

Someone outside hit the passenger window hard enough to crack the glass. Instead of cowering away, Teneil opened the door sharply and knocked the man back from her car, grunting with effort. She slammed the door closed on another man's fingers, then shut the door completely and locked it again.

Peter snapped his finger and beamed brightly at Teneil. "Laura Croft!"

"What?!" she shouted back.

"Laura Croft, you know, 'Tomb Raider'? That's who you remind me of!"

"Drive the car!" she shouted over the drumming on her little vehicle.

Peter put it in drive and pulled away from the rabble.

"You don't have to go fast. They're drunk, they can't keep up," she explained calmly. Peter slowed down a little and noticed her rubbing her eyes. "We have to go to the hospital," she added.

"It's a bright light, I know. One of the top five brightest in the world," Peter shared as he drove. "I ordered it special for this trip. But I wouldn't worry about your vision. It couldn't have done permanent damage."

She stopped rubbing her eyes and looked at him, or rather looked at the white spot where his head should be. "Not for me." She pointed a thumb over the seat. "For them."

"Did you rescue them, too?" Visions of her fighting off men with a sword in one hand and a pistol in the other flooded his mind.

"I didn't rescue anyone. I'm just the driver." Teneil's vision was slowly returning, and by the time the tires hit pavement she could make out the contacts on her phone. She dialed one and a man picked up on the second ring.

She spoke in a language that Peter had never heard. He thought she must be relaying her mission's progress to headquarters and then telling them off, because that's what superheroes usually did to anyone with authority. If he had known the language, he would have heard her call in a favor from an old friend who owned a tractor. She asked him to go down immediately and fetch the 4x4 out of the mud. It would cost her an arm and a leg, but the favor was that he does it now, and not in the morning, not leaving the truck to be pillaged by the community all night. They argued on the cost and settled for $100. $100. . .and one of the top five brightest flashlights in the world.

Arriving at the hospital, Teneil asked Peter to wait in the car while she escorted the others inside. She waited almost half an hour for the ER doctor to be woken. By then, her vision had returned fully, and she had almost completely forgotten about Peter. But Peter had not forgotten about her.

While he patiently waited in the car, he replayed the encounter with his captivating heroine over and over, allowing his imagination to add things like slow motion fight sequences and a most sensuous shade of lip gloss. He imagined she must be an international spy lying low after her cover was blown in Russia. . .or maybe she wasn't lying low. Maybe she was sent here to help him.

To help him, what? There was nothing exciting about his days, but then again that's how it was in the stories too, right? An unsuspecting scientist discovers something unbeknownst to him and then his world is turned upside down? He actually started doing an inventory of his latest data log sent back to his employers just to see if the story he was writing in his mind had any merit, when. . .

Exhausted beyond words, Teneil opened her car door and almost sat in Peter's lap.

"Oh!"

"Sorry. Are you cool to drive again?" He moved over and she climbed in.

"I forgot you were here," she confessed, her small laugh echoing in the hollow darkness of the car.

"Yeah, me too." He answered before his mind even processed what she'd said. He was so eager to agree with anything. *"Yeah, me too"?* He mentally kicked himself.

"Sorry?"

"I mean I knew I was here." He let out an awkward laugh. "I was just saying, you didn't. Didn't know. I guessed, you didn't. I. . ." He stopped there.

"Right," she agreed, too tired to process what he'd said. "There aren't any lodges open right now, but if you promise you're not a weirdo you can crash on my couch."

He laughed. "No. . ." he amended, "not weird in any bad way."

"I'm Teneil."

"Peter."

"Peter," she repeated, wanting to fill the silence, while her tired eyes stayed focused on the road. "Looks like you're out to discover Africa in that rig!"

He let out a nervous laugh. "Yeah. I had GPS telling me where to go. Somehow, I missed something. When I got stuck, I thought, 'no problem, this is why I have this truck'. But when the axle broke. . ." He trailed off, since she knew the rest of the story.

"Where were you going?" She knew there was nothing but farms past the breweries.

"To the lake."

"The lake?"

"Yeah."

She laughed, suddenly more awake. "The lake is practically half of the country. You can't miss the lake!"

"Clearly I have proven that statement false." His voice was humble, but he had a wide smile. She could laugh at him. He didn't mind; he just liked the sound of her laughter.

She laughed until she snorted like a farm animal, and he thought his heart would explode. "What is your favorite flower?" Peter blurted, unable to hold back the question.

She thought about it long enough that Peter thought he was an idiot to ask until he heard her reply: "Whatever flower is right in front of me at the time."

"Good answer."

"Why do you ask?"

"Just curious." He was a liar. But the truth would have sounded something like, "because you are the most beautiful, mysterious, enchanting woman I have ever met and if given the opportunity I would fill your life with all the things that you adore, starting with fresh flowers." But he did not think she was ready to hear that, not while she was willing to allow him to sleep on her couch.

Her house was small, and it was quite dark when they arrived. "The girls are all sleeping, so there's no talking beyond this gate," she said sternly.

"Do you have any more questions, comments, or concerns before we cross the boundary?" she added in a soft whisper.

His mind flooded with a million thoughts and queries, but he shook his head to silence them all, and she took that as a *no*. She reached for the lock on the gate, but he grabbed her arm. "One question?" he managed.

"Yeah?"

In the close space and the darkness of night, Peter could make out only a vague outline of her. "What was your nickname growing up?"

One of Teneil's eyebrows shot up, bemused. "What?"

"Like what did people call you when you were a kid?"

"That's your question?" she said, the corners of her mouth barely twitching in a small smile.

"Yup. Well, actually I have endless questions, but I could only pick one and that was the one."

"Toenail."

"Toenail?"

"I was in the first class to have computers in my school," she began to explain quietly. "They weren't good for anything but typing, really, so they made us type all the names of the students in each class for practice. Spell check was a new thing, and Teneil was auto corrected to Toenail. It got a good chuckle and stuck. That was 7th or 8th grade, I think? Anyway, Toenail." She turned back to the gate but stopped. "What did they call you?"

He shrugged his shoulders. "Peter."

Teneil burst into laughter so powerful that there was no sound, her eyes watered, and she grabbed her sides. Peter wasn't sure why she laughed, but he hoped it never stopped.

The house was quiet and true to her word, Teneil said nothing more once they closed the gate behind them. She quickly set up a bed on the couch and went to bed herself. It was not unusual for Peter to fall asleep to his own colorful imagination, but never before had he had a sleepover at a girl's house. In his wildest fantasy he could not imagine this, so he went to sleep replaying his real-life actual day in his mind, not making one up entirely.

Early the next morning, he was woken by the feeling that you get when someone is watching you. Peter opened his eyes to find a tiny person only a few inches from his face. In the deep blue of early morning, the figure in front of him was not Teneil's youngest daughter, the incredibly cute and always curious little Tapiwa. In Peter's eyes, aided by the dream he was having about zombies chasing him through the woods, Tapiwa was clearly a ghost.

He yelped in fright, throwing his pillow directly at the apparition. Tapiwa screamed too, and then went down as the pillow struck her tiny form. She landed on the dog, who also screamed.

Teneil was in the next room over. She was already awake and sitting up in bed working on her computer when she heard Tapewa get up. She'd set her computer aside, knowing the little one would be in her room for a morning cuddle. When Tapewa did not come through the door, Teneil assumed she had found the stranger on the couch.

When the screaming began, Teneil knew the stranger had found her, too. Teneil had pictured the whole scene almost as perfectly as it had played out. She should have felt badly and gone out to make introductions, but she could not; all of her air was gone. Instead, she could only offer a wheezing laugh, the kind of snickering laugh that evil cartoon dogs make.

It was good that everyone was up; she'd been waiting for some time to make coffee. She put her work aside and crept around the corner. Just before they came into her line of sight, she heard Peter talking.

"I'm sorry, again. I can't say that enough. I thought you were a ghost."

"What's a ghost?" the little voice countered, and Teneil went rigid. He would give her a lifetime of nightmares if he opened that box. There was a long silence. She had the impression that Peter was clever despite the situation he'd gotten himself into last night, and somehow, she trusted that he would know what lines not to cross with toddlers.

"I said, 'mouse'," Peter corrected himself. "You are so tiny and squeaky that I thought you were a little mouse that had come to eat my candy!"

Tapiwa's voice was no longer her fun, curious, new-friend-playful tone, but serious as a heart attack with the secrecy of espionage. "You have candy?"

"I always have candy." He reached into his pocket and pulled out a small package of hard candies. "I was told that you are not supposed to give candy to gremlins this early in the morning or they turn into little monsters."

"That's true," Tapiwa agreed. "But you did beat me with a pillow. Maybe you beat me hard? Maybe it never happened?"

Both Peter and Teneil laughed. Peter heard Teneil snort and was instantly aroused. Without thinking, he gave the little girl the entire packet of candy and got off the couch. Tapiwa had also heard her mother and the moment the candy was in hand she disappeared with her treasure before it could be confiscated.

"I believe that's extortion," Teneil observed as she came around the doorway. "I did throw a pillow at her, just in case she tries to shake me down later."

Teneil laughed. "She will, too. Coffee?"

He nodded. Though he rarely drank coffee, his mouth seemed very dry and anything she was offering sounded good to him. The long black braid from the night before was now piled high on her head, and the little makeup she wore yesterday had migrated below her eyes. She was wearing a short, light gray robe, over the pink dress he remembered.

In his eyes? She was stunning.

Had Teneil recognized that he was so handsome and funny the night before, she would never have allowed him to sleep in her home. Not that there were many other options at the time, but after a string of failed relationships, Teneil stayed away from men as a general rule. Attractive, funny men were the most dangerous.

She opened all the windows and doors to let the sunlight and fresh morning air into the house, then sighed in relief when she saw the 4x4 in her driveway.

"How is that possible?" Peter exclaimed behind her, looking out at the muddy explorer.

"I know people," she said and winked at him. His heart murmured and he thought he would crumble until she said, "It cost you the flashlight."

"B-But-"

"I know there was a special bond and I'm sorry you have to say goodbye, but it was that or leave the rig out there overnight and lose everything." She put a hand on his shoulder in consolation. Suddenly he did not care about the flashlight. He only cared about the warmth of her hand.

When a knock came from the back gate, she was gone. The moment she left his side, he felt the pain of his loss again, the darkness inside that his 6000-lumen masterpiece once lit up. He had spent countless nights looking for snakes in the trees and calling all kinds of fish to the bright light in lakes and rivers across Africa. It was his favorite resting activity and now it was gone.

Teneil returned with a fierce expression on her face. "You're in trouble. We have to go."

"Is that, like, a usual saying for you?" he asked.

But she had already gone back into her bedroom to change her clothes and give a quick wipe under her eyes. She woke up the oldest girl to tell her they were leaving.

On their way out, she grabbed a couple of shovels from a storage room and put them in the back of her small car. One thing she noticed about Peter was that he never asked all the usual questions like, "Where are we going?" or, "What kind of trouble?" or, "What are the shovels for?" He only nodded and got in the car. She liked that about him. Well, she liked that and his genuine smile. His smile, and she liked the way he always looked at her, like she was a rare, precious gem and he was a private collector.

She specifically chose not to tell Peter where they were going and see how long it would take before he asked, but he never did. To his credit, he didn't even look nervous as she took them back to the edge of the field where she'd found him the night before. Waiting for them was a large group of people, and when she opened the door, they all began pointing and shouting.

Peter remained by her side but had no idea what was being said. Even still, he was paying attention and thought he figured out most of it. This was what he saw: Teneil listened patiently to all the complaints. Most were being shouted at by one man in the middle of the crowd, who seemed to be getting everyone else aggravated as well. The man in the middle must have been a chief because he seemed very important, and the crowd seemed to listen and respond to him.

After some time, Teneil gently raised one hand and the roar immediately died. She spoke in a gentle tone, but loud enough for everyone to hear. It was clear that they loved her and that she loved them. Then Teneil responded directly to the man in the middle, and her tone and posture changed.

She was forceful and the crowd seemed to chant with her words. Tension was rising and Teneil approached the man, who lost a step. The man said something small, and Teneil stuck her hand out to shake it. The man seemed to cry a little at her touch, probably in joy or thanksgiving, Peter wasn't sure which. Then they all turned and left, many still shouting and spinning fabrics in the air, something he had only ever seen done at celebration. Maybe it was a holiday?

If Peter could have understood what was being said, he would know that the man in the middle and several others behind him were demanding large sums of money for the football pitch that was destroyed by Peter's truck. He would have heard the people argue that Peter was clearly a friend to Teneil, so they should not treat him like a bank, and also that the damage was not so bad.

If Peter knew this crowd like Teneil knew them, he would have known that the men demanding so much money were also the men who attacked them last night. If Peter spoke ChiTonga, he would have heard Teneil talk about her love of the community and how both she and Peter had brought their own shovels and would have the pitch fixed before the day's end. He would have heard her call the men that started the trouble thieves and worse.

He would have appreciated how the crowd moved to stand by her side and he would have loved it when the community, harrowed by Teneil's voice, had all agreed that they wanted the group to stop drinking or leave the village. All the people who lived in that community had had enough of the trouble caused by "spirit" alcohol.

And when the man who stood at the center finally agreed to back off the spirits or suffer banishment, Teneil made sure to shake his hand to seal the deal. She gripped his hand hard, causing him to cry out from the pain of the broken fingers that she had slammed in her car door the night before. And if Peter knew the language, he would have heard her promise worse if he ever came near her again.

But Peter did not know the words and he was even more confused when Teneil placed the shovel in his hands, until he saw the damage to the field. "You wrecked their soccer field." She smiled at him.

"Is that what all this is about?"

"Yeah, they wanted to kill you as a sacrifice to the football god. But I told them you would sponsor the next game and that you promised them a new football."

The blood drained from Peter's face and his legs turned to jello. He only started breathing again when Teneil burst out laughing. "Come on, we have to fix it." She dug the shovel into the soft ground and began the muddy job of repairing the ruts from his truck and the tractor that pulled him out.

Several members of the village came out to help and the task was done in a matter of a couple hours. Teneil caught herself several times watching Peter work. Something about a man that wasn't afraid of physical labor was really attractive. "You really know your way around a shovel," she finally said when he'd caught her looking.

"Using a shovel and pick is a big part of being a geophysicist."

"What's a geophysicist?"

"Geophysicists study the structure and composition of zones below the surface of the earth by taking measurements using seismic, gravity, magnetic, and electrical data collection methods," he replied without stopping his work.

The sentence made Teneil feel dumb, so she said, "Now I feel dumb."

He laughed and she blushed. "I look for minerals and specific layers to determine if there are good locations for the paleontologists to dig."

"Like, for dinosaurs?!" she exclaimed excitedly.

"Yup."

"That's why you have that ridiculous truck."

"Ridiculous truck?!" He laughed in mock offense. "That's been my home for almost three years!"

"That's a home? I did notice you have a fantastic imagination." She smiled.

Peter had to pause, leaning on the handle of his shovel. *Fantastic imagination?* She had called it a "fantastic imagination."

He had been called a spaz, space case, day dreamer, head in the clouds, geek, dork, dweeb, and even the dreaded "weirdo" that Teneil had mentioned the night before. He was smart and had been given a load of credit for his academic achievements, but no one had ever called his daydreaming a "fantastic imagination."

He stared at her for a long moment, the first break he had taken from work. His intense stare made Teneil feel bad about making fun of his. . .home. "Doesn't it get lonely?" she asked. "Living in a truck?"

"Not really," he shrugged, but the image of his best friend, the brilliant flashlight, came to mind and he amended, "A bit."

"Well, I looked at your truck this morning and sent an order to the mechanic. Being this far out of the city, it could take a while to get it fixed." She took a step toward him, and the world melted from his vision, leaving nothing but her. "It'll have to stay parked in my driveway." She smiled. "So, I hope you don't mind calling my house home for a while."

He shook his head to clear the dream. He was always mixing fantasy and reality. "Sorry, what did you say?"

"I said you are going to be staying with me for a while, if that's okay."

He forced all the chaos in his mind to still for a moment and said, "One more time?"

"Is that okay?" She laughed, slightly uneasy. "Would you? Like to stay? With me?"

Was this real? Was any of this real? Had he died last night and this was the "Sixth Sense" all over again? This whole time he, himself, was the ghost, no longer living half in and half out of this world but fully out? He was dead and she was his paradise.

"Peter?"

Because he was clearly now dead and the dead had no fear or insecurities, he said, "Yes. I will stay with you." In his heart he added, *always*.

Chapter Nine
IF ONLY HE WAS HUMBLE

Aaron was a man devoted to two things: his God and his work. His work, now almost finished, was titled, "A profile of faith, corruption, and the role that modern missionaries play in Africa today." Aaron Christianson had backpacked across most of Africa alone, but that was not unusual. He'd always been alone. Not that he necessarily preferred it that way, but he could never find anyone willing to go with him, and he wasn't going to let a silly thing like that hold him back.

He was the kind of man that men wanted to be, and as corny as it sounded, women wanted to be with. The kind of man that fixed what was broken and bled without knowing where it was coming from. He had started out as a hard man, but years of travel and experience had taught him gentleness and patience too. Something about his manner made elders respect him and children climb on him.

After three years wandering through the deserts and jungles of this continent, Aaron had grown restless. Something unexpected had happened: he was growing lonesome. In his thirty- eight years, he'd never really felt alone until he set foot on this journey. His latest project involved interviewing dozens of families from all over the world who had dedicated their lives to establishing Christianity in remote places throughout Africa. Seeing what they'd shared, their bond had woken something inside of him.

He *did* want someone. God help him, if he was being honest, he was depressed for days after seeing the sunrise on Mt. Kilimanjaro, and then again, when he cooled his aching feet at the base of Victoria Falls. He had seen so many wonders and each time his breath was taken away, he instantly looked down and to his left, where "she" should be. He looked at his calloused, empty hand and tried to imagine what it would feel like to experience all these things with someone. He knew that he would make a fine husband, but he longed for something more than an ordinary wife.

His attempt to place anyone he knew next to him was laughable. Aaron had met plenty of sweet girls that had no backbone. Beautiful girls who had no kindness. Strong girls who seemed to have no love in them. That was the challenge; not just any woman would do. He gave up as many times as he'd dared to hope. After several years he had begun to feel that maybe there was no one for him. And so, he would continue to wander this earth with only God, and only God knew that he still searched every woman's eyes, looking for her.

Until one unsuspecting evening in a small, quaint village in Northern Malawi. . .

From the rooftop of the hostel where he was staying, he realized that rooftops were some of the only places throughout Africa where he found peace. He watched the sky darken to evening as the endless parade of shopkeepers packed in their goods and loaded produce back in basins for the journey home, while children played contentedly in the street.

There was no parental authority in sight, except a little girl with a huge stick who seemed to naturally take on the role of mother. She played a harsh one at that, whipping any of the little ones who got too close. Kids were shouting in pain while the others laughed. Aaron laughed too, until one especially bold young man made it behind the little girl and pulled her braid. The boy was far too slow in his attempted escape, taking the little girl's stick with full force straight across the forehead. The boy was laid out flat.

Aaron's body coiled for action, ready to climb down and assess the boy's damage, but something was holding him back. *Jump,* he told his legs, but they disobeyed him. *"Watch,"* a voice whispered in his mind. He observed a woman help up the injured boy. In the fading light he could not make out her details. He could only see that her hair was dark, her skin the color of sand. She was neither small nor big. Neither was she short or tall. She was ordinary in every way but captivating.

It was her voice that held Aaron. He did not know what she was saying, but he knew the tone she used: the kind firmness of a good teacher.

Adults and children alike had seen the boy take the hit and they were all listening now. They burst out into peals of laughter that were so joyous it beckoned to Aaron, and he responded, leaning out as far as he dared. He watched as the gathering of children's eyes filled with wonder at her words. She spoke and the boy's face filled with horror. He began shaking his head and backing away. The woman was laughing when she picked up the stick and broke it across her knee. The children cheered, danced, and ran off.

Aaron sat on the rooftop until all traces of the sun had vanished. His body ached when he made his way back down into the restaurant that conveniently sat in front of the room he had rented. He grabbed a table and stared at nothing. His face wore a mix of pained contemplation and resignation.

A cheerful young man, maybe twenty years old, pulled out the chair next to him. "Teneil," he said, without any introduction.

Aaron glanced up at the man absently.

"Her name," said the young man. "It's Teneil."

"Sorry?" Aaron asked.

"The woman, with the kids."

136

He sat up instantly in his chair, shaking the echoes of her voice out of his head. "She lives here?" he questioned immediately. "What is she doing here? Who is she?"

"I'm Sam." The young man extended his hand.

"I am so sorry, how rude of me." Aaron shook Sam's hand and tried to contain himself through the traditional greeting. After a moment's respectful pause, he finally asked the question that was burning inside of him: "What did she say to them?"

Sam laughed and shook his head, remembering. He'd known Teneil for years. She had hired him as labor to help her build a water system in the mountains. Teneil kept him and several other men steadily employed building all sorts of things like home repairs, retaining walls, and currently a house for a widow and her two children. There were so many different projects, and she was always planning more. The crew liked her humor and respected her eagerness to do physical labor.

He knew that she was strong and independent. She was beautiful and had a sharp wit. The people respected her because of her willingness to listen and give sound judgment in difficult situations. She hired Sam, but she also loved him like a son. She encouraged him, she scolded him, and she was loved either way. She was like a mother to many, and because of that, Sam did not appreciate the way that this man, Aaron, had watched her from the rooftop.

Teneil had never shown any interest in any man in the years Sam had known her. Though Sam had seen many men attempt to claim her as their bride, she would graciously decline and say that her heart only belonged to one man: Jesus. He liked that about her, and he wanted to protect her from this buffoon that was looking after her like a prize to hunt and mount on his wall.

Aaron continued to pummel Sam with questions, and a plot began to form in Sam's mind. It was a brilliant and awful idea, one that he was sure Teneil would appreciate.

Sam met the older man's eyes and carefully chose which question to answer first. "She told the children that the Bible teaches eye for an eye," he began, "and that the boy who was beaten had the right to beat the girl back. But because Teneil loved the little girl so much, she would take the beating in her place. The boy refused to hit her, and Teneil broke the stick."

"What if the boy had hit her?" Aaron asked.

Sam shrugged. "Teneil would have taken it."

Aaron raised his eyebrows skeptically. "How do you know that?"

"Because she is as stubborn as she is anything else." Sam laughed.

"You really know her?"

"I do! I could introduce you, if you want." Sam smiled to himself, then made sure Aaron saw his convincing grin, too. "I work with her. We have a project tomorrow. I can show you where it is."

Aaron practically fell out of his seat, unable to believe his good fortune. Maybe, he thought, this time would be different. Maybe this Teneil was someone he could truly connect with. He was certainly drawn to her, though he'd barely seen her and her voice already, alarmingly, felt like it was fading from his memory. "Really? You would do that?"

"Oh, sure!" Sam encouraged with a grin. "I like you! And because I like you, I'm going to help you out. Some things you should know about Teneil. . ." Sam lowered his voice conspiratorially and leaned forward. As if on a string, Aaron did the same thing, pulled downward toward the table with his attention rapt to the younger man.

"She's not like other women," Sam whispered. "She really likes self-assured men, men who stand up to her and take charge of things. She tells me all the time how she feels like she is unequal to her tasks and wishes someone would not just help her but manage her work. She has always said that. She mentions all the time that she wishes men were bolder and prouder and took what they wanted."

If Only He was Humble

Aaron nodded, chewing on the precious insights that Sam had shared. It was not really like Aaron to take over, but he could be bold when the occasion called for it. And it seemed like it did now, but this sounded borderline arrogant. "Bold," Aaron mused and nodded.

"Not pushy, but not *not* pushy. . .if you know what I mean." Sam raised his eyebrows a few times and Aaron's face scrunched in confusion once more.

"I thought I knew what you meant, but now I'm not so sure."

Sam sighed. "Look, Adam. . ."

"Aaron," he corrected.

"Right, whatever. Listen: Teneil has been waiting for the right man. She has always said she would know him when she saw him. That means you got one chance at this. So, you need to think *strong*. Think, 'Rooster'. Think, 'proud warrior on conquest!' Think-"

"I think I got it," Aaron cut in with a laugh.

"Just remember, you got one shot. One first impression. I'll come by to pick you up here in the morning." He stood from his seat, but as he turned to leave, a final thought struck Sam so hard it spun him back around like a little duck in a shooting game at a carnival. "Also, Teneil hates when people use her first name. She says it's disrespectful. Everyone calls her Miss Honeypot."

Aaron smiled at the name as Sam left. It was somehow perfect, and as he laid in bed that night, he rolled the name over and over in his mind: *Teneil Honeypot.* Such a sweet name. Miss Honeypot.

And somewhere in the village in a humble house there was a man named Sam laughing hysterically as he told the rest of the crew what to expect in the morning.

Dawn was late that next day. The crew had already assembled and was busy organizing the day's tasks when the sun made its lazy appearance.

Teneil was not at the worksite just yet; she was in town haggling with the carpenter about the cost of door frames.

In the meantime, Aaron met the crew of six men, who ranged from every age and type. One old man, who spoke no English, glared at Aaron before going back to his work of cutting wire for some unknown tasks. Three men were working shovels, methodically turning a pile of sand, stones, and cement into concrete. A younger man, maybe seventeen or eighteen, was breaking bricks and preparing a foundation that looked as if it was going to be set that day.

Aaron wasn't the kind of man to sit and watch others work, so he picked up a shovel and made his back useful. The crew carried on as they usually did, harassing each other and extending that same courtesy to Aaron. He welcomed the banter and all that he was learning about Miss Honeypot in the process. Thanks to Sam's plan, the crew took as many liberties as they felt compelled to.

Teneil, Aaron had learned, was a hard woman. She liked to fight and was known to physically slap the crew members for being late or making mistakes. Oh yes, they respected her, but they also feared her. She was kind but her temper was outrageous. After a few hours, and a few horror stories, Aaron was ready to admit he had clearly been wrong about her. It would probably be best if he packed up and moved on right now. But then he heard it.

The rumble of a car's tires on the dirt road set all the men scattering back to work. *The stories must not be exaggerated,* he thought, watching them all run as if they were hiding from the powerful wrath of the woman behind the wheel.

The crew did run and hide, yes, but not because they were afraid; they were just finding optimal positions to watch the car crash of an interaction that was about to unfold.

From his position behind the building where they had just poured a new concrete floor, Aaron could not see her car, but he could hear the door close and some grunting as Teneil loaded her arms with everything she could manage before walking the distance from the edge of the road to the worksite. Sam greeted her like a dutiful second and took several items off her hands.

She laughed in response to something Sam had said, and the sweet sound called to Aaron just as powerfully as it had the night before. He began adjusting his t-shirt, running dirty fingers through his thick, brown hair, and checking his breath. The crew watched him curiously.

"I think Sam had it wrong," the older man said, "He does not want to use her, he wants to marry her."

They all nodded and grunted in agreement, but still did not move from their safe vantage points.

"This is it," Aaron murmured to himself as the woman got closer. *Why am I nervous?* Every warning bell was going off in Aaron's stomach, but he mistook the uneasy feelings for mere butterflies. He had, after all, been here the whole morning. At least he could introduce himself. "Self-assured, proud," he repeated over and over.

"Where is everyone?" Teneil sounded worried as she surveyed the ghost town and abandoned tools.

Aaron remembered the birds he had watched for hours in the Congo. The males were always strutting about with all their colors displayed. Males stomped and squawked while the females looked on before eventually flying off. It was that image he had in mind when, as he stepped a little harder than he usually would, around the partially built wall blocking him from her view.

"I," he stated boldly and perhaps in a little deeper tone than he would typically carry in conversation, "am here." And what was this puffed thing he was doing with his chest? He felt awkward and forced.

Teneil's gaze snapped to him. She wasn't really sure what to say. She instantly disliked this man. Teneil was an excellent judge of character, so when she saw his posture, his "strut" and heard the forced tension in his voice, she knew one thing for sure: whatever this stranger was, genuine wasn't it. "Who is that?" she side-whispered to Sam.

"Don't know," Sam replied, eyeing Aaron with as much of a critical stare as Teneil. "Came today, thought he was your friend. He's been yelling at the crew, ordering us all morning. You don't know him?"

Sam watched the question turn to blazing fire in Teneil's eyes. He knew how fiercely protective she was of those around her. What he had said was the equivalent to throwing a Molotov cocktail onto the warehouse of gunpowder he had been so meticulously organizing. There was nothing to do now but watch the explosion. Inside he was already looking into the future laughs that would echo for years to come. This would be his greatest prank.

"I'm sorry?" Teneil called out, walking directly toward Aaron. If he was a proud bird, she was a lioness, and he would be her light lunch. "Have we met?" She did not extend her hand but stopped far enough away from him to avoid their personal spaces from touching. Sam gave Aaron two zealous and reassuring thumbs up behind her.

Her voice he recognized but the tone was sharp as steel now. He'd half expected that after hearing all the stories about her but then he looked into her eyes. He was no judge of character, but when he looked into her amazing, brilliant green gaze that held such stark contrast with her almost black hair, he lost the facade.

For just a moment, his shoulders fell and his mouth hung agape. Had he thought her ordinary before? He fought to keep his persona. *Self-assured, proud,* he told himself, trying to keep it together. He could be, no, *would be* whatever she wanted.

"Just happened by. Looked like this project could use a man in charge."

Aaron saw in her every muscle stiffening and thought that perhaps his new friend Sam was right; he had definitely struck a chord with this woman, so he punctuated his good fortune with heavy eyelids. He'd never tried to be sultry before, but it kind of felt right.

"May I call you Miss Honeypot?" He flashed his most debonair smile; one he'd only ever used in the mirror after shaving.

Teneil felt something crack inside. To understand why Teneil did what she did next, you need to understand where she has been. You see, Teneil had not always been a Christian. At one point in her life, she was a bartender in several biker bars. She had also worked on a variety of construction projects.

She was no stranger to disrespect on a job site because she was a woman; she had endured her share of cat calls and crude comments. But she was a different person now, and this man had cut through all her years of practiced patience and compassion in less than a handful of words. There was a cool calculation that leaked from the place that had cracked inside of her.

This was Africa. There was freedom here to settle your scores and Teneil had made many friends. Could she actually kill this man? Did he have family? Would anyone ask any questions?

"Miss. Honeypot?" she repeated in a deceptively sweet voice. She needed to make sure she had heard him correctly. If she was going to rot away in a Malawian prison for murder, she needed him to sign the death warrant himself.

"How about I take you back to town for lunch and we can discuss whatever you like?" Aaron winked as he spoke, and it felt greasy. He had never acted this way before. Maybe this was what his friends talked about when they said that relationships changed a man. He didn't know if he could keep this up, but hopefully, someday she could learn to appreciate the real him.

Teneil noted how close the man's heels were to the six-inch foundation wall, filled with the freshly leveled cement that her crew, wherever they were, had set that morning. And she took a step closer. Then another slow step. And another.

Aaron's posture melted again as she drew near him. His shoulders fell slack, his demeanor softening under her intensity. *Beautiful.*

She was inches away looking deep into his eyes, fire raging in her belly. He was a dead man. Teneil had one brief moment when she thought, *pity he's so handsome. Isn't that the way of the world, though?*

The heat of her fire was so powerful that Aaron was positive it had worked. She was drawn to him as he was drawn to her, God forgive him for ever doubting. This woman would be his wife. Sure, she was a bit harder than him but maybe that would complement his mild manner. Surely, he could trust in the Lord, for surely the Lord--

Teneil pushed him. Hard. The small wall directly behind his feet stopped him from righting himself and he crashed down. Aaron landed flat on his back, in shock. The shock of her hand on his chest gave way to the shock of the abrupt shove, which then gave way to the shock of the cold, wet concrete underneath him. The fresh concrete gave, too, but only a little, and by the time he had gasped breath back into his lungs all he could see was her shouting.

Teneil's words were only half in English, but he caught some of them, "Arrogant!", "Self-righteous!" and "Tell the guys I am sorry about the foundation. I have to go."

"She's crazy!" Aaron shouted loud enough that he'd hoped she'd heard it over the sound of her tires churning dust on the road. What was she thinking? What was *he* thinking? All the stories the crew told were true; he could see it now. Several hands were there to help him up. Aaron looked around but couldn't see Sam. Sam was there, but he had fallen to the ground clutching his stomach, laughing in a way that caused no sound.

The crew, as bad as they felt for the man, were echoing Sam's torrents of laughter. They would never complain about re-leveling the foundation; they had deserved it and it was worth it.

Aaron shook off what concrete he could, righted himself, and without another word started the five-mile walk back to town. He'd ignored the strange looks and laughter as much as he could, but by the time he reached the shower in his room he was furious. How could he have been so blind? She was the exact reason he didn't go after women. Crazy, the lot of them! He imagined that even God must be laughing at him. And though he had paid for the week in advance, he packed his things and boarded a large, local taxi. Anywhere would be better than this place.

From his seat in the back of the crowded van, he vaguely overheard the taxi driver say he was headed to the border town, Karonga, a four-hour journey. *Not far away enough,* he thought, *but it will have to do.* His pride hurt as much as the rash from his walk of shame covered in the corrosive cement acid. He just let that burn add to the anger, tipped his hat over his face, and attempted to appear as if he was sleeping. Eventually his attempt was a success and when he finally woke, it was to the sound of a baby crying and the land moving quickly under the tires. He instantly felt better.

"Would you like one?" an old woman next to him offered an ear of roasted corn from her basket. He smiled and accepted her kindness. Right now, he really needed some kindness. "Are you feeling better?" she asked.

He smiled slightly and gave a quick nod but said nothing, afraid his voice would betray him.

"I saw you in town earlier," the woman said gently. His stillness was his reply enough. "What happened to you there, covered in mud? If you don't mind my asking?"

"I fell." The words came out harsh, but it wasn't a lie. He had fallen for a snake of a woman, and now he was running away.

"Did you?" She let out a little chuckle but said nothing more. Rebbeca had been married for over twenty years and had four sons. She recognized a bruised pride, and the kind of sulking that only comes at a woman's hands.

After a short time, and with a little food in his belly, Aaron's anger seemed to dwindle. He cleared his throat and began, "there's this woman. . ."

He hated that he was going to tell this stranger the crazy events of the last twenty-four hours, but it wasn't like he would ever see her again. Maybe, he reasoned with himself, if he told someone it would stop repeating like a nightmarish loop in his head. So, he talked, far too quickly, about the last few years: his loneliness, the first time he had seen the woman, the morning he'd had at her jobsite, her crew, and finally, his tender backside.

This was a long trip that Rebbeca made often to visit her family in Karonga. She was only making polite conversation with this man, looking for an interesting story to pass the time. But there were several words that caught her full attention. Words like, "building a house", "Sam", and "crazy white woman". Nkhata Bay was a small place and mostly inhabited by seven major families. In short, that meant that everyone knew everyone, and six years ago when Teneil moved in, people came from very far to see if she could help them.

Rebbeca knew several others in this van alone that Teneil had assisted in one way or another. She knew all of this, because Rebbeca was Teneil's neighbor. She also had become a good friend to Teneil, and had spent long hours talking about God, work, and the challenges for her living here alone.

Rebbeca had often told Teneil that she must find a husband. But Teneil would only laugh and say that she was not good at picking men, so she was leaving it up to God to choose for her. Rebbeca thought about all that Aaron had said and she decided quickly that she liked this man. She had only one hour until they would reach the next town and he would be gone.

"Teneil?" the old woman repeated.

Aaron sighed in exasperation, as if just hearing her name spoken was insulting. "I see that her reputation is even greater than I assumed." He laughed.

"I think you assume too much," Rebecca said flatly. She had noticed the half a dozen others in the van were all listening to the man's story as well. In her tribal language, Rebbeca stated loud enough to be heard over the rumble of the engine: "You all hear this man. You all know Teneil. She needs a husband, so why not this man? He is fine enough, I think."

One older man called back with a toothless grin from the front row, "I was still hoping she would pick me!" That brought a round of laughter that Aaron didn't quite understand. In broken English, the old man spoke up in Aaron's direction, "I know Teneil," he said with a smile. "When my daughter's grass roof burned down, and the plastic melted over everything they owned, Teneil took the whole family to the market and replaced everything. Then she paid a year of their rent in the new place."

The rest of the passengers all nodded in agreement, as if to affirm the authenticity of such a tale. Others added their own accounts of her philanthropy. Aaron, however, couldn't quite believe it. There was no way the woman he'd just fled from could be capable of such things.

The van was silent as Aaron contemplated all they had said. But there was a wall, infinitely thick, around his heart, and Aaron had already placed Teneil outside of it. All her good works were meaningless when the insides he'd seen were so ugly. Finally, the van pulled into the depot.

"This has been an interesting ride," Aaron seethed anew as he stood. "Thank you for the corn, and I'm happy to know that Miss Honeypot takes such good care of you all." He tried to be polite but also dismissive.

"Who?" Rebbeca laughed.

"Your Teneil. Teneil Honeypot." He grabbed his bag and slung it over his shoulder.

"Her name is Teneil Jayne!" Rebbeca called after him. Her words slammed into the back of his head, but it would be several more steps before they registered with him. He turned but Rebbeca was gone. What did her name matter, anyway? A rose by any other name etc. etc. He found a cheap rest house and fell on the hard bed in such exhaustion he knew he would sleep far into the next day.

But sleep refused to come. Aaron closed his eyes and saw her. He opened his eyes and could only hear the words of the passengers over and over. Finally, around three in the morning, he got up and flung the door open. He walked out into the quiet darkness, underneath the blanket of endless stars that ranged above him. He needed to be alone, but he couldn't get away from himself. He raged at God for this confusion and frustration.

He poured his heart out and finally when there was nothing left to say, he felt empty.

There was a void where his frustration had been, but he still felt wrong. *"Is that what you want?"* a voice asked in his heart, referring to the emptiness where his fury once was. It was hard to admit that the emptiness was more uncomfortable than his anger at her. *"She* disappointed *you?"* the voice asked.

Suddenly, everything became clear to Aaron, and he let the realization take him to his knees on the side of the dusty road. He saw Teneil truly for the first time. This fierce woman that had done impossible things. She had sacrificed and loved so much and fought every day, in so many ways, just to be able to help others. He could see the respect she had earned from those around her.

And, at last, he saw himself through her eyes.

All the lies he had offered her made him flinch, and then worst of all, he heard himself call her "Miss Honeypot." He understood. It was Sam. Sam had set him up. And maybe Sam was right to do so.

"I am such an idiot!" Aaron stood abruptly and in his overwhelming frustration attempted to kick a rock next to his foot but didn't realize the rock was firmly rooted. Instead, he smashed his own toes. He cried out, but also welcomed the punishment for his childish actions. She had every right to hate him. He looked out at the lights of the town behind him and into the blackness of the road going back toward Nkhata Bay.

"What are you waiting for?" the voice whispered, and an urge inside of him blossomed.

He ran, with quite a limp, back to his room in Karonga. Throwing his things in his shoulder bag, he had only a moment to make sure his toes were still attached before he began his walk. He knew it would be wise to wait for a taxi, but he couldn't stay still. She was there, and he had to make it right. He reached the edge of the quiet, dark road, like a peaceful black river spreading into infinity on the dark horizon. He had found *her:* he had never been so sure of anything. So, he walked, and he thought of all the ways he would make it up to her, if she would let him.

Teneil couldn't sleep. He was a rude, conceited peacock. She hated men like that, who assumed their privilege on everyone around them. She wouldn't have thought about him again after driving away. Lord alone knew she had bigger problems to face than this, but she was haunted. Not by his insulting nature, but that brief moment just before she pushed him.

When she put her hand on his chest and felt his heart hammering through her palm, when his posture had completely changed, when she looked into his eyes. . . Teneil had seen something different. There was a brilliance, an electricity between them that had almost made her step back.

She told herself it didn't matter; he was a creep, and he was gone. She had heard the story of his walk to town and his quick departure from many people. He was gone, but she couldn't seem to let it go. Finally, around 3am she pushed out of her mosquito net and stepped outside. The air was slightly cooler, and she drank it in big gulps. "God, what is wrong with me?!"

Aaron looked and smelled awful. He had walked for over an hour before the sky had lightened and taxis resumed their services. He tried to take the first taxi that came by but quickly realized, in his haste, he had left his wallet back in the lodge in the border town. He hadn't even cared. He laughed at himself when he realized he would have to walk the entire way back.

His toes throbbed, and his clothing chafed where it rubbed on his rash-covered backside. He was broke, dirty, tired, hurt, and rejoicing.

He was almost running when a truck with a bed full of people stopped next to him. "Are you okay?" the driver asked. "Can I give you a ride?"

"I don't have any money," Aaron huffed out between labored breaths.

"That's okay, get in," he said kindly.

And without any polite refusal, Aaron climbed into the back of the truck where he took three deep breaths and fell fast asleep. He dreamed he was too late. For what he didn't know, only that when he woke up a couple hours later the sense of urgency was only beaten by his confusion.

Where am I now? He sat up, his face puffy, hair disheveled and full of debris. Slowly, he climbed out of the truck bed. His foot screamed at him, and he caught himself before falling. He limped his way through Nkhata Bay until he recognized the hostel, where he remembered he still had the whole week paid up. He wandered into the room he had fled from just twelve hours before.

"Shower first," he ordered himself. "Then you can find her." *And say what?* But he wouldn't think about that. One step at a time.

He had a few ideas of where to look. Aaron started at the jobsite where he found the crew but not Teneil. Sam attempted to keep up his joke but found himself flat on his back in the concrete being mixed that day. Not for what Sam had done to him, but what he had done to her. Aaron had expected a fight from the crew, but they merely cheered and laughed. Even Sam, with a bloody nose, had laughed after the shock wore off.

He walked back into town to ask around. Wherever he went, they all knew Teneil and had advice on where he should look next. By the evening, he was exhausted. How could she possibly be in so many different places in one day? Did she ever stop?

Aaron sighed and muttered aloud, "God, what do I do now?"

"Rest your aching feet in the water." That seemed like the exact thing he needed. So, Aaron walked to the lake shore and, without pausing, eyes focused on the clouds reflecting sunset, he walked straight into the lake, clothing and all. The cool water was heaven on his raw skin, tired feet, and

hurting heart. He waded out neck deep and then disappeared under the water until he felt his life begging for air, and finally surfaced.

"I'm sorry I pushed you," came a sweet voice from behind him.

Slowly, Aaron turned to where she sat alone, the small waves of the large lake rolling over her toes. The orange brilliance of the sunset lit her up like fire.

"I shouldn't have pushed you," Teneil added. "Sam told me what he did, and I'm sorry. Everyone seems to think that you deserved it, but what you deserve is not mine to give. I shouldn't have pushed you and I am truly sorry."

Whatever Aaron had expected, this was not it. He slowly made his way to her until he was mostly out of the lake but remained on his knees in the water. "There is no limit to my stupidity," he admitted, and speaking the truth felt like leeching poison out of a wound. "There is no reason for you to even consider me for your apology. The way I acted, what I said. . .that wasn't me."

"Yeah, I know." Teneil smiled, recalling Sam's story.

"No, you don't," Aaron replied earnestly. "You don't know me." Tenderly, he pleaded with her, "but if you could just let me start over. I think that. . .we. . .what I mean to say is, I think that you. . ."

He paused. What was he going to say? That she was his rib?

"It's just that. . ." he tried again, "Y-you see. . ."

She smiled at him, wonder in her eyes and laughter on her lips. "I know."

Chapter Ten
IF ONLY HE WAS A HERO

The ever-dancing red dust was the only seemingly living thing for leagues in the desert. It whipped and flew high in the air, an ultra-fine powder that was impossible to keep out of anything. Teneil had heard that the red dust, being light as ash, had flown over the sea and colored the Americas, too. Eighty percent of the world was as red as Mars from space, or so she had heard. It was hard to believe anything these days, not after the world had turned on itself.

There were many names for it, but most of those still left alive just took to calling it "the rapture". After several weaponized biochemical leaks into the population, "G.O.G." was formed, a Global Organized Government, to set global standards for living in biochemical warfare zones on all continents. The G.O.G., or "Gog", had completely stopped all non-essential public gatherings.

Schools, churches, weddings, funerals, and any other traditional gathering was done remotely through video feed. To accomplish this, cameras were installed in every room of every home, on every street, and drones endlessly patrolled the skies. It was marketed as a virtual reality;

people could access global cameras to their own advantage, allowing them freedom to explore the world from their own home. It was a small trade for losing all privacy.

Not everyone complied. In fact, it was the Christians who started the rebellion, refusing to stop the small group gatherings. After six months of televised brutality against these rebels, a mass stand was taken against Gog. Seven gathering points were established at equal distances across the globe, and a call for all Christians around the world was put out. There was to be a massive religious gathering the likes of which Earth had never seen.

Looking back, it should have been obvious: the target had been painted so clearly. No one knew who was ultimately responsible for the carnage. Most blamed terrorists, saying the Christians were stupid to have publicized their coordinates so far in advance. Others, like herself, believed it was actually Gog themselves who dropped the seven nuclear warheads to solidify their global authority.

The fallout was devastating, not only to the millions who were vaporized in the twinkling of an eye, and their loved ones who were left behind, but to the world itself. The land was scarred beyond repair. Radiation levels being what they were meant that the next generation born suffered physical mutations. Most children born in the following five years did not survive, and those who did were born into an unforgiving world. Famine from the scorched land and plagues from the biochemical warfare made people jumpy and distrustful.

Those who stayed in the Magog's, the habitable zones remaining under Gog's control, lived on meager rations of 98% genetically manufactured food of questionable origin. Those who chose to leave those zones lived in "the wastes", the reported dead zones on the fringes of radioactive hot spots. Teneil was one of those people, and the ironically named Eden was one of those places.

Like everyone else in this living nightmare, Teneil traded her skills for rations and water. She was the top mechanic in several surrounding districts and people paid handsomely for her to service their water recovery devices, radios, generators, and even the occasional car. She lived with several aging widows and one young orphan boy in a cave.

It was one cave among many that was dug out of the soft sand rock. The older women never left the cave, so Teneil had worked tirelessly to support them all. The young boy she called Bart, due to his wild hair and temperament, helped with things like hauling water and on rare occasions, when it was available, cooking food.

Teneil was taking a break before she started the two-day journey back to Eden. She'd spent a long day scavenging whatever city this was; the name was long forgotten and buried below the thick blanket of red dust. She had a successful trip but walking in dust was harder than walking on fine sand. She finished wrapping the parts she'd found as well as she could to keep the dust out of them and secured them to the sled that she would drag behind her.

The next step was assembling the layers for her own protection. One hundred percent UV ski goggles came with her wherever she went. She had them coated in a film that blackened in the sun. They made things like these raids possible, and that meant that she had fought on several occasions to ensure they remained hers. Multiple layers of fabric wrapped securely around her head until she was completely covered. Her boots were laced and gloves protected her fingers from the red sun.

Ready to head back, Teneil pushed the door to whatever shop this once was open. She closed the door behind her and dragged the cover she had made back into place. It was a bit of building debris she had nailed together to camouflage her hideout. She had scavenged this city several times and this shop, with all its storage space, was the closest thing to a second home she had.

She used it as a shelter and a safe place for goods that were more than she could carry, things she knew would be stolen if she took them to Eden, and things of value that would put her family at risk. She had never seen anyone this far out. Those few who could get out here wouldn't likely find her shelter in this maze of a ruined city, and the ever-shifting dust did a good job of hiding her tracks, but even still she hid the entrance.

Teneil allowed the film to darken on her goggles before opening her eyes. Even with the blackened lenses she squinted at the brightness, but that didn't last long. The sun was quickly swallowed by a massing dust storm. An impossibly high red wall came toward her from the horizon, roaring its demands and churning with the promise of destruction. It was clear that she wouldn't be going anywhere now. She sighed deeply. Her family in Eden had enough food hidden for a week or so, but she missed them, and she hated staying alone in this graveyard.

Teneil watched the ominous lightning and swirling darkness like a gaping maw threatening to swallow the wrecked city in one bite. Through the layers over her ears, she could hear the rumbling thunder and… something else, too? Like the buzzing of a bee in the distance, it was unmistakable to her ears.

An engine revved as high as it could go, the choking sputtering of it promising that it wouldn't last for long. She could see the bike barely ahead of the monster storm. Whoever the rider was, it was clear that they wouldn't make it to shelter before the dust took them. Teneil knew she should go back inside. She could do nothing, and she didn't want to watch the stranger die. She could do nothing. She could do nothing.

There is always a way, a voice whispered in her heart.

She remembered the flare gun she had stored inside. It was useless because no one wanted to give their position away these days, but she'd still kept it. She pushed the makeshift cover away from the store entrance and ran inside. After tearing through the shelves, she rushed back outside and aimed the gun. The red, smoking flare burst out before her, but the motorcycle maintained its course toward the heart of the city.

"Idiot!" she yelled. She loaded another shell and fired. "Here!" But she could barely hear her own voice in the presence of the storm.

Nevertheless, the bike somehow obeyed her call and turned in her direction, no longer racing away from the storm but skirting along the edge. Its engine choked and sputtered before completely dying about 100 feet away. The driver dove off the bike and ran toward her. She stood at the door, waiting to open it until he was closer. By the time he reached her there was no visual, only that he had aimed his arms at her and ran blindly, hoping she would wait for him.

They locked onto one another, and she practically threw him into the small shop before turning and pushing the counter against the door, making an effective barricade. Her face covering was so thick with dust that she couldn't breathe. Teneil tore through the layers before sucking in a deep breath and hacking up the dirt that had made its way into the shop.

She ripped off her goggles, blinking furiously to see in the now-darker space, and found the stranger lying motionless on the floor. She crawled over to him, took off his helmet, and saw his face mask also caked in a suffocating layer of red. She pulled at the fabric but when it didn't give, she took out the blade at her hip, the only blade she never used, keeping it razor sharp for emergencies.

She easily sliced through the layers. The man was motionless, and visions of the dozens like him she'd lost along the way flooded her mind. She leaned in close but with the storm now crashing against the storefront like an ocean tide crashing on the rocks, she couldn't tell if he was breathing, and panic overwhelmed her. She clenched her hands together, raised them high in the air, bringing all her weight down on his chest.

"Wake- up!" she bellowed at the countless friends and comrades that wore the body of the man dying before her.

He sputtered, eyes wide and unseeing. The man reached his arms out for a blessed inhale of air that was too long coming. Finally gulping and coughing on his hands and knees, he demanded, "You trying to kill me?"

Teneil sat back on her heels in the dirty entryway of the shop. "Kill you? I just saved your life!" she yelled back.

"You punched me!" He was still gasping for air and began pulling the remaining scraps of fabric from around his head and neck, as if it would somehow help.

"You weren't breathing!" she insisted.

"So, you thought, 'punch him'?" He removed his last scarf, little more than a threadbare strip of fabric. He looked at her. His eyes, as blue as a tropical sea, seemed even more drastic set in his sun-worn face. His hair was clearly self-shaven; it grew in patchy sun-bleached tufts, some longer and some *almost* clean shaven in places, struggling to fill back in. His beard was well grown, and despite the layers of protection it was stained the same red as everything else in these Godforsaken lands.

"I should have left you out there to die!" she yelled indignantly.

He laughed heartily at that, and she joined in. He got up slowly, his spine and broad shoulders unrolling to an impressive full height. He looked around at the dust piled in the corners, the shelves holding various bric-a-brac, and advertisements depicting a life-long dead. "Nice place you got here."

"Thanks. Fourteen more years on the mortgage and it will be all mine." She lovingly eyed the room before making the small hop to sit on the counter now blocking the door.

She was pretty, or what he could see of her was. To be honest, all he could see beyond the dirt and the fabric wrapped around her head was that she had all of her teeth, and that was hard to find these days. He smiled and said, "It's gonna be a long night," then took a step toward her.

"Look, Mister," Teneil began, narrowing her eyes at him. "I just saved your life and so I'm inclined to think you owe me a favor. I would trust that for that reason alone you will respect my personal space, but if you should find that difficult. . ." She pulled a small dagger from her belt and began cleaning out under her fingernails. "I got at least one reason you might consider a more chivalrous path." She stuck the point of the knife into the countertop. "I got six other reasons hiding on my person." She smiled back at him the way a cat smiles at a goldfish.

His playful nature melted away. "I wouldn't ever do anything to hurt you." His look was grave and his tone serious.

She believed him and some tension left her body. "Come on." She jumped off the counter and walked through a beaded curtain to the store's back room.

He didn't hesitate before following her away from the vicious roar of the dust storm, not until she moved a few boxes from where they covered a cellar door. She carefully brushed the dust away without stirring it up, lifting open the door to a hole with a ladder that descended into blackness. "Get in."

"What's down there?" He swallowed hard and she saw herself through his eyes. The world was full of gruesome troubles, and he didn't know her from Eve. Clans relying on cannibalism were common in many of the fringe areas, and hadn't she already threatened him with a knife?

"Suit yourself." She flashed a grin at him and disappeared into the blackness.

Stupid. He knew it was stupid to trust a full set of teeth. Rolling his eyes at himself, he followed her against his better judgment.

"Shut the hatch, would ya?" she called up, and he obeyed.

The blackness was total, the air stale and musty. It was deeper than he had guessed. He stuck his arms out and found a wall directly in front of him. "We need to get the dust off here before we go inside." Her voice was like music in the darkness somewhere behind him. "So, take off your clothes."

"Take off my clothes?" He laughed. "What about *my* personal space?"

His laughter in the tight dark area was deep, joyful, and playful. When was the last time she had been allowed to be playful? The smile that stretched her face felt foreign and good. "Slow down, lover boy, not all of your clothes," she laughed. "Just the dust layer."

"Right." He coincided, still laughing. Slowly, as not to stir up the dust, they both took off layers. His soft apologizing when they accidently bumped into each other made Teneil feel more comfortable. Was he really a gentleman? Down to a tee shirt and his boxers, he was truly feeling the fool. In a mere few minutes this clever girl had completely disarmed him and had him practically naked in her basement. He was sure this was the dumbest thing he'd ever done. This was the wastes. Where was his mind? He was a dead man.

The latch on the door was rusty and he could hear her struggle to turn it before it clicked open. "Give me your hand." She called out to him, and without any question he reached toward her voice. Her hand was warm, and her calloused fingers slid between his with perfect ease. Less than an hour ago he was skirting a storm on a failing engine, sure of death, and now he was in the dark, in his underclothes, with a full toothed maiden holding his hand.

Not a bad day after all, he thought to himself.

She pulled him into another room and her hand slid from his. It was an effort not to grip her; he couldn't remember the last time he had held a woman's hand. But the thought was broken by the sound of her closing the rusty door again and latching it. "Wait here" were the most unnecessary two words he had ever heard, but he obeyed. Two loud cracks rang out in the space and a fluorescent blue and yellow sparked from her hand. She shook the neon sticks and the room lit up.

She stood before him in a small tank top and short set that may have been white once but now were a few shades darker than her pale skin. She was thin but not weak, her muscles, like most these days, spoke of hard labor. Her face was mostly still covered in dirt and shadow.

"Welcome to my humble abode." She turned and walked into the bunker, tossing a light stick on either end of the room. He could see it was almost the size of a single wide trailer house. The bunker was impressively clean and organized. Labeled barrels stood sentinel and two bunks hung from chains on one wall. He let out a low whistle.

"Home sweet home. Hungry? Of course, you are." She crossed the room and sat on a rug. "Come, dine with me," she said in a dramatic accent, and held out two small airline packages of moist towelettes.

"Are you for real?" He tore the edge of one packet open and held the washcloth to his nose, the clean soap's perfume radiating through the plastic. He sat and brushed his hands reverently on his shirt before taking out the little towel and washing his face, giving a small sigh of pleasure when the cloth slid over the back of his neck.

Teneil watched him for a while before taking care of her own face and hands. The way he'd appreciated her gift made her want to give him more.

When both cleansing wipes were as used up as they could be, he opened his eyes and saw her sitting across from him, still working on her own face. Her hair was short, no doubt sold in the market like most women, but it looked good on her. He watched her hands move the towel over her neck and shoulders before he'd realized how far his thoughts had gotten.

She cleared her throat in a knowing way. Her eyes were bright and curious and all for him. He almost said, *beautiful,* but caught himself. She was beautiful but he didn't want her to feel uncomfortable. So, he focused his attention elsewhere.

She had a hard time not blushing at the intensity of his gaze. His eyes like ice in the dim lighting chilled her core. She had not thought about anything other than survival in so long, but she was still a woman, and he was handsome. When he'd turned his head bashfully and respectfully, she saw the scar that ran from the temple down his neck and under his shirt.

Other scars were now visible on his hands, arms, and face. Both on his forearms, *defending himself*, and on his knuckles, *fighting back*. She had the same ones. She popped the top off of a container next to her and threw something at him. "Here ya go." She spoke kindly, like a person would when tossing scraps to a stray.

He caught a bottle of water and felt every muscle in his body get tense. This was *a bottle* of clean, unopened, 100% pure, priceless, water, and... "MRE?" he exclaimed in awe. The old military issued food rations weren't as rare as water but still, he was in shock.

"Make sure yours isn't toilet paper before you bite into it," she warned, then chuckled at his stunned expression. She had several food caches throughout the city and only accessed them in emergencies. Emergencies and holidays. She'd unlocked several old bunker warehouses in the last couple of years, but this one was her favorite, not just for the bed it offered but also the family photos on the walls. She didn't know any of the people, but it still made her feel less alone.

She knew it would never last. She had relied heavily on her storage to feed her community, and she would never be able to come this far if not for the food waiting for her here. When the stores were finished, she would no longer be able to come here. She had no idea what she would do then but tried not to think about it.

He pulled out a hard, white square and sniffed it before taking a small bite of the corner. *Bread? Maybe it was toilet paper.* The bunker was quiet; only rarely could they hear the booms of thunder from far, far, above. All storms had plenty of lightning and thunder, but no rain. Never any rain.

"Where are you from?" she asked him, cutting the silence.

"Nowhere, really. Just a drifter." He wasn't trying to be evasive; he truly had no home.

"If you don't mind my asking, what are you doing chancing the wastes in March? This is the worst of the storm season. Everyone knows that," she said through bites of salty MRE gruel.

"Is it March?" he asked, perplexed.

She pointed to a calendar on the wall that read, "MARCH 1993".

He chuckled and shook his head. She had shared her food with him, shown him her extreme wealth, and saved his life. If he couldn't trust her, he couldn't trust anyone. "I'm looking for someone."

"The city is empty. I have been coming here for years and you are the first person I have ever seen out this far. First living person, anyway." She continued on with her meal.

"Not here," he explained further before savoring a bit of water from his bottle, running the liquid between his teeth and over his dry gums before swallowing. "A settlement a couple of days walk from here. A place called Eden." He saw her stiffen but resume her eating. "You know it."

"Yeah, I know it. Full of widows and beggars. Looking for someone you know? Relative of yours?" She tried to act disinterested.

"No, I don't know him, I've only heard of him." He reached into his jacket and pulled out a metal box, then handed it to her. She turned it over in her hand and noticed a bullet hole and rust on one side. *No, not rust,* she thought. *Old blood.* "I'm looking for the mechanic," he added, almost in a way of questioning her.

Teneil set the last of her food down and took the small box to a worktable. She donned a headlamp and after switching it on, she reached for a pair of magnifying lenses to inspect the object. She had only ever seen one of these before, and that had been at a distance. But even still, she knew exactly what it was.

This was a key to a Gog supply and storehouse. There was only one in each settlement. There were scraps of rumors about what exactly they stored there, genetic testing and weapons were always speculated, but everyone agreed that each one held a large supply of food for the Gog military forces.

"You know what it is, then?" he asked, while watching her deft hands work delicate instruments.

Finally, Teneil put her tools down and switched off her head lamp. "What are you going to do with it?" she asked, trying to withhold any excitement from her voice.

"I'm going to raid the stronghold and then I am going to destroy it," he said flatly.

She knew who he was then. Word had spread quickly when he had taken out the first stronghold. When the second one fell, Gog was forced to abandon the city in the north, and the people in the fringe were free to move back into their homes. "They call you Robin Hood, you know?" She looked at him closer now. He was a legend, a hero. "I thought you would be taller," she said with a smile.

"And I thought you, the esteemed mechanic, would be a man." He laughed.

"Guess we're both disappointments." She winked.

"Can you fix it?" he asked, hopeful.

She could. She had everything she needed to fix it here, right now, in less than one hour. She thought about little Bart with a full belly, and pictured him sleeping in an actual bed, not in some sand cave. She would make sure that the people of Eden would get their portion of fertile land, too. She said a silent prayer of thanksgiving.

"Oh, I can fix it," she said, looking deep into his eyes with no question in her voice. "And I'm going with you."

Chapter Eleven
IF ONLY HE WAS KIND

Teneil had been looking forward to this all week. Avocado, like all veg and fruit (less bananas), was a seasonal item. When she had spotted the first head-sized fruit in the market, she quite literally squeaked. Her hair, uncut for several years, had made its way down her back. She had thought of cutting it on multiple occasions, since she was unable to properly care for such a mane. The ends were frizzy and sparse, but this avocado would make all the difference.

She also picked up a lemon, a papaya, a bag of local raw sugar, and a couple eggs for her weekend treat. It was a rare occasion to have the house to herself. Her girls were all visiting family or away at school, and Teneil decided that instead of burying herself in work, she would enjoy a little self-love.

Self-love was a tricky concept in Malawi. For example, if she wanted a hot bath, she had to start the charcoal and boil enough water to qualify as "hot," hauling bucket after bucket into a larger basin. It wasn't large enough to get into, but big enough to hold a "lather, rinse, repeat" amount of water. Self-love was often more work than her usual to-do list, and so days like this were extraordinarily rare. Her love tank was definitely flashing a red "E".

When Teneil arrived back at the house, she shut the gate behind her, lest anyone think she was home. She set her bags on the floor of the entryway and leaned her back against the heavy wood door. She took a deep breath through her nose, noting the musty undertones of her three dogs, and the sweeter peanut butter-crayon smell of children. She lit a stick of incense. Blessed silence filled the small room. She set her playlist on high and her hands to crafting her treatments.

The hair conditioner consisted of a mashed-up avocado and one egg yolk. The oils of the avocado and cholesterol of the yolk were better than any salon product she had ever used. It

made her hair shiny and sealed up the split ends. But if she was being honest here, the best part was her inner child being set free to mix the bright green slime into her long mess of hair.

The face mask was mashed-up papaya, great for lightening dark spots, (not that she had any, mind you), with a spoon of raw sugar mixed in for exfoliating. But if she was being honest here, the best part was licking the spoon.

The lemon was for her water.

Teneil donned her favorite well-worn, threadbare, and stained blue dress that at one time had been beautiful but was now barely suitable for sleeping in. She liberally applied her concoctions and did what any sensible woman would do: she picked up a Francine Rivers book and got lost in a world of blushing romance. She settled onto her patio chair, what she called her "happy place". The back of the house was a large, open space where everyone played and meetings were held, but the front of the house was much more private. It was a small yard that Teneil had filled with the different flowers she collected.

A high brick wall around it gave her complete privacy, and a little porch with the shade of an awning kept her outside the reach of the sun.

Adjusting to a routine of alternating seating positions, hours passed this way.

The sun was dipping behind the trees and just like any avocado that has been left out for any amount of time at all, the green mess in her hair blackened and began to smell like the back of a communal refrigerator. The fruit and sugar all over her face (well, except within licking distance around her mouth and what had dripped down the front of her dress) had dried to a delightful, orange-ish, fruit leather.

Her stiff neck was the ultimate alarm that it was time to put the book down and prepare her hot bath. The dogs gave her a wide berth after a quick sniff. She paid them no mind, her eyes already on the large basin in the corner of her washroom. There was no grumbling about filling the basin today, she picked up the bucket and walked to the outside water tap to make the first trip hauling water into the bathing room.

She was looking forward to having a bath that didn't involve phrases like, "I will be finished in a minute!" or "Get out!" She was going to take her time, using the back scrubber that hung unmoved like a royal guard on her bathroom wall. She might even lose a pound or two shaving her legs, which was more than overdue.

Teneil placed her bucket underneath, turned the handle, and ... nothing. Two frustrating drops sputtered out in a rush of air. *No, no, no,* she thought, then like a light switch and a burned-out bulb, she closed and opened the tap again, and again, desperately hoping for a different result.

Clearly the water had been shut off at some point in the afternoon. Her head was beginning to itch now, maybe it was just panic. She frowned or tried to with her face hardened by a solid layer of sugary mess.

"Ode!" A man's voice called out from her back gate. The greeting basically translated to, "Excuse me!"

Teneil shouted back a proper response for, "I'm coming!" but she did not. She went in the opposite direction to glance in the mirror at her disgusting hair and face. It was bad. Her eyebrows were glued at odd angles and yesterday's mascara, which she had been too lazy to take off, had run down her face during a particularly touching scene in the book she had just put down. She looked like a villain in a comic book.

She wanted to shout that she was ill and that she wasn't taking visitors, but that was not the truth, and she knew that most people only came to her house when they were in need. It was likely that the person who was out there was in fact ill and needed help. It was late Sunday afternoon, and the village knew that she only entertained emergency needs on Sundays.

So, she took a deep breath, turned her back on her horrifying reflection, squared her shoulders, and walked to the back gate.

Of course, he was gorgeous. He was tall, dark, and handsome in all the classical ways. He was smiling with casual confidence. He was beautiful. He was. . .what was he doing here? *WH-Y-Y-Y*? Why now? When she went back in her house, she would have some respectful but strong words with her Lord and savior, Jesus, whom she could almost hear laughing in her head.

"Hello, good evening." She smiled and attempted to act like nothing was wrong. Nothing at all. As long as this dashing stranger stayed upwind from her, she was only visually disturbing. But if he smelled her, too? Resignation washed over her more successfully than her nonexistent bath. Instead, she thought, *yup, buddy, this is what it is.*

He hesitated, obviously struck silent for a moment, which was fair, his beautiful smile melting off his face, and she knew why. Teneil allowed him a moment to process what he was seeing. She even held her arms out as if to say, "yes, see me. See all the luck and splendor that is this poignant moment!"

"H-h. . . Ugh. . .Hi," he stammered. "I'm your new neighbor. I got in last night, and I just wanted to introduce myself."

Of course, you are, she thought. *Handsome and thoughtful.* "It's just a real pleasure to meet you right now, in this, my finest moment." She smiled and bowed her head in respect.

"Oh! God!" His strong face contorted, and he defensively reached for his nose. "What's that smell?"

"Would you describe it as a 'salad bar' kinda smell?" she asked.

"A salad bar in, like, a bad neighborhood." He nodded, unwilling or unable to drop his hand from his face.

"On a hot Thursday afternoon," she agreed, nodding.

"During a power outage." He grimaced, but forced his hand down, perhaps realizing the threat was not lethal.

"That's me."

"Nice. That's like a perfume? Or a lotion?" His brilliant smile returned but held a hint of mockery.

She pointed to her hair and said nothing, instead pressing her lips in a tight line.

"Why on earth would you do that?" From his tone, she could tell that he genuinely wanted to know, and oddly she felt like he deserved an explanation. Hadn't he paid for it with the assault of his senses?

"It's not supposed to be this way," she explained, feeling a blush rise on her cheeks underneath her nightmarish mask. "The water is off, and I can't go to the lake looking like this to wash it out, so I'm just waiting for the water to come back on, and here you come. With your 'I wear clothes during the day' and 'my hair smells like a normal person' attitude and judge me. Well? Welcome to the neighborhood, friend."

"Pleasure is all mine, I am sure." He smiled at her, and an awkward silence ensued. "I'm just. . .uh. . . going to go now. I'm gonna go."

She nodded and sighed, "Yeah." Then she turned her mortified self around and walked back into her house. Teneil marched straight to her desk and let her nasty head fall into her hands, instantly regretting it when her fingers slid into the foul, crusty black icing on top of her cake.

A few moments later, there was another, "Ode!" At the gate. Of course, there was. She took a deep breath, choked a little on the fumes that wafted around her, and walked back out to find her same new neighbor with a hose in his hand. She blinked at him, not sure where this was going.

"There's a water tank on the side of my place," he began. "I got to thinking that I should probably drain it before I use it anyway. So, I borrowed your hose and was thinking if I hold the hose for you, you could wash your hair."

Teneil was at a loss for words. But the setting sun was baking the muck into a hard shell as she stood there contemplating. She pulled open that gate and said, "You can't just borrow my stuff without asking." But she was smiling.

"I'm begging you, please. I could smell you from my house!" he laughed.

She smacked him on the arm but quickly ran inside to get her shampoo.

Chapter Twelve
IF ONLY HE WAS WILD AT HEART

It was ridiculously hot, but the heat was nothing compared to the irritation of the flies. There were small black ones that swarmed around and often into the eyes. Brightly colored yellow flies that almost resembled paper wasps turned out to be nothing more than gentle body salt lickers. "Horse fly" isn't the proper term for the large, biting fly that could be seen from far off on the horizon. "Elephant flies" perhaps? Tsetse flies was the true name.

Earlier that year, 500 elephants had been relocated to Malawi. It was meant to be good for the economy, good for the elephants, and good for the morale of the people who had been suffering from the corrupt government elections and a solid year of rioting that followed. In all fairness, the elephants did all of those good things for the people of Malawi, but there was also a high cost that no one had anticipated.

Teneil was one of the world's leading entomologists. She was a peculiar person that spent most of her time analyzing and categorizing bugs. Teneil had chosen this exact spot, in this exact season, for this exact reason: the Tsetse fly. You see, the elephants weren't the only thing that was brought into Malawi. Soon after the elephants arrived, locals began getting sick, complaining of headaches, weakness, and body pain. Trypanosomes were a tiny parasite that spread by the bite of the Tsetse fly, better known as "sleeping sickness". It was notoriously difficult to treat.

Teneil had left Cambridge University with all her best equipment and her quiet but brilliant assistant, Thomas. They headed deep into the jungle, each team member carrying all that would be required to procure samples from the infamous fly that was causing the trouble. Teneil had some new theories and she needed confirmation. Unfortunately, the local guide that they had hired had gotten sick and was forced to turn back three days ago. Teneil, however, was unafraid.

She had enough protein bars to last for several weeks. She intended to do her job and find a better way to deal with the Tsetse fly infestation.

After an entire afternoon of slashing, mucking, tripping, and ducking through the dense vegetation, Professor Teneil Jayne was exhausted. She was, of course, in incredible, peak physical condition, but she had been a bookworm for the majority of her life and her perfectly carved gym muscles were not suited for field work. They set camp next to a small pool of water. It was still early in the evening, but when Thomas and Teneil came upon the clear pool, neither had to convince the other; they simply dropped their bags.

Teneil decided to make use of the early camp by checking her delicate equipment. When the guide had turned back, green, sweating, and vomiting profusely, Thomas and Teneil had been forced to manage his share of the pack mule haul. Teneil had fallen several times under the added burden, and she was sure at one point she had heard glass break. That became her primary concern: she needed everything intact if she was to accomplish her mission here, or this was all for nothing.

Soundlessly, the camp was set up within half an hour. It turned out that only a couple slide lenses had cracked, what sweet mercy. Stress leaked out of Teneil, and she decided that she had earned a proper bath.

"I'm going to the pool," she told Thomas, who was busy checking his own equipment and only grumbled an inaudible reply.

She almost cried when the cool water hit her blistered feet, but she settled for a deep moan. The rocks were slick underfoot, so instead of walking out into the water she simply reached out her arms and fell backward. She relished how the cool water ran over her scalp and face. Water had been limited to drinking only during the last week of their journey, and her body itched with the need to be clean. She had no soap but instead found a perfect stone with a good texture and began polishing off the layers of dirt and sweat.

He had been tracking them, the three of them, for over a week now. The largest of the two men he knew; he had seen him before. That one was a brute and a thief. He had seen him play the guide time and again, taking people into the jungle only to rob them and leave them stranded. He never got involved. He assumed that if people were stupid enough to follow a stranger into this jungle, his jungle, they got what hard lessons they deserved.

But he had never seen a woman like her. She dressed like a man; at first, he thought she was a man until they had made camp the first night and she took her hair down. He sat transfixed while he watched her tie it into a long braid to keep it out of her equipment. Strange equipment it was, too. He watched her spend evenings turning knobs and writing in a book.

He wasn't completely ignorant of the world. He just didn't see much sense in it. People were always searching for what was obvious to him. People liked to talk about less being more, but the truth was abundance in nature and people simply survived indoors. Out here, he was surrounded by food, entertainment, medicine and friends. The people he saw were so disconnected from nature that they didn't even know how to see anymore.

She was different. One afternoon a few days ago, he'd watched her have a conversation with a beetle. An actual conversation! "Well, hello there!" she had said with more courtesy than most people offered when talking to each other. She had gone on to ask the beetle its name. He didn't even know beetles had names.

She told the beetle all about her search for a certain type of fly that was making people very sick and asked the beetle if it knew where to find the elephants. Apparently, the beetle didn't know or lost interest in the conversation because it flew off. He couldn't hear the beetle, though he had strained to. She was the most fascinating thing he'd ever seen, and for that reason, he rarely took his eyes off her.

He'd spent his whole life in this jungle and the beetles hadn't ever talked to him. If he was being honest, he was a bit jealous at first, but ultimately came to the conclusion that it would be better to make friends with this woman so she could teach him. He had followed their party of three until he noticed how the big man was looking at the woman. He'd watched the guide attempt to spy on the woman while she changed her clothing and hated the look in the man's eyes.

Finally, one night when he couldn't take it anymore, he dipped a freshly dead poisonous frog in the man's tea. The big man was gone by morning, and he, himself, had decided to lead the group. Using animal calls and occasional path suggestions he had successfully navigated them to one of his favorite pools. The jungle was full of them, but this one had a certain blue-green algae that seemed to make it glow, very few leaches, and in the evenings, it came alive with fireflies.

He was delighted when she dove into the spring. In his mind clothing was a ridiculous tradition. It was the hot months, rains were not due for several weeks yet, and he didn't know how she'd managed every day to wear her leather and cotton ensemble. He had thought to do her a favor on multiple occasions and just take her clothing while she was sleeping. He was sure that she would thank him the next evening.

But he'd decided that theft was no way to start a friendship. He would let her have her silliness and when she had finished teaching him how to talk to the bugs, he would teach her the joy of running through the jungle without clothing. They would be best friends.

He watched for a while, enjoying the view from his perch in the tree canopy. He watched her scrub her body red with the stone he'd left for her at the entry to the pool. He watched her dive, swim, and brush her hair out with her fingers. By tomorrow he would lead them to the elephants. There were several different herds, but he knew she was looking for a sickness, and he knew she would get no answers from the other beasts.

He didn't really know how to speak to women, or people in general. He also knew that allowing her to simply stumble onto this particular herd of elephants would be her death, and he could not allow such a tragedy to fall on the most interesting, no, the *only* interesting person he had ever met.

She had finished her bath and put on a white dress. He had never seen anything like it before. Her dress was so light that every delicate movement set it dancing like the newest branches in the treetops that swayed with even the lightest breeze. There was shape to the garment; it wasn't a formless pillowcase that he had seen most women prefer. Her arms were bare, the back and neckline dipped low, and the hem fell just below her knee. She sat on a rock and attempted to wash her day's clothing in the pool. He watched her arms flex and extend as she dipped clothing into the water only to then wring it back out. He decided this work was dumb, and if she listened, he would convince her that if she *had* to have a dress, the one she was wearing was all she really needed.

And then she began to sing. Her voice was nothing that would ever earn her a penny, but in the stillness of the jungle, even the bird's song wavered and listened. She was quiet, but the way her voice echoed off the bare rock filled the space with her music. She washed to the rhythm of her voice and the jungle watched the song and dance unfold.

When she finished, there was a booming silence. She looked embarrassed, but actually curtsied to the jungle and said, "Thank you for your attention" as she blushed.

And as the bird song picked up again, she whistled back. *Of course, she can talk to the birds too,* he thought, rolling his eyes. That was less impressive; birds had always given him trouble. He was searching the branches trying to find the particular bird she was singing to when she screamed. It was the most frighteningly horrific sound he had ever heard. Within a moment he was willing to fight whatever beast was threatening her. He scanned the clearing, panic rising in his chest. "*What, woman?!*" he cursed under his breath. He briefly glanced at her to get a direction on her fright. . .and found her eyes locked with his.

Teneil was working in her nightdress. It was still early evening, but she just couldn't stomach the thought of putting those trousers and boots back on in this heat, not after the coolness of the pool. She only had two sets of clothing and a nightdress, so she took the opportunity to wash, or at least rinse out, one of her sets.

She felt as if she was being watched, but she'd had that feeling for a week now and thought it must be the hundreds of eyes that lived in the jungle. When Teneil saw *him* up in the tree, it took a moment for her to recognize what she was looking at. She hadn't even realized that she screamed until the sound woke her out of her daze.

A man, a mostly naked man, was up there watching her. Her body sprang with reaction like a spooked deer. She ran through the jungle, which to her surprise was soft, spongy, and cool under her bare feet. Her white dress billowed around her as she jumped off one tree root, reaching high for a low branch to aid her in her descent. The branch broke and she was left gasping for air flat on her back.

But before Teneil had even gotten that blessed first inhale that comes when the wind is properly knocked out of you, she was already on her knees, eyes scanning the trees and the ground, too aware of everything. She got back to her feet but knew she wasn't fast enough. There was a cluster of roots tangled high enough above the ground that could be a small shelter, though not for long. Perhaps, it would buy her enough time to come up with a plan. She had prepared for seemingly everything but had never taken a feral man into account.

She was faster than he had suspected, but she was no match for him in the treetops. The canopy of the jungle was his home. While she ran barefoot and dodged through trees, he sat and watched her dress dance with great appreciation. She reminded him of the deer on the plains, lively and quick. He wanted to run with her. He wanted to do everything with her. She belonged here, with him, and he would never let her leave. When he watched her reach for the dead branch, he wanted to shout. Hadn't she noticed that the tree itself was almost dead, let alone the lowest branch? Perhaps she was not as intelligent as he had once thought.

From her ground nest, Teneil couldn't see anything. She could not hear anything but bird song, a tune she used to love but now was hiding the malevolent noises she was searching for: sounds of a mostly naked man swinging through the treetops. She was barely breathing, trying to calm the heartbeat in her ears. Every one of her senses was alert and ready.

Then she felt the tickle on her back. It wasn't a light touch but something heavy snaking across her shoulders. She instantly regretted her hiding place, which had seemed so perfect only a moment before. She had her suspicions before it crawled over her shoulder and into view: *ethmostigmus trigonopodus*, the giant African blue-legged centipede.

Only once had she been bitten by a giant centipede. She'd been trying to extract the creature's venom when the minion, lightning fast, twisted around unnaturally and bit her on the hand. The pain had been excruciating and lasted for days. There was no anti-venom for this, one of the most painful bites known to man.

The centipede in her laboratory was only a baby in comparison to the monstrous creature exploring her neck. Now, Professor Teneil loved *all* of God's creation. To her, God gave life and so life was sacred. She respected this creature as God's creation and also for the combination of neurotoxic proteins and peptides loaded in its fangs, but she would respect it a lot more once it was off her body.

To her credit she did not scream. . .it was more of a song and dance. Her wail was like a mournful opera, her dance like a hillbilly spoon jig. The creature was long gone by the time the show was over, but the echoes of her cries carried on. Wait. . .that wasn't an echo, *laughter?* She scanned the canopy, suspecting the source, and found him. He was far enough away but in perfect view of her, holding his sides while the tree he was perched in rumbled.

She may have laughed, too, if the embarrassment hadn't given away to such red-hot anger. How incredible is the power of wounded pride! She no longer cared about this man or whatever danger he may be to her. She would get herself back to camp and, for heaven's sake, get her regular clothing back on. She would talk to Thomas, who was much more fluent in the local dialects, and tell this man, whoever he was, exactly what she thought about this whole situation.

The problem was that she wasn't sure which way she needed to go to head toward camp. She couldn't see the sun through the dense vegetation, and she had no idea which way was north. She thought briefly about scaling one of the trees, but she didn't want to encounter the man she knew was up there.

The floor of the jungle was soft with rot and moss, but the occasional thorn or stone caught her. Her pride made its best attempt to bind the wounds and forced her spine to stay rigid. She swallowed her whimpers before they were even born. She had no direction, but she marched on as if she knew exactly where she was going. The jungle floor got dark quickly at nightfall. The moon was full but so little light made it through.

Surely, she didn't intend to spend the night exposed on the jungle floor, did she? He didn't think this was bravery or stupidity, but something else entirely. She was seated on the floor of the jungle. Her white dress, though not truly white anymore, was still such a stark contrast to the dark around her, it was as if she glowed. Her perfume, faint as it was, filled the jungle air around him. He appreciated the ethereal beauty and the scent of her, but he also knew that if he could see her and smell her, so could the rest of the jungle.

She sat with her face buried in her knees, arms wrapped protectively around her ankles. And ... was she crying? His face fell. He realized then that she was not okay, and some instinct told him that it was his fault. His stomach rumbled and he knew she must be hungry as well; he had watched her march for hours and never stopped for food or water. Without ever setting foot on the ground, he was able to gather a feast of fruit and greens from the canopy of the trees.

Silent as a whisper, he descended and slunk to the ground only a few feet across from her. He set the banana leaf platter of food between them and said nothing. He mocked her posture, bringing his knees up to his chest and wrapping his arms around them. It was comforting and he thought to himself that he should sit this way more often.

"Oh, what have you done now?" Teneil sobbed into her dirty frock. "Stupid, stupid! Why didn't you just go back to the camp and get Thomas?

I'll tell you why: because you are so. . ." She froze. She felt a shift in the atmosphere before her. Something big had joined her.

She was afraid to lift her eyes and see her own death in the eyes of the wild man. So she sat, motionless, barely breathing, until she was too exhausted to be afraid any more. Her body ached and she knew she had no defenses. If she was going to die tonight, she would not die a coward.

Teneil lifted her eyes and saw him. The mostly naked man was only a few feet from her, sitting just as she was, chin resting on his knees, looking at her with dark, soft, compassionate eyes. Fear and courage leaked away at the same time, replaced with curiosity and frankly, a touch of bashfulness. His stare was so intense; there was nothing shy about this man.

Very softly she said, "Hello."

He stiffened but only grunted softly in reply. Without moving his body, he slowly reached out and toppled the pile of fruit toward her. She hadn't even thought about food until it rolled to her feet. Where had he gotten all of this? She had spent the last week living on nuts, dried meat, and protein bars. Her stomach growled loudly in reply. Embarrassed, she clutched her stomach and gave a huff of disapproval.

"Rarr!" The man mocked the sound, then laughed and grabbed his own stomach.

Was he laughing at her? Some combination of the last week and this day that led her to being lost, crying in the jungle with some wild man in nothing but her nightdress, thickened her resolve. She picked up one of the dark, soft fruits, did a few calculations in her mind, and chucked it at his head.

Teneil had never been a sports enthusiast. But there was no need for talent when her target was a mere few feet away. With a loud, wet splat, his laughter died. He sat in stunned silence before the fruit slid down his face and into his lap with a sloppy plop. When he looked at her, she knew it was the worst possible thing she could have done. Satisfying as it felt, he was the only help she had, and she was throwing precious food at him?

When the fruit hit his face, he knew he had done something wrong. He sat waiting for her to tell him what it was, but when he saw the anger in her eyes, he knew it would be a combination of a whole day that pushed her into a food war. He had no idea what to do or say. He sat stone still but the fruit refused to respect the situation and it slid, slowly, down his face and into his lap.

Her face changed so dramatically from rage to horror that he burst out laughing even louder than before. He hadn't remembered the last time he laughed so much, but now in the dark of night, the sleeping jungle was woken. He was a wild man and he laughed like a wild man.

She could feel the sound of his laughter beating through her and she understood the utter ridiculousness of what she'd just done. The giggle that bubbled up to her lips was replaced by a soundless peel of racketing, joyous heehaw. They had both fallen to the ground clutching their sides, tears streaming down their faces and gasping for breath. When the moment had passed, she opened her eyes and found him staring at her, only inches away.

"OH!" She tried to scoot back. For every inch she retreated, however, he advanced, until she could go no further, her back digging into the soft moss of a tree's trunk.

He had never been so close to a woman. He wondered briefly if they were all so nice to look at. No. He concluded that she was not like anything, much like he was not like anything. He wanted. . .he didn't know. He wanted *more* of her, somehow. He inhaled her, closing his eyes and picking apart the different scents of the oil she put on every morning, mixed with her fear and joy. He wondered if she wanted to smell him too. He wondered what he would smell like to her.

She felt she should slap him. Wasn't it rude to smell someone? Before she could think to move her hand, he had opened his eyes and was staring so intently at her she was no longer sure she did want to hit him.

Unbidden, heat rose in her. "M-my name is T-t-ten-" Huskily, she stumbled over her own name, cleared her throat, and gave her head a little shake. "Jayne," she finished much more confidently.

He took her hand and held it against the bare beating of his chest. "You, Jayne. Me, Tarzan."

Chapter Thirteen
IF ONLY HE WAS DASHING

"I still like the red one." Debora pursed her lips in disapproval.

Teneil turned to evaluate the back of the purple cocktail dress she was currently trying on. "The red one was a bit too much."

"This one is a bit too little." Debora left the fitting room and went back into the gallery to keep looking. "I found it!" she called out, reappearing with yet another option.

The new dress was cut perfectly; it was not revealing nor was it modest. It was a blue so deep that in some lighting it would look black. It was not desperate or flashy, but classic and glamorous. Perfect for a thirty-*something*-year-old, single woman.

"It's perfect," Teneil admired, until she looked at the tag. Her entire body stiffened, and she held her arms as far away from the dress as possible. "Very slowly, Deb ... I need you to, very carefully, unzip this dress."

"Why, what?"

"Why?! Why did you bring me a dress that costs more than my monthly rent?"

Debora laughed. "It's a company party, so we'll put it on the company card."

"Don't be ridiculous, I don't work for your company. You'll get fired."

"No, I won't. You are my plus one, and I have a yearly budget for things like this."

Teneil let her arms and posture fall in defeat, and a smile rose on her lips when she glanced at herself again in the mirror. "You have the best job in the world."

"I know." Debora smiled. "Let's go play in the shoes!"

The evening was clear and cool. Teneil had never spent much time in New York City, and she was often teased for gawking at the towering buildings that climbed endlessly into the sky. It didn't bother her that everyone laughed at her, and it didn't stop her from craning her neck either. Teneil thought that even if she lived in this city for years, she would still gawk. It was inspiring, what men had made.

The party itself did not matter so much to Teneil; she was only in the city to see Debora before heading back to Malawi. When Debora told her that she had a work party she couldn't get out of, Teneil was more than happy to be her date. Getting ready was the fun part anyway. After a spa day, hair, nails, and makeup all artfully done, she put on the absurdly priced dress and the low, black heel on which they had compromised.

"This dress demands at least four inches in heels!" Debora, the fashion savvy and catwalk worthy city girl had insisted while waving a sparkly stiletto at Teneil.

"If any dress needs those shoes, it's the wrong dress," Teneil had countered. "Besides, stilettos are made for dainty feet like yours, not my flat, fat, duck feet. I wouldn't last an hour walking in those, and I don't think I would be well received if I took off my shoes before dessert."

"Point. Good point." Debora nodded, and Teneil kept her two-inch high, unadorned, black shoes.

They let a valet park the car and entered a particularly impressive Manhattan sky rise. The outside of the building was a monument to man's architectural achievement, classically decorated with gargoyles and intricate crown molding. But the inside was a stark contrast to the cement jungle.

Pristine marble and polished steel met in seamless junctions. Everyone inside wore fitted uniforms and most had clean, white gloves, a testament to the impeccable upkeep of the staff. Teneil awkwardly fell in behind Debora and the man escorting them both to the first of two elevators that would take them to the uppermost floor.

"You know I love you, right?" Debora said as doors silently slid closed.

"Aww. I love you, too, buddy." Teneil tried not to fidget with her hair or makeup, feeling out of her element with layers of powders on her face and pins holding the twist of her hair frozen in place.

"You know I would do anything for you?"

Teneil hesitated, eyeing Debora carefully. "Yes?"

"I only want the absolute best for you."

"You're freaking me out."

The elevator chimed and the doors opened. On the 25th floor, they disembarked. Across from them was an attendant who held the door to a second elevator. He got in with them and turned a key to unlock the penthouse level. Teneil tried to hold herself tall, like getting on the penthouse elevator in one of the most beautiful cities in the world was no thing, like she belonged here.

Standing next to Debora, who towered a full six feet tall in her stilettos, didn't help. Debora's long, blonde hair was artfully cascading around one shoulder, her eyes bright with excitement and promise. Teneil was made very aware of the things a beautiful dress and blush could not hide, like the callouses on her palms from hauling water, and the deep tan lines on her shoulders from long days working in the sun. Debora belonged here. Teneil was just using a day pass.

Debora had a strange look on her face, all pride and love, like a mother who was sending her child off to the first day of preschool. Teneil silently mouthed, *"What did you do?"*

Debora silently mouthed back, *"You look beautiful."*

Teneil rolled her eyes and began to fidget. The elevator was too hot. It was actually not hot at all, but at that moment Teneil felt like wild game being flushed into a trap. She glared at her old friend until the doors opened and she reflexively put her polite smile on. The elevator attendant walked them through the entryway to a set of remarkable double doors. Then their guide stopped, at the end of his tether.

If gawking was what Teneil had been doing to buildings from the street view, ogling was what she was doing now. Debora continued to walk into the room while Teneil stood in the entryway, transfixed by the crown molding, rich art, crystal chandelier, and flowers. Everywhere she looked there were flowers. Massive bouquets surrounded her that must have been arranged by a florist on the spot. The scent of jasmine and countless sweet roses filled the air. She noticed that she was all alone and took a few tentative steps into a world she did not belong to.

Piano music played softly in the corner, while men in tuxedos silently served drinks and *hors d'oeuvres*. The small, grand front room Teneil had just entered was only a taste of the splendor that waited in the main area of the penthouse. The far wall was covered in ceiling to floor windows that folded open and out to a large patio that called to her, promising the view of a lifetime.

Teneil noticed all the eyes in the room honed in on her at some point or another. *You don't belong here, and they know it*, she told herself, *but you are here now so you may as well enjoy it.*

Newly resigned, she walked through the small groups of richly clad people and directly out into the night air. The air was cleaner up here than it was on the ground, and she breathed it in deep. She looked down onto the city below and noticed how the sky had somehow been flipped over;

all the gleaming stars were now house lights, and the milky way was a river of taxis.

Someone walked up next to her, and without looking up, she commented casually, "I suppose in New York you have to get very high up and look down to see the stars." There was a hint of sadness in her voice, understanding the natural beauty that these millions of people had sacrificed for the opportunities a city offered.

"I didn't know there *were* stars until I was eleven. My parents took me to the French countryside for a summer."

The voice that responded to her was rich and deep. Teneil heard ice clink in his glass as he took a sip of some golden liquid.

"That's. . .like. . .really sad." She laughed and looked up at the stranger on the patio beside her. He was significantly taller than she was, but his presence was taller still, almost commanding in nature. To say that he was well groomed would be an understatement. Everything about him was impeccable, from the cut of his suit to the sharp, defined lines of his dark hair. He was a walking Fortune 500 cover, though his broad shoulders said that he very well could have also belonged on the cover of *Men's Health* in nothing but a swimsuit and a towel. . . *or no towel.* She swallowed hard and stood a little straighter.

He smiled a bit at her comment. "I suppose it is."

She knew she should have excused herself from the conversation before he discovered she didn't belong, but curiosity got the better of her. "But you chose to come back? Even after knowing the truth?"

"What truth?"

"The truth that this is all part of something infinitely bigger, and you are not the center of it?"

The chiseled lines of his face somehow grew harder. That was exactly what he had learned that summer. He was small. He had been raised by his family to believe that he was a great mountain but looking up at the night sky far away from any city was the most humbling thing he had ever witnessed. He was not a great mountain; he was only a man.

"I was eleven," he defended in a way of dismissal.

"I would have run away."

He laughed, "I don't doubt that." He was handsome and confident, and Teneil felt cornered.

"Sorry, I seem to be missing my friend." She excused herself.

Debora was where she usually was, at the center of the party, surrounded by "friends". By "friends", she meant every available bachelor at the party. Debora had always loved too easily, in Teneil's opinion. She was always either on top of the world in love or on the bottom of life mending a broken heart.

Teneil observed her closest friend flashing endearing smiles at the men around her and thought about how Debora would have approached the handsome man on the patio; no doubt, Debora would have had him swooning. Teneil loved too deeply to fall so quickly. Broken hearts took Teneil years to heal, and so she thought it would be best if she just stayed away from romance all together. Teneil was content to watch and live vicariously through Debora's letters.

After a moment, Debora glanced over at Teneil and made her way through her harem like a queen. "Let's get a bite to eat," she said, sliding her arm through Teneil's and guiding them into another room.

The room was full of heady spices, tables covered in silver trays, loaded with every delicacy. Teneil reached for one, but Debora stopped her. "That's Foie Gras," Debora explained softly, "mushed fatty goose liver." She stuck out her tongue and they moved on. "Fish eggs, snails, intensely molded cheeses-"

"We should have had pizza before we got here," Teneil muttered under her breath.

"How about we stick with the dessert tray?"

Teneil nodded in agreement. After all, they were adults, and as adults, dessert was a perfectly acceptable dinner substitute. Teneil knew this because she did it regularly and it always seemed to work out alright. Chocolate cake in hand, Teneil suggested they go out on the patio to enjoy it.

"But there isn't anyone out there," Debora argued.

"And?"

"And, you know me. I can't be satisfied alone." Debora winked at a particularly handsome man that had been flirting with her.

"Okay, I will go outside. You stay and enjoy," Teneil smiled.

"But you are my plus one!"

"Yes, and I am having a wonderful time. You should, too." Teneil gestured to the man Debora had rarely looked away from and then nudged her in that direction. Debora didn't need any more persuading, so Teneil walked back out to the patio, alone.

She sat on one of the many empty chairs, and because she was alone, she brought the cake to her nose and inhaled. Sensuous dark chocolate filled her senses. She took a massive, *way too big* bite. The dark cake was richer than anyone at the party, and Teneil moaned as she rolled the delicacy around in her mouth.

"Impressive bite," the same rich voice commented from a table in the shadow of the window's light.

Teneil froze. Her cheeks bulged like a full-on fall harvest chipmunk, chocolate frosting adorning both corners of her mouth, the consequence of exceeding her lip's clearance. She tried to swallow her enormous bite, but the cake was too rich, and her throat protested. She looked down at her plate, finding half of the piece remained. She lifted the plate to him in offering.

"Oh, no thank you." He waved a hand in protest. "Not that you didn't sell it well. I just find it to be a little rich for my taste."

Teneil nodded in earnest agreement, but still her throat refused to let her swallow, let alone speak.

"Would you like some champagne?"

Teneil shook her head.

"Water?"

She shook her head again and tried to say one word: "Ilk?"

"Milk?"

She nodded and he chuckled in understanding. "Follow me."

He led her to a staircase on the far side of the patio. It took them down below the party to a kitchen bustling with men and women plating trays and calling out orders. Now these were her people. Teneil wanted to tell them that when they all stopped their work and watched the two of them enter.

She wanted to shout, "I'm not with him! Please, don't stop working on my account!" But the cake had fused her mouth shut.

He walked with purpose through the mess of people that only resumed their work once he had passed them. He led her to a fridge the size of a walk-in closet and opened the massive, stainless-steel doors. Bulk meats, wheels of cheeses, and crates of various vegetables lined the shelves.

"Help you, sir?" came a call from behind.

"Oh, yes. Thank you. We need to get this young woman a glass of milk."

"Milk, sir?" He glanced at Teneil, who nodded adamantly. "Right away, Miss." And he returned with a large glass of ice-cold milk. Teneil took the glass and drained half before breathing deeply with relief.

Everyone around them in the bustling kitchen paused to watch her, questioning expressions on their faces. "Oh." Teneil sucked on a tooth, looking at her half empty glass like a fine vintage scotch. "That's good milk," she declared with a contented sigh.

"Good milk, Miss?" the chef asked.

"Perfect. Exactly what I needed. Thank you so, so much."

The man blushed. "No need to thank me, Miss."

"I disagree." She kissed him on the cheek, instantly regretting the chocolate smudge she'd left behind.

Her escort laughed. "Should we return to the party?"

"I could use a mirror, I think," Teneil said, rubbing at the corners of her mouth.

"There is another door through here." He took her to the far end of the room to another unassuming door. With a small push, it opened into an empty but elaborately decorated hall. It was quiet and private, and Teneil felt uneasy.

"We can't just walk around here like we own the place," she hissed.

He gave her an amused look. "Why not?"

"Because we are in someone's home," she whispered, as if this were obvious. "And they probably have guards or cameras or a dragon hiding somewhere in this castle!"

He laughed again, and the sound echoed into the empty hall. "I don't think there are any dragons." He kept walking until they reached a set of doors. He pushed them open and stood aside for her to enter. Before them was a warm but simple private study. The walls were lined with books and plush furniture sat in the center of the room. Off to one side there were even more doors.

"Pretty sure one of those doors leads to a powder room."

"How do you know this?"

"Just a guess." His dark eyes sparkled with mischief.

"You're lying."

"Okay, call it an educated guess. I'll wait for you here."

She pulled open the door and found what she was looking for. Closing the door behind her, she ran to the mirror, devastation spreading over her face. She not only had chocolate on the corners of her lips, but she also had the chocolate between her teeth like coal dust. Mortified, she went to work on putting herself back together and wondering if Debora had noticed that she was missing.

Worse yet, she had dropped a glob of chocolate on her dress. "Oh no!" What should she do? The dark chocolate was almost black, and no doubt would stain the delicate fabric. "This is why you don't have nice things," she scolded herself.

"Are you alright?" His voice, full of concern, echoed to her from the door.

"Um. . ." She hesitated. "Yeah?"

"Can I come in?"

"No!" She panicked and yelled a little too loudly. "I mean, I'm coming out."

He was leaning against one of the study's couches and stood when the door opened. "Sure, you are alright?"

She could not make herself look more foolish, could she? "I dropped that death by chocolate cake on my new dress and I have no idea what to do." She drew his attention to her bosom where an ink black stain had been smudged in the soft, deep blue lace.

He swallowed hard and cleared his throat. "That's not a problem." He took her through another door that revealed an elevator.

"Where are you taking me now?" she asked, each step taking them farther from the party.

"You'll see."

She only looked at him suspiciously as he stood alone on the elevator. "You don't trust me?"

"Should I?" She gave him a blatant stare, holding his gaze. To his credit, he didn't look away.

"Yes. You should."

He said the words with such serious conviction that, despite her better judgment, Teneil did trust him. But that's not why she got onto the elevator; she got on because she was having more fun sneaking around behind the party than she ever would have had at the party itself.

He hit an unmarked button and the doors closed.

"What's your name?" she asked when the silence was too great.

"Steven."

"I'm Teneil." He only smiled. "You already knew that."

"Yes."

The door opened and they switched elevators to continue their descent. "What aren't you saying?" Teneil had a way of cutting through nonsense.

He looked at her for a long moment, then said, "Your friend, Debora, works for my company. She told me about you when we were looking for non-profits in which to invest. Unfortunately, your organization does not qualify, as it is out of the country. Shame, too. I've been watching you over this last year and I'm truly impressed. I told her to invite you to this party. I thought you could rub a few elbows and maybe leave with a purse." When the doors opened, he added, "I didn't expect you to hide on the patio all night."

"I was not hiding." She strode past him into a poorly lit utility hall. He just stared at her and let the silence hold for a few heartbeats. "Okay," she admitted, "I was hiding, a little. I'm sorry. Those aren't my people, and I would rather be poor than kiss up to some upper-class yuppies to get to the money they hide where the sun never shines." When she realized who she was talking to, she added, "No offense."

He laughed. "Should I take offense, as one of those yuppies?"

"Maybe, maybe not. Why were *you* hiding on the patio?"

"I wasn't hiding," he insisted, and when she attempted the same convicting stare, he had used on her, he added, "Truly, I was not hiding. Why would I hide in my own house?"

"Your house?!" Teneil missed a step, or some ghost had tripped her. Either way, she stumbled but he caught her arm before she went down.

"One of them, yes."

She couldn't stop a small scoff that escaped her lips. "Bragging?"

"No, not at all. Just being honest." He winked at her.

They entered a large room, loud with machines and the people working them. Everywhere there were people ironing and starching bedding and towels, as well as dry-cleaning laundry. A man in a nice suit approached, Steven whispered in his ear, and the man eyed Teneil once over. He left but quickly returned with a toolbox of solvents and a garment bag.

"You'll have to take the dress off." Steven smiled at her.

"Not a chance." She folded her arms and looked between the two men.

"This," Steven said as he handed her the garment bag, "should fit fine, in the meantime."

She took the offered garment and was ushered to a small room to change. After several moments, she poked her head out and waved Steven over.

"What's the problem?"

"My zipper is stuck." She looked like she was on the brink of tears.

"Let me see."

Delicate fabric had gotten wedged deep into the metal zipper. He tried all he could to free the material from between the tiny metal jaws, but it was well and truly stuck. "I'm going to have to force it."

"Don't you dare!" She stepped back from him like he was a poisonous snake.

He sighed. "If I break it, I will replace it."

"That's a good point." She turned away from him and added, "But please don't break it."

"I will do my best."

He gave a count down and she held her breath: "Three, two, and o-" He forced the zipper down and felt the fabric of the dress give. A loud ripping sound made Teneil's teeth clench, but the cold air on her entire exposed backside was what made her yell in surprise.

"What did you do?" She whipped around quickly, trying to keep the fabric on in all the places it counted the most.

His eyes were wide and he stuttered, "I, um, I didn't mean to, I. . ."

"Don't just stand there!"

Without another word, he left the room.

She let the fabric fall to the floor and quickly opened the garment bag. The dress that hung before her had a few stones shimmering in the harsh lighting, but she didn't take any time to look at it before letting the liquid gold cascade down her. It was a tight fit and she was glad she had only eaten half the cake. There were no mirrors, but there were also no alternatives. The dress was floor length, but the top was a wide-open French neckline and Teneil felt incredibly exposed. She took the pins out of her hair and shook out the long, dark curls to cover her bare shoulders and chest. She cracked open the door again. Steven stood with his face in one hand, leaning against a large work table.

"Well?" Her voice was timid as she nudged the door open, exposing herself to his ridicule.

His head shot up at her voice. She stood in the doorway, looking for all the world like a storybook princess. The dress had been made from silk and it moved like liquid, only slightly weighed down by small crystals that snaked around it, mimicking wisps of smoke.

She looked down at herself and back at him. "This is not a cocktail dress. This is a ballgown."

"Then let's get you to the ball, Cinderella." He smiled and offered his hand with a small bow that held no hint of mockery.

As they walked back out of the mechanical room, she said, "My shoes look awful with this dress."

"No one will be looking at your shoes." He took her hand and ran it through the crook of his elbow as they got back onto the elevator. "I am really sorry about your dress."

Her senses were overwhelmed in this close space, and he hadn't dropped her hand. "That's alright. Truth is Debora bought it for me using a company card so technically, you paid for it in the first place." Realizing what she said, she added, "Please don't fire her."

He laughed. "Not to worry."

"Where did this gown come from?"

"I honestly don't know. I told the man to pick something that would work."

"So, this belongs to someone?" she asked incredulously.

"We'll return it tomorrow, so try to stay away from any chocolate." He winked.

"Funny."

They made their way out of the common elevator and down a small hall to the private residence elevator, walking fluidly with each other. Arm in arm, they stood in front of the finely polished steel doors, waiting as the numbers slowly chimed their obedient descent.

"Would you look at that?" he said more to himself, but Teneil did stop fidgeting and looked up. The image took her by surprise; the two of them, perfectly framed in the polished elevator doors reflection, looked like a painting over a fireplace in some ancient castle. They complemented each other perfectly: his statuesque manor, hard and strong with her looking so delicate and dazzling beside him, like a jewel. They were both silently taken with the couple looking back.

DING. The doors silently slid open and perfectly divided them, breaking the trance. In silence they entered the elevator.

"What if the woman who owns this dress is at the party?"

"Not likely."

"How do you know?"

"Because it's my party and I don't know anyone who lives in this building."

"There are hundreds of people who live in this giant tower and you don't know even one?"

"No."

"Doesn't that bother you?"

"No."

"What if you need something?"

"Like what?" he mused.

"Like, I don't know. . .like, a cup of sugar?"

Then she remembered the small supermarket that was one floor below his massive penthouse.

"I'm not concerned with things like how much sugar is in the house."

"Right, you probably don't even know where they keep the sugar."

He looked at her, amused. "Besides, this is a work function. And I know all of the people I work with."

"What about your friends? Are they at the party?"

He chuckled a bit, and they made their way back down the long corridor toward the main hall and the sounds of music nearby. "I don't have *friends*."

"Maybe someone in this building could be your friend?" She smiled innocently at him.

He rolled his eyes. "There is nothing that the people in this building can offer me."

She looked at him, observing how his proud stature filled the wide halls. He looked for all the world like a storybook prince, handsome and strong, and this was a castle. But without companionship? He was both a prince and prisoner.

Her silence warranted a look from him, and her eyes were wide and sad. Her mouth was set in a gentle frown. "Wait, are you pitying me?" The absurdity was a slap to his face. "People want to be me," he tried to compensate, but the words sounded shallow and thin in his own ears, and he wished he could take them back.

"Maybe because no one knows what that really means. Does anyone really know you?"

"People know me. Everyone knows me."

"Then why do you hide on the patio?"

"I wasn't hiding." His anger flared. "I was- I- just didn't want to be around anyone."

With those last words, he dropped her arm. As he opened the doors to the great study, she felt the wall of his defenses raise. She recognized that this must be the pattern of his life. She followed him in. He sat in a large wing back chair and let out a long sigh.

Teneil remained standing and folded her arms.

"Why did you throw a party if you can't tolerate human interaction?" If he was going to shut her out so readily, she had no need to tiptoe around his narcissism.

There was a long silence, and finally, looking at her, he said, "For you." Only the slightest quiver at the corner of his eyes betrayed his emotions.

"Me?" she asked incredulously.

She had taken a step away, and doubt filled him. This was not how he had expected the evening to go. She said nothing more and the silence became deafening. "So, you could come and maybe make a few friends that could help you with your organization," Steven went on. *Not true.* "You know, bat your eyes and make some money."

The look on her face was as if he had struck her.

"What kind of person do you think I am? You think I have so little integrity?"

"I didn't say that. I just wanted to help." His tone was not remorseful but irritated. Truthfully, it was neither; it was calculated. He'd made a mistake and the best thing for him to do now would be to drive a wedge between them, and the flush in her cheeks told Steven that it was working.

"I might be the one person you know who doesn't want to be you, Steven. I don't need your help."

He scoffed. "Please, Teneil, I have seen how you live in Africa. No kitchen, no running water, sleeping on a bit of foam. You barely survive." He went as far as to laugh at her, but the laugh was clearly forced; he had nothing but respect for her.

She was not mad at him or hurt by his words. She had already seen through his facade. He thought that he was going to push her away after all this? She was unwilling to play his game and decided to cut to the real reason she was here. "At least I'm free."

"Are you saying I'm not free?"

"Are you saying you *are* free?"

He originally brought her here because he pitied her. Only now, with her standing in front of him, did he realize why this was his mistake. She held her head high. This woman who lived in a brick hut would not grovel for money. Gown or not, she was not a princess; she was a queen, and he was little more to her than a successful merchant.

She came to his side, but he held tight to his mask and refused to acknowledge her, so she went to a small table that sat next to another chair. She took the lamp and various other knick- knacks off the polished surface and put them on the floor. She picked up the small table and sat herself knee to knee with Steven.

He looked at her sitting on the small 18th-century tabletop as if it were her throne, then at all the contents she had put on the floor. The Tiffany lamp alone cost more than she'd probably earned in a year. "You are a unique woman," he murmured, more to himself than to her.

"Come with me." She leaned forward, searching his eyes.

"What do you mean?" His laughter was soft and uneven as he moved uneasily under her stare.

"Leave, all this, and come with me." There was nothing playful in her voice; she was serious. "I can't-" she started, then stumbled over her words. After looking at her hands and then back at him, open and tenderly she continued, "I can't offer you any of this life that you have. What I can offer you is uncertainty and adventure. Chocolate cake that you can actually eat, people you actually want to talk to, and a night sky filled to bursting with countless stars. Come and be free with me."

He leaned forward and reached out. Gently, he took a lock of her hair between his fingers. When she did not shy away, he brushed her cheek with his fingertips. It was so remorseful. This was his goodbye. "I can't." He dropped his hand.

Her skin burned where his touch lingered, and the resignation in his voice cut her deeper than any of the jabs he had intended. "You brought me here to trap me," she whispered, "didn't you?"

He was no longer looking at her eyes but at her lips. Wishing she would walk away so he could reconstruct his hard exterior, being this close to her had made him weak. *Didn't she deserve an answer?* "Yes," he breathed.

She could see his need for her; not just physically, though that was clear. He needed her in his life, or he was in jeopardy of never truly living. She tried to picture herself waking up in this cold stone and glass kingdom. She knew she would never really have him as long as they were here. The best she could think of would be to share him with his work, but hers would no doubt be the smaller cut. And she would be left in this big house alone, except for servants.

"Steven, I can't live like this."

"No, I could see that the moment you walked in. You were so beautiful, so full of life. And all I could think about was a lioness in a cage. So, I stayed outside, away from you." He smiled wryly. "But you just kept following me."

"Wow." She tilted her head to the side. "You got it pretty bad for me."

He scoffed and shook his head with laughter. She reached both of her hands up to cup either side of his face. There was a smile on her lips but a seriousness in her eyes. "Come with me."

A promise of great adventure and passion lay in her invitation. A love that would be for always. All the freedom that she'd promised. She was offering him water, air, food, and some critical other element that he had been lacking and therefore dying without. She was offering him the keys to her kingdom of color and spice and laughter. He could picture himself wrapped around her on lazy mornings, walking, reading to one another, growing old with deep lines on their faces and still more laughter.

Then a heavy gray door slammed down on his vision. His company. His father's company. The suits. What would they say about him? That he'd cracked? He would lose everything he'd ever known.

They looked into each other's eyes for a long while before there was a quick rapping on the door. Steven grabbed her hands from his face but held onto them. "Yes?" he called back.

"A one, Miss Debora, is searching for her friend, sir."

"We will be right there." Steven dismissed the man and looked back at Teneil. Her eyes were large and pleading like she was talking him off a bridge. "Teneil, I-" He hung his head in defeat. "I can't."

She stood and took her hands back from his grip. There were tears forming in her eyes, but she felt foolish. She didn't even know this man, not really, so why would his rejection be so painful? What was he to her? But that was not the reason her eyes threatened to betray her. The question that bothered her the most was, what he could have been to her.

"For all your money and power, Steven, you're a coward."

"A coward?" He stood, instant anger on his brow.

"God gave you wings, but you would rather rot away in your tower than fly? You could do anything, but you choose prison. And for what?" She waited, but when he made no reply, she went on, a bit colder now, "I can see myself out. Thank you for the wonderful party. It was lovely meeting you." She turned and left the room.

She caught up with Debora, still the center of attention in the grand setting of the main hall. That was, until Teneil walked in and the room quieted to low, stunned murmurs.

"Teneil?" Debora began, wide-eyed.

Teneil had forgotten how she now was incredibly overdressed for the party. "I need to leave," Teneil said, fidgeting with her hair over her bust.

"What happened to you?" Debora stood. "You look incredible!"

"I will tell you all about it if we can just go, now, please."

"Yeah, of course." Debora ran her arm through Teneil's, and they left the party without even saying goodbye. "I take it you met Steven," Debora said in that hushed tone that girls use when they talk about boys.

"What were you thinking, Debora?" Teneil was not mad; she was hurt, but they sounded eerily similar.

"I was thinking that my boss is one of the most amazing, rich, handsome men I've ever met and you two would be perfect for each other! What? He's a great guy!"

Teneil hung her head. "Yeah, he's something, that's for sure."

"So, what happened?"

Teneil's eyes filled with tears, but she bit back her sob. "Nothing."

"Nothing?" Debora pushed, "Doesn't look like nothing. Looks like a sure something to me."

"Deb." Teneil silenced them both with the nickname, and that was that.

The next morning Teneil packed for her trip back home and had the cab take her to return the dress before she went to the airport. She hesitated in front of the elevator. How could she show him what freedom was if he didn't have the choice to go or stay in the first place? So, after leaving the dress at the front desk with no note, she turned around and left.

She made it to her gate at JFK but inside herself she was already far away. She sat down in one of the lounges and a young man came by serving drinks. "Cocktail, Miss?"

"No, thank you," Teneil said, and the man moved on.

"Do you know why they call it a 'cocktail'?" asked a voice like satin steel in the chair next to her.

She stiffened. "I hadn't ever thought about it," she said without looking up.

"Because a rooster crows in the morning and at the tail end of the day, he has a scotch."

"Is that true?" she laughed and looked up to see Steven sitting next to her.

"Maybe. It should be, anyway." He shrugged. "I took the liberty of upgrading your ticket to sit with me in first class."

"Steven, that's not really how I-" she began to protest.

He held up his hand to calm her. "Baby steps, Teneil." He winked. "So, my Queen, what's next?"

"Next?" She couldn't help but laugh, and then she kissed him.

Chapter Fourteen
IF ONLY HE WAS A MIGHTY WARRIOR

Daniel had studied nothing but Teneil's file for almost two weeks. Her photos hung throughout the office and bunks of the small hut set deep in the jungle, where Daniel and his team of five other men had set up base. He saw her face every hour of the day; there was nothing else his elite team focused on. It should come as no surprise that she haunted his dreams, too. During the day they worked on tactical advantages, searching for the best possible way to get her out of the incredibly hellish situation she was in. At night Teneil tormented him in different ways.

It was the same dream over and over:

She always stood on the top of a hill, or in a field of wheat, or at the end of a long dirt lane, waiting for him. She wore a thin white dress of lace, and her long, dark hair was artfully braided with delicate white flowers. Always, he was running after her. She would turn toward him with love and joy in her eyes. She would reach out her hand and he would push with all he had, knowing he had to get to her. Nothing else mattered. Always, she would fade before he reached her, and he would wake up in a sweat with his heart hammering.

To Daniel, the dreams were normal; they would happen frequently when he was hyper- focused on a job. He wondered if the others were also dreaming about her. For some reason the thought made him jealous. He had worked with his team for seven years, and he knew saying less about his own dreams was better.

They were U.S. Special Forces, or at least they all had been at some point in their careers. Highly decorated and finished with their individual services, they stuck together and used their skills in other ways. Still, they were the best at what they did: search and recovery of U.S. citizens taken captive in foreign affairs. Their job was primarily based in Nigeria, West Africa.

They had shut down several extremist groups in the last three years, but no matter how hard they worked, it never seemed to make a dent.

The latest plague they faced was called "Ayanfe", which translated to "the chosen ones". The extremist group did not focus specifically on Christians but all believers of all faiths. Their goal was to show the world that God was a lie, and they had begun migrating east spreading like a virus across the middle of Africa, to the coast of Mozambique. The group sculpted fear like an art medium, with public executions and random acts of violence. No one was safe. The people avoided them at all costs, and so Ayanfe ran free like a fire consuming everything in its path.

Daniel thought about Teneil's beautiful face, her public humanitarian work, and her community presence that benefited so many around her. She was no doubt a great prize to these ruthless trophy hunters. They would not kill her right away, but he shuddered to think about what she'd been living through in the two weeks since he'd received her file. He knew that these operations took planning, and planning took time, but he had never felt such an urgency before. He had to get to her.

Teneil was in an earthen box. No light penetrated through the blackness of where she was being kept, underground, somewhere. No one had come for a long time. At least, she thought it may have been a long time; there was no way to tell since night and day looked the same in her prison. She had begun wondering if her life before the box had been real. Did she actually have a family that was free out there, or were they also in boxes now?

Her ears rang with silence, but she no longer strained her swollen eyes to see. There was nothing, not even a vague outline. Only complete and total blackness. She had been back and forth on the hard packed floor, along all the walls, and even examined the low ceiling, but there was nothing except herself and the stirring of cockroaches that bit her if she held still for too long.

There was a soundless trickle of slimy water that she licked from the rock wall, though it tasted foul and made her sick. She was cold to her bones. The small flow of water made the room damp, and she no longer had the strength or the means to warm herself. They had taken her clothing and laughed at her skin. She thought that they would kill her then, or have their way with her, but instead they called her a walking disease and beat her to unconsciousness. From the way she felt waking up the next day, they had not stopped when she blacked out. At least they had cut her hands free before condemning her to this tomb.

It hurt to breathe, it hurt to stand. After almost a week in the darkness, it hurt to hope. She had replayed the events over again and again in her mind. She was in the market, as she always was in the early morning. She'd bought her daily veg and turned the corner to go out of the back of the market, as usual. Then everything went black, and something hit her in the stomach so hard she couldn't inhale. A bag had been shoved over her head and her feet had been kicked out from under her.

She wanted to scream but there was no air. She began gulping, trying to swallow oxygen, when she was thrown to the floor. There was instantly a knee in her back pinning her to the ground, forcing out what little air had been left within her. Her body screamed as the sound of a zip tie forced her wrists together behind her back. Just as she was ready to surrender to blacking out, the weight was lifted off of her.

BREATHE! She gasped and felt the ground shift under her. She rolled to the side, unable to hold herself with her arms tied behind her. Completely disoriented, a sharp corner sent her flying across the small space. Her back slammed into a wall, but Teneil didn't feel the impact that dislocated several of her fingers. She was too focused on breathing through the thick canvas that sucked against her face every time she opened her mouth. Desperate, she breathed through her nose in greedy need.

She lay in a ball, anxious for whatever came next. Over-alert, she could only listen, but she couldn't understand anything over the roar of an old engine. Tears fell from her eyes, but she didn't waste her air on crying out. *Just breathe. Just keep breathing.*

Now she lay on the floor in one corner, farthest away from the bolted door and drifted in and out of consciousness, continuing her mantra. *Just keep breathing.* She was grateful that she prayed to the unseen God. She wanted to cry but her eyes were hot and dry as sand, and so she only whimpered. Not for her situation or pain, but for the wave of peace that surpassed her understanding continually wrapping around her. Live or die, she knew she was not abandoned; she was not forsaken. She sat in her peridox, beaten, broken, and yet still loved and saved.

There was noise outside. Teneil didn't know the language, but she was grateful for any interruption in her relentless thoughts. The door opened and revealed a man holding a flashlight as bright as the sun. He looked at her, spit on the floor, and kicked her hard where she lay. His boot connected with her hip, and she opened her mouth to cry out in pain, but only a breathy sob came out. Her voice had long dried up. The man laughed and left the room.

Another man came next, younger than the other. He wore a mismatched military uniform that seemed far too large for him. He carried a jug of water and a bowl of some kind of gruel. He looked at her and almost vomited. She thought it was from her wounds, the smell, or maybe the inhumanity of it all. She didn't have the energy for shame at her filthy naked state. She crawled to the bowl at his feet. He stepped back with fear on his face. *Too young for this horror,* she thought. *Poor boy.*

"Thank you," came a tiny, weak whisper from the floor.

The young man hung his head in shame and slammed the door, sliding the bolt back in place. The sound was like a nail in a coffin.

With numb fingers in the darkness, she carefully picked her way through the food. It was rotten and several times she felt something move before she bit down, but it was still one of the best meals of her life. The water, mercifully, was clean. She half expected it to be something more malicious, but the fresh water tasted like sugar on her tongue. Something about it still disturbed her. The jug was large. How long did they expect to keep her alive here? She used a small amount of water to clean herself as much as she dared, not knowing when or if she might get more.

Part of her energy was renewed, and her mind was sharper from the food. The reality of the hard boot in her hip had actually helped her divide dream from fact. She would have thanked that man, too, if her voice had not betrayed her. Physical pain she could handle, but losing her mind was worse.

Teneil inspected her face and body with her hands. Her face was still tender in a few places, her ribs did feel a bit better. She had one gash on her leg that was swollen and was extremely tender. She drained the infection as best as she could. In the darkness of the box, she was not sure how many times she lost consciousness as she wrestled with the agony that came from cleaning out the infection. Finally, she rinsed it with water and settled back into her corner and slept.

She dreamed she was wearing a white dress made of lace. She was on a mountain top, and she was waiting for someone. When she turned around, she saw him running toward her. Her heart filled with joy. She put her hand out to him.

"Hurry!" she called.

"I'm coming!" he yelled back.

But the image faded back into blackness as she woke up lonelier than before. With new water in her body, her eyes could fill with hot tears. No one was coming for her. This was her life. This was her end.

"I'm coming!" continued to echo in her mind. She knew it was pointless, but she clung onto that thread like a lifeline. She whispered prayers and recited Scripture and her family members' names over and over. She sang old hymns and cursed her mind when she forgot the words, finally making up her own. But after another week without any more food, water, or light, inside Teneil, where there once was a blazing fire, only an ember dangerously close to snuffing out remained.

He dreamed about her again, only she was no longer in a lace dress. This time she was broken and bleeding, hanging on the edge of a tall building, her body trembling, fingers slipping. She cried out, "Daniel!"

He woke, sitting up straight, dripping in sweat. He took some deep breaths and laid back down. The moment he closed his eyes, he saw her again. She was in a river of ice, the ice slamming into her body as she continued to surface for air. She was being pulled down stream, where he could not follow. "No!" he yelled out, waking himself from the nightmare.

"Dude, you okay?" his bunk mate, Jonah, called out in the darkness.

"I-I don't know." Daniel's voice was shaky as he swung his legs over the edge of the bed, running trembling hands through his tousled, dark hair. The air in the small bunk room felt heavy with foreboding, despite the cool night breeze that shifted through the small windows across from him.

"Dreaming about her again?"

There was little privacy when you slept three feet away from each other, and Daniel often talked in his sleep. "Yeah, but it was different this time. Something's wrong." Daniel got up and turned on the light above the table in the corner of the small room and began looking through papers he had already memorized.

Jonah knew that Daniel often had dreams that were impossible to explain. They had frequently changed operations on his hunches, and that was partly why they were so successful. The team originally laughed at his nearly prophetic dreams. They ignored him once, years ago, and Jonah took a bullet in the shoulder for it. After that, Jonah had claimed the bunk next to Daniel and even kept a journal of Daniel's dreams.

Jonah sat up in bed. "Talk to me."

"She's in trouble. We have to move, tonight." Daniel pulled out a duffle bag and started loading it.

"You know we can't do that--" Jonah started.

"I'm not asking." There was no room for compromise in Daniel's voice.

Jonah hesitated for only a moment. Everyone higher up in the chain of command would not admonish his team leader if they were able to bring Teneil home alive, and the waiting was killing them all. After getting dressed, he went around to the others still sleeping. "Get up, we're moving."

No one made a sound. No one protested. They were trained for this. Daniel was proud of each of them; they had been through this again and again and there was no one he trusted more. With them he felt 100% confident that they would get her out. . .but would she be alive when they did?

Teneil heard the bolt slide open and prayed for a quick death. The starvation, solitary confinement, and fever from her leg had made her ready and even hopeful for the end. A young man stood in the doorway with a fresh bottle of water in his hand. The light was dim, but she still shied away from it.

He crouched in front of her and held her head while he gently tipped the water into her mouth. She gagged at first, sputtering and choking, but then her mouth recognized *water* and she drank quicker than the water came, swallowing gulps of mostly air before she coughed.

"Slow down," the young man spoke with a thick accent.

She inhaled deeply, then whispered, "Thank you."

"Please don't do that." The man's voice was a soft rebuke.

"I'm sorry," she whimpered.

"No," he replied, "I am sorry."

"You didn't do this." She looked into his young face, into his sad eyes.

"Yes." He hung his head. "I did."

"I remember you." She smiled weakly. "You gave me food."

"I gave you a bowl of trash that was not fit for the pigs." Tears filled his eyes.

"I would be dead if it was not for you." She reached out and grabbed his hand.

Her palm felt too hot and out of place in the cold damp cave. "You will still die. Soon, I think," he said, not in hate, but comforting her.

"Thank God." She smiled at him.

He took off his ill-fitting jacket and wrapped it around her. "I am so sorry." He began to cry in earnest, and she could see how young he really was.

"Don't be." She smelled the detergent on his jacket, sweeter than any flower. "God bless you for your kindness."

"How can you serve a God that would do this to you?" He shook his head.

"God did not do this." She reached up and wiped away his tears with filthy hands, and he did not shy away but leaned into her touch as if she was his mother. "God is not inside those who would do these things. But I'm sure He is with the one who would share his jacket with a corpse."

Her gentle smile only cut him more. Her head fell back, and he picked up her small frame.

Taking her body off the cold, wet floor, he sat beneath her and held her like a child. "Surely if your God exists, he is not a friend to me."

"I forgive you." She closed her eyes, "And if I can forgive you, God already has."

"I cannot free you." He said this as much to himself as he said to her.

"I could not walk away even if you did."

He sat on the cold floor and rocked her in his arms. "All I can do is be here, so you do not have to die alone."

"That is enough for me," she murmured, and she slept in his arms.

"What's going on, Daniel?" A severe-looking man named Zach asked as he loaded equipment into a bag.

"She won't make it another day," Daniel said flatly, loading his handgun into a holster at his ankle and another into the holster behind his back. No one argued with him; every man in the room owed Daniel a life debt and it looked like he was calling that in. "Let's go over it one last time," Daniel ordered.

Jonah unrolled a map and the men gathered around the table. "There are at least thirty men between us and the target, maybe more."

"Hardly seems fair," a man named Levi spoke up. The others laughed but Jonah went on.

"Daniel and I will run point. Levi and Uriah will take the ridge. Do not fire until you hear fire." Levi and Uriah were the best snipers Daniel had ever witnessed, and they nodded in unison. "Zach and Tim will circle around and make the brush fire."

Zach took out a Zippo with an American flag on the front and flashed a wicked grin. He was always the first to volunteer as the diversion. If you asked him why, he would say, "More action that way."

Less than ten minutes later they were loaded in the Jeep, headed into the lion's den. Daniel, knowing they were all likely putting their careers on the line for what felt like his own vendetta, said, "Thank you."

They all gave a grunt or punch to his arm. Each man had seen Daniel change over the last few weeks. Daniel was always obsessed with his work, but something had snapped when he opened the file that said "Teneil Jayne". Somehow this was personal and because of the bond that they had shared, the battles they had fought together, what was personal to Daniel was personal to all of them. They acted as if it was their own little sister being held captive behind enemy lines.

In position, they waited for the smoke. A coolness spread throughout Daniel. Finally, he was here. Within the hour she would be with him. "This has to work," he said, not to anyone but himself.

The smoke rose in the air behind the camp and several shouts echoed through the trees.

Jonah put his hand on Daniel's shoulder. "Let's go get your woman."

At his words "your woman", a strength and rage burned inside Daniel. His woman. *His woman.* That was how Daniel had come to see her. And the need for retribution that waited for those who had hurt her resolved into an unstoppable inferno in his gut. They would pay for what they had done. Today there would be a reckoning.

Their feet moved but no sound was heard over the surrounding shouts of alarm at the fire. Most of the enemy line was untrained, and quickly left their post in search of the source of the smoke. Only one guard remained at the entry of the underground storage where their intel had stated Teneil was being held.

Jonah had made quick, silent work of the guard as they entered the shelter. A set of stairs immediately headed down, the only direction they could go. Gunfire had begun popping overhead, and Daniel did his best to ignore it. There was a short hallway with several doors. The smell of rot and excrement overwhelmed them. The flashlights mounted on their rifles were cutting through the darkness and illuminating the nightmare. Daniel almost ran when he heard the weeping coming from the open door at the end of the hall.

"Go," Jonah said beside him. "I will check the others."

When Daniel walked into the room, he saw a man sitting on the floor with a pile of bones in his arms. Daniel held his gun on the man for a long while. "Identify yourself," he seethed.

"I'm a friend. Have you come to help her?" The man, little more than a boy, was rocking back and forth, tears streaming down his face.

Daniel suddenly realized that he was holding Teneil. Her eyes were closed, her face pale and gaunt, but there was no mistaking her. His gun fell to the floor, and he sank to his knees before her. He picked her out of the man's arms, finding that she weighed nothing.

Her eyes fluttered open. "It's- you." She rested her head against his chest.

The hospital had induced a coma when she arrived. Teneil's wounds were too great, it was the closest thing to mercy they could offer. They kept her that way while she burned through the fever threatening her life. She had several fractures, including her skull, hip, and three ribs. Several dislocated fingers and a broken eye socket were also treated.

The doctors did not expect her to live through the night, but Daniel did. He would not allow himself to doubt. He sat by her bed, Jonah often by his side, but even when Jonah left, the other members of his team would come in to keep him company. They often just watched her sleep without saying a word. Only once the doctor had told Daniel that she was being moved out of the ICU and into a bed for observation, did he finally leave her side to take a shower and change clothing.

Daniel and his men were not the only ones to stand vigil over Teneil. The young man Daniel had found her with was never far either. Daniel had been the first to question the sixteen- year-old, Jayamma.

Jayamma was brought into the organization after his family was murdered in Nigeria, only six months before, when he was still fifteen. They sent him to the camp where Teneil had been held captive, where he would know no one and have little chance to get back home. This was how they grew their ranks so quickly. After a few years, Ayanfe would own the minds of countless young boys. Most of the recruits were much younger than Jayamma; eight years old was preferred. They were abused and made to do awful things to break their spirit.

Jayamma willingly told Daniel everything, starting with the first time he'd seen Teneil in the dark. He had been sick all night. He still had nightmares about how she had thanked him and cracked the blackness that was swallowing his soul. He knew it would cost his life, but he didn't want to go on in this life anyway; he would rather die than sell what was left of himself into such evil. He would not let her die alone. Ironically, that had been what had saved Jayamma's life the night Daniel's team arrived.

After her rescue, Jayamma refused to leave Teneil's side and questioned anyone who came too close to her door. Daniel liked him; in fact, the whole team liked him, especially when he described every stop they had made on their route to Malawi, exposing the entire inner network of Ayanfe.

"Why don't you take six months off?" Jonah said to Daniel one night, cutting through the quiet rhythmic beeps and murmurs of various machines.

"I'm fine," came the automatic response.

"I'm not asking." Jonah smiled.

"You know I can't do that."

"I have never seen you more distracted, Daniel. There is no way that you are going with us until you figure some things out." He looked down at Teneil. They had removed her breathing tubes and color had returned to her cheeks. Her frame was still too thin, but she was clean and any day the doctors were hoping she would wake up. "You can't leave her," Jonah added, also not a question.

Daniel rested his elbows on his knees and itched at the dark stubble on his face. "You're right," he sighed. "I know you're right. I don't know what to say."

"To me or to her?" Jonah gave a knowing smile. "Listen, with the intel from Jayamma we were able to get several forces combined to lead the raid for the next six months at least. Looks like we'll have somewhere around 10,000 international troops at our disposal, so you won't be missed." He winked and Daniel laughed. "Besides, we leave in one hour."

Daniel looked up sharply. "When were you going to tell me?"

"I did tell you. Twice," Jonah chuckled. "This is why you're staying. Besides, don't you want to be here when Sleeping Beauty wakes up?"

Daniel smiled and shook his head, his eyes immediately going back to Teneil's face. "Well, that's one I have never seen before." Jonah said and stood.

"What?"

"A blushing Daniel." He gave a wicked smile and left the room.

Daniel felt the red creep up his neck and rolled his eyes as Jonah walked out. Now that the room was empty, he moved back to his preferred seat, a smaller, more uncomfortable, blue chair closest to her bed. He knew every scar on her knuckles and every freckle on her face. Her lips were dry and cracked but at his request the nurse had applied a balm and they were healing beautifully.

The balm melted at the warmth of her skin and left her lips looking glossed. Her thick lashes looked painted, and her hair fell in perfect waves around her shoulders. To Daniel, she looked like she was just having a rest before going out, if not for the cuts and bruises that had faded into a yellow green all over her body. He rested his face in his hands and sighed deeply.

"I think blush is a good color on you, soldier," she whispered.

He looked up sharply but said nothing. Had he imagined her talking again? "Can you turn the lights down?" Teneil said with a painful squint.

He jumped up and took the room in two strides, shutting the overhead lights off. Leaving only one lamp dimly illuminating the corner, he was back at her side.

"Thank you," she croaked.

Daniel grabbed the water that he kept next to the bed for just this moment. He had kept vigil over many soldiers, and he knew the first thing they usually asked for was water.

Teneil moaned as she drank in small sips. "Oh, you're good," she said with a half-smile.

"They do say that about me," he teased.

She laughed and sucked in a sharp breath. "The pain says I'm not dead."

"No, not dead," he confirmed. "You sound disappointed."

"Well. . ." She closed her eyes, peace relaxing her brow, a small smile on her lips. "I was pretty ready to go." When she opened her eyes again, looking up toward heaven, tears formed, and Daniel caught them before they could fall. She looked at him then and smiled.

Her eyes were not haunted. There was something light and warm in her expression. His mind stopped and his mouth went dry. "Well, I wasn't ready." He smiled back.

Chapter Fifteen
IF ONLY HE WAS COMPASSIONATE

It was one of "those" days. I don't mean the "everything goes perfectly", "serendipitous", "delightful" kind of days. One of those *other* days, the black holes in the timeline of existence.

Simultaneously, it was one of the best days of Teneil's life.

She woke up like she did most mornings, to the sound of the dogs erupting in response to the calls of the fishermen coming home with their catch off the lake. The men shouted alarms to the other boats, indicating shore in the blackness of the water's edge. Other times the cries had little to do with warnings, similar sounding but more jovial, signs of a good catch and/or a long night of drinking. Village dogs that seemed to understand the language were eager to join the revelry. Teneil didn't mind; it was like waking up to a colorful celebration instead of a blaring alarm.

Today began at 4:15am.

Even the dark of early morning couldn't keep away the heat of October. She sighed deeply, looking out at the small city of fishing boat lights on the horizon as they made their way in. Then, she moved on to the hot water kettle, easily sliding into the only routine in her everyday life: coffee.

She could hear the clicks and hisses of the electric kettle starting to gain momentum. She stood, much like the walking dead, eyes half open and body seemingly under a greater gravity than the world around her. Still, she was acutely aware and ready to spring into action at any sign of life. Such as:

1. Cockroaches
2. I don't really need to add anything more to that list

That ever-present cockroach awareness was how she knew the instant that the kettle clicked off prematurely. The dark void where the neon orange glow should be emanating set her reflexes into action. Teneil's eyes opened in a flash, spine straight, she pounced on the kettle like a zombie on a brain. And much like a brain-dead zombie, she flicked the switch over and over in her denial of the reality that the electricity was now off.

Next, she tentatively felt the kettle and found it warm, not-hot-coffee-hot. *"Try it anyway,"* the voice of Determination sang in her mind. *"It's still coffee, right?"*

Instant coffee, which melted in mere humidity, had no problem accepting the warm water. Nor did the sugar. It was the powdered creamer that denied the unholy union. Not hot enough to melt the palm oil in the prude powder, the creamer floated at the top of the brown liquid, spinning like the laziest of Susans.

God help her, Teneil tried to drink it. But because it was neither hot nor cold, but lukewarm, she spat it out of thine mouth.

She was running out of time; the second alarm was about to sound. The local women would be getting to the lake, haggling with the fisherman over the night's catch, filling their baskets, and then fanning out into the community shouting, "FRESH FISH!" As one would imagine, this usually caused some issue with the local dog community as well, earning the title of "second bell" or "the snooze alarm", and occasionally, "Here! I'll take fish today!"

This was also the call that woke the rest of her house.

"Just get the charcoal going and hop in a shower. We can salvage this," Determination shouted over the voice of Defeat that was slowly marching its way to center stage in her mind. Resolve stepped in, and the next thing Teneil knew she was digging through the charcoal bin unperturbed. Then she heard the giggle.

It was the most amazing sound in the world that made things like no coffee both not matter and simultaneously seem very detrimental. "Hi, pumpkin," Teneil smiled, and used the back of her charcoal blackened hands to hug the bright and energetic girl.

The rest of the morning chores and breakfast flew by without much note, until, still covered in charcoal dust and sticky from the humidity and her own sweat, Teneil attempted a shower. A rattle and a thunk teased her, but no water came forth.

"No, no, no." She sighed, knowing she would have to use one of the bottles of water she kept for storage. The charcoal and dirt along her body seemed to laugh at her feeble attempt to bathe, but at least she knew that if she didn't have water, no one else did either. Everyone would stink together. And she did smell badly, that is. It was as if the bottle of water she'd used had only made it worse, turning an old, dirty, dog smell into an old, dirty, wet dog smell.

What happened next was. . .well, just imagine a typical house in the morning with two teenage girls and one toddler getting ready for school. Now multiply the typical teenage eye rolls and frustrated mom grunts by the Tower of Babel language barrier.

After Teneil dropped all of the girls at school, she went to the job site, which was currently a stone and cement potable water storage tank, being fed from a natural spring in the mountains. It was an exciting project and one she was really happy to be doing. Building was always satisfying work and she liked the idea that this water tank would supply hundreds of individuals with clean drinking water. Her secret side project was making a large shower stall so that folks could bathe at the water source instead of hauling the water back to their own homes.

The location of the water storage tank was quite the hike, and all of the work was basically done in the mud. That part was usually a pleasure on these hot days, except for the animals that also sought relief from the heat at the natural spring. Snakes and biting flies filled the canopy of the trees. The flies played a game of making one slap oneself with hands covered in mud. The snakes, playing no games indeed, continually kamikazed themselves, falling on unsuspecting workers with shovels already in hand. Malawi boasted of sixty-six different varieties of snakes. It was the proverbial box of chocolates.

When Teneil considered these things and added them to the swarms of mosquitoes, massive spiders, poisonous frogs, and a loose, rocky creek bed hike… She was *really* stoked to go there, every day, for months.

If you are great with foreshadowing, you will already have guessed at the swollen and excruciating ankle, black eye, and bruised ego that are waiting for you, dear reader, in the next sentence.

Teneil fell, hard, with a full case of tools in the pack on her back making sure her impact would be remembered. Not wanting the work to stop on her behalf, she sat in the mud for seven hours, while her face and leg swelled and throbbed. Her cuts bled dry by the time the workday was done. Then she proceeded to hike out proudly on her bum.

Finally, home, still with no water or power, Teneil found that she was unwilling to start the charcoal again, but the weight of responsibility of parenthood meant she could not *not* feed the girls. She convinced them all that eating dinner in town would be a real treat! After popping several NSAID tablets, Teneil had just enough umph left in her aching, bitter, bruised, caffeine- deprived, muddy, bloody body to sit in the car while they went into the marketplace searching out fried potato and plantain stands.

HONK!!!

The car behind Teneil was making it perfectly clear that he was unhappy. He was also making her aware that *she too* was unhappy. She was clearly parked in a space reserved for the market with plenty of room to go around, but that incessant HOOONNNKKK!!! still blasted behind her aching eyeballs. Again. . . and again.

Suddenly, every heavy piece of that awful day hit her at once. The sun had set, and she was finished. The back of the camel done broken, and all the straw was about to come crashing down.

"You know what?!" she snapped and tore her keys out of the ignition. Resolve, Pride, and Ego teamed up, while the fruit of the Holy Spirit spread out in a game of red rover. She forced her battered limbs out of the car.

At that point, she did look more than a bit like the aforementioned zombie, but a real one standing in the middle of a busy market with a confused and frustrated expression. Teneil's clothing was torn, and her face battered. She now had a grotesque limp, as well as charcoal smudges and dried mud mixed with sweat and blood all over her. She even smelled like an old, dead thing.

She achingly clung to the side of the car while the entire marketplace rolled to a stop. It reminded her of a scene in an old western brothel, when the unwanted villain's spurs were heard entering the romping, cheerful room and the music abruptly died. Every pair of eyes went wide, taking in all she had to offer.

Teneil raised her hand to get the attention of the car behind her, unaware that the honking had stopped. She gestured to indicate that the car could go around, and she would guide him, if that was what they required. She put a little weight on her leg and bellowed out in pain and fury at her own idiocy. Apparently, her lack of distinguishable words, erratic arm language, and a final verbal wail of great pain were the conclusive evidence that confirmed her to be of dark and hellish origin with clear determination to feast on the brains of the living.

Children cried. Mothers tried to comfort them but also hid behind them. All of the people and even the stray dogs on the street took a step back. Those who had never trusted in the Lord crossed themselves like practiced Catholics. Vaguely aware of herself being the problem, Teneil attempted to take a step forward and explain, but her leg buckled and instinctively she braced herself for what would surely be a painful impact . . . but the pain did not come.

"My God, are you alright?" Asked a deep, smooth voice, in an urgent and serious tone.

Strong hands had picked her up, holding her fast against a powerful chest.

One unfocused eye, that's all she had to offer the man. That, and a moan that bordered on a whimper. He set her down on the steps into the market, and for the first time in his medical career noted that he didn't have to say things like, "make some room" or "step back".

"Who did this to you?" His tone was oddly stoic, like he would defend her honor. Obviously, he didn't realize he would be defending her from *herself.* "Are you okay?"

"Yeah." Teneil shrugged one shoulder casually. "Why do you ask?" She attempted a smile, but showed teeth encrusted with mud, the results of sitting downwind of the sand pile all day.

"Is that not obvious to you?" There was no humor in the question, only genuine concern. He must have thought she had a concussion. Maybe she did? He attempted to get a boy who was selling ice water from a cooler to come over, but the boy only stared back with wide eyes. "Wait here," the stranger added.

Teneil thought snidely, *no, I don't think I will. I feel rather like going for a run just now.*

But she rested her back against the wall and closed her eyes. Moments later, there was a cold, firm hand on one side of her face and an ice-cold shock against her blackened cheek. "Who did this to you?" he asked again, with slightly more compassion.

She sucked in her breath and grabbed the ice from his hand. "Just me. I am all that is required to look this good."

He chuckled. After a quick exam and a huff of approval, he declared, "Not broken," and wrapped three of the ice bottles around her ankle.

Teneil opened her swollen eye to the best of her ability. The man's eyes were big and brown, and full of soft humor. Another ice water was waiting for her to drink. She swished the first mouthful of grit and spit it out, then took a deep drink.

"How many of these did you buy?"

He laughed, pointing to the kid showing off a large wad of money to his friends nearby. "I just bought the cooler."

She looked at him, sitting on the side of the dirt road with her while the entire community watched, and couldn't help the blush that bloomed on her one good cheek.

Chapter Sixteen
IF ONLY HE WAS ADMIRABLE

Teneil was toweling her hair off when the thought struck her like a lightning bolt. *A Biblical archaeologist!* That kind of man would be the perfect fit for her! Think of all the things that they could talk about and living in Malawi wouldn't scare an archaeologist.

She dropped her towel unceremoniously on the back of her chair and sat down. Putting "Biblical Archaeologist" in the search engine of her computer, she scrolled through the results. Some big things were happening in the field, and it all seemed to be focused around one man. The headline read, "Malachi Young, two-time recipient of the 'Gold Medal for Archaeological Achievement' award."

"Hold up," Teneil gasped, pushing a piece of wet hair out of her eyes. "Is that his photo? My goodness, is he ever dreamy!" The archaeologist who currently held the attention of the world was a cup of tall, dark, and hand me that pick-ax. *Okay, I can work with this. Let's check the stats.* She typed "Malachi Young" in the search bar next. It looked like he lived at the university where he taught. Married to? His work. Pets: one medium-sized mutt rescue. That was really all she needed to know. He would be hers. Oh yes, he would be hers.

He was doing a lecture at The George Peabody Library in two weeks. She could make that work. *Wait? Where is The George Peabody Library?* Another quick search revealed. . . *Baltimore?* Yeah, she could make that work. She booked the ticket in one hand and in her other hand she had her literary agent on the phone to book the lecture hall of The George Peabody Library, located in Baltimore, for the time slot directly before her dreamy professor was meant to speak.

From there the dance could begin. The first few steps were easy: a simple matter of phoning a few friends. Step, step, slide, Teneil had friends everywhere. Step and twirl, find the perfect dress. Step, step, kick, print some photos to boost subtle self-promotion. Step, slide, clap, social media and marketing so everyone knew she was coming. Step, stomp, clap, clap, now... she waited.

During her lecture at The George Peabody Library, Teneil talked about all sorts of things. It was easy to talk about all the amazing things happening in her life. And, actually, as a side bonus, she was able to raise enough money to complete the road she was working on!

After her talk, she retreated to a small, private study reserved for speakers. Now that the work was finished, she was free to dream. There was a two-hour time slot between speakers. She looked in the mirror and tried not to fidget, tried not to roleplay, tried not to panic. The dress was perfect: royal blue and classy, it had a modest cut neckline, but it held her curves nicely and even flattened out the notorious third curve that most women struggled with. Her hair was artfully swept on top of her head. Her jewelry was minimal, delicate, and sparkly. She was sophistication in heels, and frankly she looked a little like a classic movie star, or a James Bond love interest.

She waited for her cue, the applause that would tell her that he had arrived. Waited like a punk kid waits to light the grand finale firework. She waited, but there was nothing patient about it.

The parking lot was already full when Malachi arrived. "God give me strength," he chuckled to himself, remembering blizzards on mountain tops, colleagues being forced to turn back, and knowing that death was around the corner. But this? Talking in front of hundreds of his peers? It was almost too much.

But he also knew how funding worked and when he was unanimously chosen by the university to speak, he didn't have much choice. He hated the attention and frankly the boredom of a night in a tux answering the same questions over and over.

"Sir, we have arrived." The driver shook him out of his brooding.

The lecture hall was an architectural marvel. He had been here several times before, but he still gawked at the beauty. There was an added attraction this night in addition to his presentation, it would seem. A ten-foot-tall poster depicting a beautiful landscape in Africa was arranged at the front door. He had always loved Africa. As he made his way up the stone steps, Malachi saw another poster of a different kind of Africa: not the jungles and wildlife but the poverty. Only there were no downcast faces in these photos. The people were laughing joyously. Another poster showed a whole family dancing in an open spigot of clean water. Again and again, he walked past more displays, every so often, all slightly varied but with a similar feel: rejoicing.

"Curious," he murmured to himself when he read the poster that stated they were presenting right now. There was no way he would make the ongoing lecture, but he might have some interesting people to talk to if they stuck around.

The last poster in the series was a close up of a smiling child. Malachi was trying to pick out a reflection in the poster child's smiling eyes when a greeter spotted him and escorted him into the main hall. He was welcomed properly by many in his field. He knew that there would be a crowd, but this was a black-tie affair. The applause, though muted with satin gloves, was still thunderous.

He mingled into the crowd easily enough, his responses were almost automatic at this point. They drifted from topic to topic, and Malachi's attention wandered to the conversation of two women standing directly behind him. It was not his intention to eavesdrop, but they were talking so loudly that it couldn't be helped.

"Isn't she just fabulous? You know she lives there alone, don't you?" one woman said to another.

"Oh, yes! The poor dear."

"Poor dear?! My heavens, no! That girl can wrestle a lion and fix a sink without chipping her nail polish. Poor dear, indeed. I never met a more capable woman in my life. Funny, too!"

"And beautiful! Goodness me, I can't believe she doesn't have suitors lined up!"

"Turns 'em all away, I heard. Says she's looking for-"

"Heavens, ma' boy!" A booming laugh shocked Malachi back into the conversation at hand. "Where on earth did you go?"

Malachi glanced back at the group currently gathered around him, all holding cocktails and expectant expressions on their faces. "I apologize, I'm a bit tired from my trip. Excuse me, I think I will get a cold drink." He walked toward the lounge, where even more were ready to receive him. He was met with great pats on the back and offers of cigars and scotch. He politely declined and settled for a tall drink of ice water. As soon as this was over, he would be a free man for six months. He didn't know where he was going, but he hoped it would be somewhere that no one would have heard about his discoveries.

"What did you think?" A middle-aged woman in a large hat lightly laid her hand on his arm.

"I'm sorry, I didn't catch the question?" Malachi fumbled.

"I was asking what you thought about Teneil Jayne's talk?"

"Ten-teneil?" he questioned, still lost.

"Teneil Jayne. . .she just finished speaking?" an older woman with a kind face and a walking stick smiled at him.

"I'm afraid I only just arrived. I didn't have the chance to listen." He was happy to talk about anything that didn't have anything to do with himself, so he added, "It went well?"

The older woman interjected, "Are you single?"

"M-me? Um, yes. I haven't had much experience with women, I'm afraid." He blushed, caught off guard by the scrutiny of the old woman.

"But are you willing?"

"Willing to meet someone?"

"Well, sure. Seems a proper first step." She smiled brightly. Malachi chuckled at the older woman's boldness.

"Mom-" the woman in the hat started, but the old woman cut her off with a simple hand motion.

She was so much like his own grandmother, who was also a very direct woman, that Malachi figured this woman likely preferred when folks spoke plainly as well. So, his next response was quite honest: "I'm afraid the woman I'm looking for does not exist."

"Oh, I don't believe that." With a scowl at the woman who was clearly her daughter, the old woman added, "Come, escort an old lady outside for some fresh air." She took his arm and led him away from the noise out to a small patio, not giving him a chance to object. The moment the door closed behind him she turned and said, "If God made you, he made her, too." She winked at him, and something tightened in his stomach. "I'm going to tell you something that might sound a bit nutty, but I want you to keep an open mind."

"Of course," Malachi said with a smile. He was enjoying her company and getting away from the mass of people.

"In a few short moments a lovely young woman is going to come and greet you. I'm not supposed to tell you any of this, but I like you and Teneil is like a granddaughter to me, only I like her more than I like any of my own. There is no reason why you two can't make it work. She seems to think that you are her match, and standing her in front of you now, I can see why. She came all the way from Africa and put this all together just to have a chance to meet you. I have no doubt that once you meet her you will agree. All I'm asking is that you be good to her." She glared at him.

Malachi felt his smile falter with each of the woman's passing words. "I'm sorry, I'm a bit confused."

"I told you it might sound crazy, but I'm serious. You better love her and treat her right because if you don't, I will see that sweet Jesus allows me to come back and haunt you until the day you die."

Well that certainly took a turn, he thought, finding that his throat had gone dry. "I, I um-"

"I like you. I don't think you will mess it up, but I'm adding my own insurance. Now you promise me, young man."

"Promise what, exactly?" The seriousness in her gaze forced him to contain his laughter.

"Promise that you will love her."

"Okay?"

"No, not good enough."

"I promise that I will love her?"

"Good." She nodded in seriousness.

He did laugh a little then. "So. . .this Teneil is my match?"

"You will know it when you see her." And with that she turned and left him to find his own way back into the party.

Teneil heard the applause when he entered. She was not afraid of crocodiles or hippos, and she would not be afraid now. She took one last look in the mirror, prayed to God that, if nothing else, she could add this to a list of hysterical stories for her next book, and left the private room.

It was time to gather her courage and play out the last act of her brilliant plan. This was her ingenious moment; she knew exactly what she would say, what *he* would say back, and how she would casually and nonchalantly clamp a ring on it. She had given him ample time to mingle in the crowd, which gave her friends ample time to talk her up. Teneil thought of it as a "soft introduction". Only now, when she stepped into the crowded hall. . .she couldn't find him. She was searching for him in every face but when her eyes connected with strangers she was forced to mingle.

Where is he?

He saw her enter the room. Everyone saw her. It was almost like a bell had rung when she walked in, and people automatically looked for the source of the music. She moved like water through the crowd. He followed a few steps behind in her blind spot, watching, listening. Her laughter was contagious and everywhere she went laughter cascaded around her, but all Malachi saw were tears.

People cried and so did she, but no matter how serious the discussion, she seemed to know exactly what to say to lift the spirits of those around her. The thing he liked the most about watching her was the way he noticed her never stop looking for him.

It was clear by the way she treated others and the way that others treated her that she was genuine, kind, clever, and truly everything he had never found, aside from the fact that she was absolutely the most beautiful woman he had ever seen. He thought about what the old maid had said on the patio: *"You will know it when you see her."*

And she was right; he did know it. But there was no way that he could allow this farce to carry on, to allow himself to be manipulated into meeting her. He was flattered that a woman of her caliber was pursuing him, but it also gnawed on his ego. How was he supposed to introduce himself to her? How could *any* man willingly walk into a trap?

And so, the hunter became the hunted.

When the lights dimmed indicating that Malachi was about to speak, Teneil's heart broke. In all of her careful planning, not being able to locate him between their speeches was not even a possibility. It seemed that she was always one step behind him. Everyone had just seen and talked to him. "He was here a moment ago," she was told countless times. It was as if he had purposefully hidden from her all evening. But that was impossible, because he wouldn't even know who to avoid.

She listened to him, though she had no seat. Forgetting, of all the things, to get a ticket to his lecture. She watched him from the balcony. So close but so far away. He was given a standing ovation for his talk as Teneil made her way to the main hall to greet him on the way out. She had one last chance to find him. She waited for almost an hour, politely talking to everyone as they left, but she never saw him. When she finally got up the nerve to ask, she was told that he had left directly after the talk.

Teneil's laugh was sardonic. This was by far the most foolish thing she had ever done, or so she told herself for the next forty-eight hours as she journeyed back to Africa. The night replayed over and over in her head for a week solid. For days she'd refused to get out of bed, overwhelmed with her own Greek tragedy. Despite what she'd considered a fool-proof plot, the whole thing had turned out far too embarrassing.

Finally, back at her home in Malawi, she screamed into her pillow until there was nothing left. Eventually, kicking and thrashing like a child, she pulled herself into a shower and then forced herself out into the sunshine.

She attempted to justify her foolishness by focusing on the funds she had inadvertently raised at the library. And with each bag of cement she mixed, she felt better and better.

Teneil was almost done with the road that stretched into the remote mountains. For an entire year she had been working on it, and when it was done, she was going to take a break. She didn't know where she would go, but she felt the need to hide away and lick her wounds. She couldn't shake the feeling of loss, which was irrational because she had never even met the man.

Mostly she felt shame. It had been a long shot in the first place, but she was used to getting her way, not because she was spoiled but because she knew how to work hard and she was clever, yet still, somehow, she had failed. What was worse was the fact that everyone she had talked to about her plan was constantly bothering her for relationship progress. Failing was one thing; failing with an audience was an entirely different box of rocks.

She got home that night, exhausted and covered in mud. She began boiling the water for a much-needed hot bucket to pour over herself. Her hands ached from the acid in the cement, and when she took her hair down, only half of it actually fell. The other half was plastered in place with mud. Her feet were soggy from her work boots, her eyes red and tired.

She looked long in the small mirror before her in her bathroom. She could not be farther from the glamor she had worn in the lecture hall. It was probably just as well that he never met her, then; if he'd known what she really looked like on a daily basis, he would have been extremely disappointed. She kicked herself for allowing Malachi to slide into her thoughts.

A horn began honking, over and over. She ignored it at first, but her house was a way off any main road and honking like that usually was for her. The truck she found parked outside was large and weighed down by bags of cement.

"Evening!" She shouted at the men who were unloading the truck into her driveway. The driver shut off the engine before greeting her in return.

"I think you are confused," she laughed. "I didn't order any cement."

"I have the paperwork here." He handed her a receipt and she looked it over. The paper said 300 bags of cement for her "road project", signed by "M.Y."

"There is a mistake! I didn't buy this," she insisted at the driver, who shrugged his shoulders and told her,

"Just the driver."

"Wa- I'm not stealing someone's cement!" Teneil burst, unable to stop a confused laugh from leaving her lips.

But the driver only repeated, "I just drive the truck where I am told." And the men continued to unload into her driveway.

Teneil rubbed her face with dirty hands and gave a deep exhale. It would seem her day was not yet done. Now she would have to go down to the hardware store and sort out this very expensive mistake. It took quite a while before they finished, and when they were done the pile of bags was so high, she could not see the road anymore. She had a moment to think, *I kinda like that. I should build a privacy wall there.*

Malachi had been standing in front of the truck the whole time, but she hadn't seen him. It wasn't until the truck had left that he decided to speak up from where he stood next to the cement. "Excuse me, ma'am?"

Teneil spun toward Malachi. She stood with her mouth slightly open, her mind and body frozen. *Malachi?*

"I hope that it's okay, that I'm here." He began his rehearsed speech, but the look on her face was unraveling him; not the joyous reception that he had expected. "I would have come sooner but it was a lot to organize. The trip over here, I mean. It wasn't a big deal. I just. . . I hope I'm not intruding. I didn't have your number, or I would have called." He let out a weak laugh. "I mean, of course, I wanted to surprise you. But-" He trailed off. He'd spent plenty of time planning what he would say when he met her, and the collection of words that just spilled out of his mouth was *not* it.

Teneil still stood, not saying anything, staring at him, disappointed? That's when Malachi realized that this whole thing was a bad idea. He shouldn't have played with her this way; he should have introduced himself that night in between their lectures. He thought he would have the upper hand, surprising her this way, but instead he felt like a selfish fool.

She looked so incredibly beautiful covered in dry mud, standing barefoot. She had been breathtaking before, but this was something else. She was raw and real. There was no mask here; the natural beauty that he saw now had muddled his mind from crisp apples to applesauce. He had thought to come here and "claim" her as his own. But the look on her face said he'd be lucky if she even talked to him.

He wanted to make her smile and laugh like she had done so easily in Boston. She was not smiling now, and all the bravado that he had built up in himself over the last couple of weeks had melted away. He had gotten it all wrong. She had risked so much to get to Boston, and he had left her there alone, for his own pride. Would it have been so bad to let her win?

She recognized him and fought the urge to turn and walk away. In her mind, she had weaved him into a monster so that she could move on. Maybe it was childish for her to do, but I'm just relaying the facts: that's what she did. Now, seeing him here in front of her, she struggled to keep her minimal defenses.

"What are you doing here?" Teneil's tone was not playful. It made him feel even more foolish for thinking that she would be flattered by his attention.

"I came to see you."

His tone, the quiver in his voice, and his posture told her all that she needed to know. *Malachi Young was smitten.* She had miscalculated. Something in her plan had failed miserably, and yet somehow it had come back around. "What am I missing?" she quietly asked herself.

"Sorry?"

She looked at the cement and then back at Malachi. ". . .Is this a set up?"

The irony was a little too much. "*Me* setting *you* up?" He laughed. "Isn't that the way of a guilty mind?"

"Guilty?" She stood a bit taller. "Guilty for what?"

"For what you did in Boston!"

She could have gone either way; she could have paled and acted nonchalant to hide the deception, or she could have done what she actually did, which was to turn red-cheeked and accuse him: "You *knew*?"

He also had a choice: play it cavalier and offhand, or the actual path he chose. "You're honestly mad because I didn't fall into your trap?"

"That was not a trap. That was a … clever introduction." She waved her hand in dismissal.

"It was a trap," Malachi insisted with a small smile. "One I narrowly avoided, thank you."

"Avoided?" She laughed. "Look where you are!" She held out her hands to emphasize the fact that he was standing on her doorstep in Africa. She looked at the receipt in her hand and the signature. "Is this your cement?" She handed him the receipt.

"Um, yes." He flushed red. "I thought it was better than flowers?"

"I believe my trap worked perfectly."

He smiled. "Your *introduction*, you mean."

"That too." She turned to go inside, then looked back over her shoulder and added, "Well?" Her smile grew wide, and her eyes sparkled. "Would you like to come in for tea?"

"Tea?" He laughed. "Tea would be nice."

Chapter Seventeen
IF ONLY HE WAS TENDER

The rain had been falling for days. In other parts of the world, the soft drizzle would have been little more than an annoyance. While consistent days of soft rain in places like Malawi were great for crops, rains often came at a price.

The most common type of house was self-made by burning the mud found onsite into bricks, and some homes had better quality clay than others. Then, water is used to mash that same mud into a sticky mortar. The typical roof was a thin sheet of plastic with the same feel as a cheap garbage bag, covered with dry grasses.

When the rains fell heavily, the walls and roof held up alright, but in slow drizzles like this? Almost every house became a sponge. The mud walls drank in the water and swelled to such a degree that window shutters and doors no longer opened or closed. And, if the rain continued to fall on the bricks, eventually they lost their form and crumbled. With the rainy season being around seven months long, structural collapse was always one of the leading causes of death.

It was on just such a night that our story takes place. Rain had been falling for several days now. The river was running at full capacity and had washed out completely, turning the usually clear, beautiful lake into mud and hippo soup. The rain-soaked ground and wind gusts had uprooted several trees and knocked down power lines. Power was not likely to return until the rains stopped. . .whenever that may be.

Everyone else who relied on solar power had drained their batteries days ago, leaving the evenings dark and quiet. The usual cacophony of birdsong, dogs, goats, motorbikes, car horns, blaring broken speakers, and people hawking their wares was replaced with the white noise of steady rain on the upgraded tin roofs.

Many Malawians believed that the rains brought disease. The rain itself was what carried things like malaria, and so the schools, businesses, and street vendors were all closed. The rains did bring out more mosquitoes and therefore malaria cases always went up with the rainfall, so the logic was sound.

There was little in life that Teneil loved more than the rain. Having grown up in the high mountain desert where it only rained a few times a year, weather like this was a miracle to her. The rain she had experienced as a child was light and usually ice cold, even on the hottest days.

But the rains in tropical East Africa were awe-inspiring. She breathed in the comforting smells of warm, never-ending sheets of water. Even after years, Teneil would stay up all night to watch the lightning. She often stood (where no one could see her, lest they think her insane) with her arms wide open and her head tilted back, feeling the rain on her skin. The warm droplets pouring over her washed away all the damage that no one could see.

Rain, to Teneil, was a shower for the soul.

She was sitting under the cover of her porch, reading a book in the fading light. Her attention was pleasantly balanced between the book before her, and the music of the water drops accompanied by the occasional thunderclap. The rain wasn't meant to stop for another week and there was little to be done. Even if she wanted to go out, no one else would be willing. But she did not want to go out.

Rain was her guilty pleasure; not the rain itself, but the peace that came with it. The rarer a thing, the more valuable, and the silence of the village with the lack of visitors was golden. No one would be at her gate today. Her three children were away in the village for the midterm break, and her dogs were content to keep her toes warm, snoring and grumbling together. Peace.

The storm had been picking up as the sun began going down. It would be a long night for many in the village. Teneil said a prayer as she stepped inside and filled her tea kettle, placing it over the charcoal cooker that sat just outside her back door. The air was growing chilly, and she put her sweater on. Her sweater was an everyday item. She wore it in the early morning like a hug, and when the air grew hot, she shared it with the back of her chair. She hadn't washed it in weeks and had no plan to; the last spray of her perfume still lingered in the fabric.

It was the last of her things that she valued from her old life, and at almost $100 a bottle, it had been a very rare splurge. To her it smelled like America and everything and everyone she missed. Every morning she would get up right before dawn, make a cup of coffee, go outside, and sit on the cement slab of her porch to watch the red sun rise over the mountains of Mozambique.

And while she waited for her coffee to cool enough to drink, she would smell her sweater, think about the life she left behind, and cry. It wasn't because she was sad; she was where she wanted to be, but that didn't make it any easier. She cried because. . .I mean, seriously. Wouldn't you? I'm crying right now as I'm writing this. Maybe it's a girl thing. Anyway, she put the sweater on.

Teneil went from window to window, shutting them as tight as the swollen wood frames would allow. The sky had grown dark quickly, not just from the evening sun but also from the mounting storm. She began lighting the lanterns and candlesticks that she kept around the house. She heard two booming sounds: one was the distinct sound of thunder, but the other ...that was something else. Her heart sank. It took precious seconds to run to her bedroom to quickly put on her shoes. She grabbed a small flashlight, for the little good it would do, and ran outside. She stood in the middle of the mud road in the rain, waiting, then she heard the mournful cry, muffled by the gathering wind. Teneil guessed the direction and ran.

The muddy road was slick and rivers of rushing water had carved deep grooves in their attempt to reach the lake at the bottom of the mountain. Teneil found the small house that she knew belonged to a large family. Half the house was gone.

The mother stood screaming helplessly in the street while the father and two other men dug frantically through the piles of rubble. Teneil put her flashlight between her teeth and dug with her hands.

Glass, splintered wood, and clothing were entangled in the heavy bricks. As she threw aside jagged pieces of the family's home, Teneil prayed for help. Several others joined the scene, both in digging and in screaming. Her knuckles were in tatters, and she had several deep cuts from broken window panes, but the screams of the mother kept her motivated.

Slowly, one by one, people were pulled out of the rubble. Teneil had no idea how many exactly stayed in the small house, but she knew that if there was still shouting there were still others missing.

"Please, God. Please, God. . ."

And she felt it: a small arm under a pile of wet blankets. Teneil heaved more weight off of the tiny form until she could lift and cradle the child to her body. She stretched the open front of her sweater to share it with the limp form.

"The hospital!" she cried over the rain.

Several people pointed and shouted toward a small truck being loaded with several injured persons. Teneil didn't ask who the truck belonged to; she just got in the front seat.

Someone climbed in the driver's seat and the truck trudged forward through the deep mud.

Teneil refused to look at the tiny body in her arms. There was nothing she could do but pray, and she hadn't stopped doing that since she'd left her home. She did her best to support the child through the hard ride. The hospital was a fifteen-minute drive away, on a good day, and all she could think was, *I should have checked if the child needed CPR first,* but she knew that there would be no ambulance coming. Getting to the hospital was the best she could do. She felt sick as they fought their way down the water-logged road. The urgency only built painfully in her stomach; they weren't going to make it.

"Can you drive faster?" Her voice came out harsh and demanding in the dark. She knew it was a foolish request, but she heard a grunt of approval from the driver and the engine did speed up, if only a little.

It gave her comfort, even though they were driving recklessly and the people in the back of the truck were surely having a hard time. She couldn't think about anything except the charge in her arms. They were doing everything they could, even if that meant putting their own lives in danger.

The hospital was being run off a large emergency generator, and the lights were like a beacon through the dark storm. The gate of the hospital was open, and they didn't slow down. They pulled up to the emergency entrance and were greeted by several staff members. Teneil was in shock, and they had to pry the child from her arms. They did not allow her into the exam room.

Teneil stood suddenly alone, bleeding, soaking wet, and covered in mud. A stark contrast to the sterilized white and mint green of the hall around her, and unable to keep her feet, Teneil crouched down and buried her face in her hands. She instantly felt everything in one powerful, overwhelming wave: the pain in her hands and the reality of how drastically the last thirty minutes of her life had shifted. She felt the strength leaving her legs and decided this was a good place to sit down.

"Up you go."

Arms slid behind her and lifted her back onto her feet. Teneil turned to see the driver, covered in mud and blood, much like she was. "Let's not ruin this clean hospital by sitting down. Follow me."

Numbly, Teneil let him lead her to the casting room, where two large sinks ran both hot and cold water. They both silently began removing their outer layers and unsuccessfully washing the mud off.

Red clay mixed with red blood and swirled down the drain in unison. Teneil was not crying but fat, hot tears somehow kept rolling over her cheeks at their own will. The silence was palpable, until Teneil tried to wring out her sweater and hissed in pain.

She let the man next to her grab her hands and study the damage. "Come on," he said, taking her gently by the elbows and guiding her toward the emergency room.

"No, I can't." She stopped when she saw where they were going.

"You need stitches."

"I can't."

"Why not?"

"Because look!" she shouted at him. There was only a small window on the door that led into the ER, but they could see the chaos of every available member of the staff rushing around tending to serious injuries. "I can wait," she said stoically, even as fresh drops of blood fell to the floor.

"Okay, hero," the driver scoffed. "Let's go." He changed their direction and led her to another area of the hospital instead. A sign caught Teneil's eye: Surgery Ward.

Her eyes grew wide, and he saw the need for further explanation. "I was a 68W, a combat medic, in the ARMY for six years." He looked in

242

each room before shutting the door again. "I did three tours. I don't think anyone will mind if I stitch you up myself."

"Honored, I'm sure," she groaned, but was too out of her senses to do much more than allow him to lead her.

He laughed at her bitter words and opened the door to an empty operating room. It smelled of harsh disinfectants and the fluorescent lighting made her look green. No, it wasn't the lighting: she was actually green. "Are you doing okay?" he asked seriously.

"I've seen stitches," she began, "where they put the needle right into the wound to numb the area? I don't know about that. It's really bad, isn't it?" Her eyes were large and red, and he wanted to tell her that it would be alright, but he knew the process all too well. And he wouldn't lie to her.

"Never had stitches before?"

"Probably should have a few times," she admitted. "But no, I haven't."

"They do say that is the worst part."

He couldn't keep the smile from his face at her apprehension. He had been sitting on the porch of his friend's house, counting himself the only person around who was enjoying the rain, when he saw her. Like a madwoman in the rising storm, she ran out to stand in the middle of the muddy road. He almost called out to her from his dry seat to see if she was okay. It was only then that he had heard the cry of distress.

He saw her run and followed her, not sure of the exact direction himself. When he saw her digging in the ruins of the house, he fell in the mud beside her, also plunging his hands into the rubble. He'd known she needed stitches because he had been next to her when she cut herself on the broken window.

When he saw the child's limp form as she pulled, he wanted to stop, but she didn't. He watched her fold the child in her sweater and knew that it was already too late. He'd seen enough war and death to know that there was nothing that could be done for it, but he could do something; he could take care of her now.

"Have a seat there." He gestured to the operating table and rummaged through drawers and cabinets until he found what he was looking for.

Teneil sat politely, dropping her soppy sweater on the floor as opposed to the nearby chair.

"Let's have a better look." He very gently turned her hands over.

One hand had deep lacerations across the palm and several of her fingers were cut to the bone. There were more gashes on her arms, and even one high on her cheek. He had witnessed much worse, but this still hurt him to see. "Let's start here." He handed her a couple pills for pain.

"Oh, no thank you."

"Okay, but this is really going to hurt."

"It's okay, just do it," Teneil insisted.

He hesitated but put down the pills and grabbed the syringe containing the local anesthetic. "You'll want to look away."

"No way!" she laughed. "I don't know you from Adam and I'm not sure I trust you enough to be doing what you're doing."

"Lucky for you, my name is Adam." He smiled, but her face did not change. "Seriously?"

"Seriously." Her eyes peering out from behind muddy tendrils of hair were pained but hard.

"Alright, fine. Watch if you have to." He placed the injections directly in each of her wounds. She whimpered a few times but never flinched. He was finishing up the stitches on her palm when he glanced up into her face. Eyes downcast, she was looking through her hand. No doubt in her mind she was far away somewhere, kneeling in the mud with a tiny body in her arms. Her eyes were rimmed with tears and her lip trembled slightly.

"He's dead, I think." She said the words as if in echo to the thoughts that were screaming in her mind.

Adam did not stop working. "He could be," he replied tenderly, then moved to work on her fingers. "Would that be so bad?"

Suddenly her eyes were sharp and focused on him, searching his face for the answer to his question. "What?"

"I mean, of course his family will grieve, but what about him?" He never paused in his work, tying the closing knot on another stitch as he spoke. His words were filled with a kind of passion that a blues singer reached when they rehearsed words written on their heart. He was not just saying the words; he was feeling them: "'To the one who is victorious, I will give the right to sit with me on my throne, as I sat with my father on his throne when I was victorious.'" He moved to the next finger. "No more pain. No more suffering. Just an eternal moment, sitting on the lap of God, looking into the eyes of love Himself."

He finished her stitches and began rubbing ointment into her other wounds. When he touched the wound on her cheek, her strong expression slowly melted into tears. He sat with her, not attempting to fill the silence; there was nothing that could be said.

She took a deep breath, and with a still-quivering lip, she lifted her chin again. Her tears had made fresh tracks in the mud still clinging to her skin. He grabbed a warm, wet cloth and gently cleaned her face. In the privacy of this room, she could allow herself to be vulnerable.

He added a butterfly stitch to her cheek and, wrapping her hands in gauze, he said, "I think that about does it." He looked up and smiled almost proudly at her. His look made her blush. His sureness about the way he moved and spoke made people naturally follow him. She had never before let someone take care of her, and most definitely not to this magnitude.

"Thank you."

"Thank you," he said back, "for what you did out there. Let me get your sweater." He picked up the garment from the floor and, without flinching, hung the bloody, muddy rag over his arm.

They walked back to the waiting room to find that the rest of the family had arrived. The family jumped at the sight of the two and didn't hesitate to hug and thank them both. Teneil searched the room and finally found the boy's mother. She cried and hugged the woman. "I'm so sorry."

The woman wiped her tears and kissed Teneil. "It was just a house! If it wasn't for you, I would have lost my boy!"

"He's *alive?*" Adam was shocked.

"Yes!"

Teneil stared at Adam, who just shook his head. "He's alive," Teneil repeated the words a few times to help them sink in.

"He's alive," Adam echoed again in wonder.

After some time, they finally began heading back to the truck. It looked as if a war had taken place inside the cab. "Might clean this out tomorrow," Adam laughed, and Teneil climbed into the passenger seat. The rain had let up a little, and the sky was lightening, close to dawn. She sat with her better hand picking at the loose strings of her damaged garment. She put the sweater to her nose and inhaled deeply, but only the warm smell of clay and the copper tang of blood touched her. Defeated, she dropped it back in her lap.

"Special sweater?" Adam asked as he started the engine, wiping some chunks of mud off the steering wheel.

"Something like that."

"Was it a gift or something?"

She laughed quietly. "No, actually. I got it about a year ago in a used clothing market. It's the only sweater I have, but mostly. . ." The scent was gone. "It's dumb and petty. It's just that it smelled like home. It sounds stupid, I know, but. . .I had this perfume for years and. . ." Her tears were dangerously close to the surface.

She trailed off. It sounded even more ridiculous after the night they'd had. Should she say that she liked it because it made her cry?

Adam nodded and said nothing. He helped her inside her house when she couldn't grip the key. He tucked her mosquito net in for her, and he even fed her dogs who clearly thought they had been abandoned forever.

They both paused when he saw her pajamas sitting on the table next to her bed. He blushed furiously when she laughed and said she would figure it out herself.

"Thank you for everything, Adam. Really, thank you."

"It was an incredible night, and I am blessed to have met you." He hesitated, wanting to hug her, wanting anything but to leave her there alone and hurt. But he bowed his head, said goodnight, and left.

The next morning Teneil had a hard time getting out of bed. . .literally. She could not get the mosquito net untucked from the bed. Her hands ached, and they felt hardened like they had been dipped in wax. She had almost given up on starting a kettle for coffee when there was a knock at the door.

She was greeted by a small, round, redheaded woman, with a large smile, and a brown paper bag. "Good morning, dear." She pushed past Teneil.

"Can I help you?" Teneil asked, bewildered.

The woman looked at Teneil's bandaged hands and disheveled, muddy hair and said kindly, "Not likely, but I can help you." The woman took a quick look around. "I bet you would like some coffee?"

Teneil nodded dumbly. The woman took off to the kitchen and began brewing two cups. "Who are you?" Teneil managed to ask as she followed.

"My name is Naomi, but that isn't what you want to know, is it? You want to know what I'm doing here."

Teneil nodded again.

"Adam sent me." She sat down with Teneil and the coffee. "I've been hired to be your hands." Naomi smiled and waved her fingers at Teneil.

"I think I can manage," Teneil said, even while it took several adjustments to grab her coffee cup.

"I can see," Naomi said with a smile. "In fact, Adam said that I could expect you to say no less. But if it's all the same to you I would rather not turn down the little extra income." She set the brown paper bag on the table, then pushed it toward Teneil. "I was also told to give you this."

Teneil opened the bag to find more bandages and cream, with a note that said,

Naomi is a retired nurse, the only woman I have met more stubborn than you. Let her help you. - Adam

Naomi had a way of taking over and Teneil was extremely grateful. She scrubbed the mud out of Teneil's hair and off her skin. She changed the bandages on her wounds and the muddy, bloody sheet on her bed. She made way too much food and told Teneil stories, some true, some not.

The second day Naomi arrived with another brown sack. "We have plenty of bandages," Teneil protested.

"I'm just the delivery boy." Naomi dropped the bag in Teneil's lap.

Teneil sighed and opened it. Inside was a bundle of fabric tied with a ribbon. The note simply said,

I guessed – Adam

Teneil pulled the ribbon and the soft fabric melted in her hands. The material was a knit of blue yarn so rich in color that she'd almost mistaken it for black. It was cut much the same as her last sweater, except the quality was a large step up.

Teneil's old sweater had been well loved long before it had ever made it onto a dusty tarp, in the middle of a parking lot, on a market day in Malawi. This new sweater was just that: brand new. It fit her perfectly, and from the moment she put it on she'd refused to take it off, because it was so soft. . .mostly.

On the third day Naomi had yet another brown bag, this time smaller and slightly heavier. Teneil was excited when she saw it, and she offered no protest when Naomi handed it to her. The note said,

The child is being discharged today, let's celebrate! –Adam

Inside the bag was a container with a large slice of chocolate cake, where she discovered another note that said:

PS: I took a bite, poison control. – Adam

And sure enough, there was a corner marred by the distinct markings of a fork. Teneil laughed.

Even Naomi chuckled. "Think that boy is sweet on you."

"Do you know him very well?"

"I've worked with him here and there for upwards of about ten years."

Teneil's eyes grew wide. "What do you think of him?"

Naomi thought in earnest for a while. She sucked on one of her teeth a few times and said, "Greatest man I ever met." She flashed a smile. "Just don't leave him alone with your cake."

On the fourth day, when the knock came at the back door, Teneil was ready. She had been up all night, her mind racing with questions for Naomi. Instead, she found Adam himself standing there with a brown paper sack.

"Adam!" Teneil exclaimed, startled. She had only ever seen him that night, covered in mud and gore. He was in a suit now, clean and smiling. His dark auburn hair, she would never have guessed from that night, was cleanly groomed and matched his full but well-groomed beard.

Dark eyes were bright when he saw her in the sweater that he'd picked out for her, wrapped around her like a hug. His smile was wide and proud as he took in the sight of her. Her hair was down in dark morning tangles and her skin was no longer sallow green but flushed pink.

"I just thought I should come by and check on you."

"Would you like some coffee? I mean, you'd have to make it and make mine for me too, but. . . would you like some? Please say yes." She smiled and stood aside for him to accept her offer, which he did, with a great bout of laughter.

They sat outside in the early morning sun on her patio. "I have something for you." He handed the bag over to her. She took it confidently; glad her hands were healing as well as they were.

"Every day?" She blushed and hugged the knitted fabric she was wearing. "By the way, this is beautiful. And what was left of the cake was delicious! The bandages were thoughtful. I wonder what delight awaits in bag number four?" she mused, opening the bag. She froze and tears ran down her face. "How?" she whispered while looking at him with awe.

"It's a long story that involves a spy named Naomi finding an empty bottle of perfume still on your desk," Adam confessed, "and a perfume store in South Africa, with a few bribes."

Teneil took the bottle out and sprayed her new sweater. She buried her face in the fabric and breathed deeply. Her face twisted up and she began to sob.

Adam moved quickly to her side. "Oh, I'm sorry! I didn't mean to make you cry!"

She wrapped her arms around his shoulders and continued to cry, even leaving a bit of snot on his suit jacket. "It's good," she squeaked out.

"Really?" He looked at the mess she left behind. "*This* is good?"

"Really good," she confirmed through a twisted "ugly cry" face, leaning into him again, holding him tighter. "Really, really good."

Chapter Eighteen
IF ONLY HE WAS PASSIONATE

He kissed her.

Wait, let me backup a bit…

She shot him, and then he kissed her.

That's still not far enough; let me step back just a hair more…

She had married him, then shot him, and then he kissed her.

Maybe I should start at the beginning. . .

David was an international man of mystery. As an undercover member of a secret Intelligence Agency, he was currently trailing behind the scum of the earth. He had tracked a dozen British socialite elitists through several African countries. For months, he had seen them at their parties, full of drugs and prostitutes. They never seemed to grow tired of consuming life.

But David didn't care about their minor offenses; it was the rumors of child trafficking that kept him up at night. Monsters like these would only get a slap on the wrist for drug charges, but David could serve better justice than that: he would see them rot serving life sentences in prison for their black hearts.

David was leading a small team of only two other officers, Ben and Eli. The three of them had worked together off and on for a decade and made a formidable brotherhood. When the private yacht they had been tracking landed on Mozambique's shore and only half the criminal party exited, David had split the team in two.

He followed the group of men headed inland while Ben and Eli stayed with the others still on the boat. One week later, David was alone in some tiny, poor country in East Africa and had gathered enough intel to start the process of taking out the trash. He had called the other two officers in for the arrest, but they were still days off. Within the week, some very bad men would be going away for a very long time.

David was staying at a lodge in a quiet village next to a beautiful bay. He happily played the undercover role of a missionary. He loved Scripture and his mom always said that if he wasn't a man of the law, he would have been a man of the cloth. David saw the two jobs as different branches of the same higher government. The cover was perfect; it allowed him freedom to talk to anyone he wished and go wherever he wanted.

Under this cover, with his Bible in hand walking through the beautiful fishing town, he learned much about the area as he waited for Ben and Eli to arrive. Over and over, he heard of a woman named Teneil. While trying to get information on child disappearances, people kept insisting that he needed to contact her and that they should work together. He had also heard from multitudes of little old ladies that she was in great need of a husband.

That made David snort with laughter. He was not even remotely interested in meeting women, not when the greatest break in his career was about to take place. But he listened like a good man of God would and, after a few days, to save time, he started by saying, "Hello, I'm a friend of Teneil. Can you help me?" People were very willing to talk to and even feed him.

Enjoying the hospitality that came with this mysterious woman's name, David got a little too comfortable. So far, he'd learned the "when", but not the "where". Five days from now, a boat was coming across the body of water that stretched between Mozambique and Malawi. He knew that five young girls were taken from Mozambique's side of the giant lake. He'd learned that was a common way to traffic youths; by taking them across the lake, they wouldn't know the language and there would be no road to follow back home. Children rarely ever ran away from their captors. Even if they had the chance, where would they go?

He knew the names, ages, and even the cost of each, but he did not know the "where" and he was getting desperate. That's why, one afternoon, he was acting like a nosy neighbor and not a trained professional. David found himself listening directly under the windowsill to the three men he'd been tracking since they disembarked from their boat. He had taken to calling them "Larry, Curly, and Moe."

Being careless and stupid got him caught.

Without a warning, a thick stick connected with David's ribs and then his head before he was hauled to his feet by several pairs of thick hands.

Maybe it was the pain in his ribs that clouded his judgment. He would most definitely blame it on the pain later that night when he replayed the day in his mind. But when one of the men shook him and demanded to know who he was, "I'm Teneil's fiancé!" blurted from his lips. The men had laughed at that. . . well, all except the bigger one.

"I don't believe you," the large man, whose true name was Aleze, seethed.

The man was a force. His gaze like steel matched his iron grip and both of those attributes complemented his cold, dead insides where most humans kept things like mercy and compassion. Aleze was more like a reptile who could only be warm by stealing warmth from someone else.

The tension in the small room was palpable as the laughter from the other two died abruptly. Birds and the crashing waves were the only sounds as the two men assessed each other, mutual malice burning in the air between them.

"I have heard that Teneil had a friend in town, a missionary guy friend." The thinner of the three shifted nervously on his feet and looked David over with new suspicion. "I didn't know anything about a wedding, though. . ."

"I've only just asked her," David reasoned, sounding more confident than he felt. His primary concern was the trafficked girls, but a fork of concern broke off in his heart for this woman. Whoever she was, once word of this got out, she would probably have to leave town.

David had no regrets about that. There was only the success of the mission: inconveniencing one woman was a small sacrifice that David was happy to pay for her.

"You lie," the big man choked out.

"Let's go ask her," suggested the third man. "I saw her doing that floating thing in the lake on my way here."

David's body stiffened as they all looked at him. "Great!" he agreed with false enthusiasm. "I had been heading to meet her on the beach when I ran into you guys."

The three men looked confused at one another; had they run into him? He'd said it with such confidence that it stopped them for a moment.

"Let's go," Aleze smiled in a knowing way.

Tourists played in the water where only a dozen yards away mothers and children washed their laundry and bathed. Teneil never spent much time on the beach. It was beautiful, and she understood why people came here on holidays. She was not avoiding the tourists, exactly, she was avoiding those who preyed on the tourists that frequented the large beach. There were about a dozen in the gang of thieves and vagabonds that occupied this length of the lakeshore.

She had spent her first year in Nkhata Bay fighting them off at every corner and falling into their traps. She had been manipulated out of a good portion of money before she understood what had happened to people like her who came to live here. They had finally backed off after running through all the games they knew how to play. That didn't stop them from harassing her every time they crossed paths. Finally, she had cut a deal with them: if they left her alone, she wouldn't say things like "That guy stole my shoes!" every time she saw them with another foreigner. But she still avoided the beach when possible, except for this day.

Today, she needed to be in the water.

Teneil left her dog in the shade of the tree. Sanji, the name translated to "jealousy", the massive Rottweiler-Rhodesian Ridgeback mix was her constant shadow, unless the path involved anything that looked like a bath. But Sanji was content to lay in the flowers with one eye open while Teneil walked into the lake.

The bottom dropped out from underneath her feet and she continued on. At its deepest, Lake Malawi was about half a mile, which was quite deep for a lake. It was rare to know how to swim here, and those who did rarely went that far from shore. Teneil continued swimming until her arms burned. By now, she was far enough out that the sound of the beach had dwindled to an indistinct murmur.

Then she rolled onto her back, letting the sun beat onto her face and the water in her ears drown out any other sounds. The water was calm, and she breathed shallow and slow, holding enough air in her lungs that she wouldn't need any extra effort to keep her face above water. She closed her eyes and sighed. This was her secret place. A quiet place, without distraction or obligation, a place where no one could reach her but God.

The week had brought her one awful thing after another. She had supported a family with a small business, by getting a bundle of clothing to sell in the local market. Someone from the neighboring village had stolen the new bundle, and when the family discovered who it was, they'd brutally killed the thief. It only got worse when it was discovered they had killed an innocent man. The family of the man who was murdered retaliated and killed several of the original attackers. This caused a small civil war. Almost a dozen people were now dead, and even more were hospitalized.

Tears made a short descent from the corners of her eyes into the lake. She exhaled and the water closed in over her head, burning into her nose. She watched the light reflect on the surface as she sank deeper and deeper. *Just feel. Feel the water. Feel the ache for air.*

Teneil let the physical discomfort of needing to breathe overwhelm the constant loop of tragedy playing through her emotions. When she couldn't take it anymore, she frantically kicked for the surface, gulping in air, overwhelmed now with gratitude at the need fulfilled.

Often when life seemed too much, she would do exactly what she was doing now. More times than not, when she left the lake things seemed right again. Unfortunately, that was not the case today. When she finally made it back to the shore, she felt no different.

The hike back up to her house was steep, and she decided that since she was down by the water so rarely, she would enjoy it a little before leaving. If the water could not cure her of her foul mood, maybe the hot sand could. The lake often looked like a sea, the water clear and blue. The beach, though littered with trash and broken glass, was still beautiful. The lush, tropical growth and large, black granite boulders made it look like a screensaver.

This was paradise, albeit a broken one. Maybe she could play the tourist for a little while. Would it be okay to forget everything and just enjoy, even for a moment?

She laid back in the hot sand, the sun burning away the water left on her skin. Teneil couldn't remember the last time that she had laid in the sun like this. It felt good. She inhaled deeply and tried to focus on the brilliant color the sun made when it shone through the backs of her eyelids.

She was well-aware of the sudden cacophony nearby. She was neither trying to block it out or listen to it, but let it wash over her. *I will not open my eyes; I will not open my eyes. Relax, relax. . . just folks playing on the beach . . . relax.* She chanted this over and over to herself, but the sound continued to draw closer.

It wasn't easy, but Teneil was forcing herself to at least act like she was not incredibly highly strung right now. Then the steps pounded up to her, stopped, and a person fell onto the ground next to her. She smiled as her mood lightened, wondering which of the children had spotted her on the beach and ran to see her.

"Teneil, I promise I will explain everything. Please just go along."

The deep, male voice that met her ears was low, hushed, and rushed. She tried to open her eyes at the stranger's words, but the intensity of the sun almost blinded her. As she blinked, the world was washed in a deep blue haze, like a twilight shadow in midday, made even more dark by the three large figures that appeared to block her connection with the sun. Whatever peace she had managed to secure was quickly washed away with the bile rising in her throat.

She propped herself up on her elbows. She didn't need to see all the details of these men's faces to know who they were.

Aleze, Marcus, and a man who called himself Chicken Biscuit (and had actually got mad when Teneil had laughed about it) stood above her. These three bullies had a tendency to drink far too much on the beach, and her house was on the way home. The larger of the three men, Aleze, had repeatedly asked her to join him for things like dinners and walks, but she never accepted his proposals.

At first Aleze had laughed about her refusals, but when she insisted she wasn't interested, he got mad. Repairing all the windows and flowerpots they had broken at her home over the years had been expensive, but when she had finally told Aleze that it would *never* happen, it had cost her the life of her closest friend at the time: her sweet dog, Koinonia.

But Teneil was not afraid of these thugs. Maybe she should be, but when she looked at them, she did not see men but slithering, gross things. And she did not fear slithering, gross things.

She groaned and lay back down against the hot sand.

"Teneil, there is a problem," Aleze began in a comfortable but serious tone, like they were old work colleagues. The familiarity of his words made her sick.

She laughed, raising one arched eyebrow. "Everywhere you are, Aleze, is a problem." Marcus snickered and Aleze gave him a grave look.

"I'm serious," Aleze snapped.

"So am I." She turned her head away, dismissing him. "You are blocking my sun."

"Do you know this one?" He ignored her obstinate rejection, kicking sand toward the man at her side she had almost forgotten about.

Teneil finally glanced at the man lying next to her on the beach. She would have loved to say "yes" because he was handsome, and there was a look in his sharp, gray-green eyes that said he needed her. Teneil was not traditionally a liar, but she said, "Yup," mostly because, whoever he was, he was clearly some kind of annoyance to Aleze and that was enough for her.

"Says he's your fiancé." All three of the men towering above her laughed.

"Yup." She was so full of seething disdain that the shock of what Aleze said could not register.

Aleze ground his teeth and growled at her, "Answer the question, Teneil."

"I already did." She stood up. She was still shorter than him by quite a bit, but she felt better on her feet, facing him head on.

"You may want to rethink that." Aleze took a step toward her, the tension palpable between them.

She smiled calmly and brushed the sand from her arms. "Didn't notice I brought a friend with me today?" With a subtle nod of her chin, she gestured to the area behind her.

Aleze scanned the brush to find large, dark eyes burning into him from the shadows. The beautiful, sleek, deadly, Sanji was truly only half domesticated. She was Teneil's replacement for the small mutt she had lost thanks to the bullies before her now.

Ridgebacks were lion dogs, used to guard the diamond mines in South Africa. Mixed with the overprotective American Rottweiler, meant that if Aleze put a hand on Teneil, he would likely lose it. From the uncertain, frustrated expression in his brown eyes, Teneil knew that Aleze was well aware of this fact.

"Sanji. . ." she whispered, looking into the eyes of Aleze with a challenge clear in her gaze. The bush behind her responded in a low, reverberating growl. Teneil's smile grew into a sweet grin. "Sanji. . ." The dog's thick muscles coiled. Her growl, one of pure bass, was like a warm hug to Teneil's midsection, exactly where these men were also feeling it, but what they felt was cold. "I would go, slowly." She winked.

Teneil knew that if one of these men ran from her in that moment, there was no word or command that she could use to stop her dog from attacking. It took a long time to get used to having an animal of this magnitude. Sanji was not a beast that she could fully control; she was very capable of killing a full-grown man. Teneil kept Sanji because she had proven to be an excellent judge of character; the massive dog that loved children and hated cockroaches in all forms. Today, Sanji would get a whole chicken for dinner.

"See you soon." Aleze took several steps backward before turning slowly and walking away, his two lackeys in tow.

Teneil watched them retreat for a while before she allowed herself a breath. As grateful as she was for Sanji, she knew there would be times when the dog was not around to protect her. But that was a day that would worry for itself; she had enough on her mind right now. Speaking of current problems, she looked down to find her "fiancé" staring down the barrel of her monstrous guard dog.

Before the handsome stranger was a mouth that could easily clamp down on an entire head. Drool ran out of her jaws, her focus pinpointed on the snack in front of her. Wisely, the man refused to move from his crouched position. "Um, Teneil?"

"Yes, my love?" Teneil stood unmoved, her hands on her hips. She said nothing else, calling the dog's name now meant that she would likely set Sanji on him. So, she simply walked away, knowing that the dog would follow her.

David couldn't take his eyes off the woman whose name he'd known and reputation he'd used for the last few days. When he first saw her, she was soaking wet, fresh from the lake. She had no towel, laying directly on the sand. Her dark, knee-length dress clung tightly to her body, her hair a mess around her shoulders, white sand lingering on her sun-darkened skin. She was breathtaking.

Somehow, with everything he had heard about her, he hadn't expected that. The moment he saw Teneil, he'd began to pray that God would open her eyes, not for his sake but for hers.

How had he been so stupid to involve her in this? He was going to rely heavily on her reputation for kindness and her clear distaste for the three thugs. She was anything but soft: instead, he'd witnessed a woman who was strong to almost cruel. Calculating, clever, and confident.

The way she talked to the stooges. She'd known exactly who they were, and she'd hated them. She was not playing games with them, there was no need; she knew she had already won. During the whole exchange he'd just sat there dumbfounded. He had always admired strong women, but this was something else.

She was brilliant. And her dog? Her dog was another story. Teneil's dog had finally snorted in his face with disapproval before stomping off after her.

David was left speechless on the beach for some time. Ultimately, he decided that he would use her hatred of the three men to convince her to keep up his ruse for five more days. In exchange he would contact the Malawian government and make sure the stooges would serve a prison sentence somewhere far from Teneil's home. David was good at getting what he wanted and now had a way to manipulate Teneil into agreeing with his plan. The five girls: that was all that mattered. The job, his job, was the priority.

As he stood and brushed sand from his legs, he thought he had everything lined up perfectly. What he hadn't expected was the handful of people who had overheard the exchange and ran to share the gossip in town.

Teneil was getting married!

He found her house easily enough; it was the only one with a high brick wall around it. Sanji lay dutifully at the only gate. With as much confidence as possible, David cooed, "Hello, beautiful."

Sanji lifted her head and wagged her tail.

"Oh, that's a good girl!" David let out a surprised chuckle, not really expecting the dog's gentle, lazy act after her aggressive display at the beach. Lucky for him, "good girl" was Sanji's equivalent flowers and chocolates. "Yes, that's a really, REALLY good girl!" David slowly reached a hand into the gate and Sanji, the cheap date, rolled over like a Thanksgiving bird and gave him the full view of the gate key (her belly) that needed scratching.

Teneil saw her dog prostituting herself at the gate and wondered which neighborhood kid brought bones this time. When she came around the corner, her smile died. "Oh." She folded her arms and cocked her hip. "It's my would-be husband." She rolled her eyes. "You never even asked my dad."

David leaned against the outside of her fence. "Ask your dad what?"

"For my hand in marriage. Call me old fashioned but there's quite a few steps you missed."

"Could I just have a moment of your time? To explain myself?" She stood unmoved, so he added a sincere, "Please."

"Fine." Teneil was cold, but it was an act; she was actually very curious. This was a story that she wanted to hear. He wasn't hard to look at either, but she also wasn't sure that she shouldn't be mad at him, so she played it somewhere in between. "But I'm very busy," she added as she opened the gate and let him in, "so you only got a few minutes." That wasn't true at all; she had nothing going on today, but the best defense is a good exit plan.

"Yes, of course." But then David added, "Do you mind if we go inside? It's a very private matter."

"Yes, I do mind," Teneil said flatly, sitting herself on a small wooden chair outside. "I don't allow strange men in my house."

"Right, perfectly reasonable." He sat opposite her.

"I'm all ears!" She smiled, not entirely disingenuous.

He told Teneil who he worked for, what he was planning, and how he knew who she was. He told her about the five trafficked girls and the sale that was set to take place that Thursday. He told her everything, then he went for the final, crucial piece: "And so, Teneil. . .I am, in fact, asking for your hand in marriage. Just until Thursday, to help secure my cover so that I can help these girls and hundreds that will no doubt come after them if I don't nail these guys. What do you think?"

"You're a *spy*?" she questioned doubtfully.

"Not a spy. I'm an intel-"

She held her hand up, cutting him off. "Yeah, yeah, I heard you."

"These are bad people," David insisted, leaning urgently forward in his seat. "I've been building this case for two years. This isn't the first time they have done this, and it won't be the last. Please-"

Sanji began to growl and ran to the gate. There was a ruckus building outside, and Teneil sighed as she stood up.

"Hold on just a moment." She went to the gate and found the *whole village* waiting for her. A great cheer went up, and, bewildered as she was, Teneil laughed and cheered with them. "What's happened?" she asked.

But no one answered. They just pushed the gate open and came into her yard. Several grandmothers gave her flowers, and the old men kissed her hands. Finally, Teneil spotted her good friend, Esther. "What is all this?"

Esther jumped on her friend. "I cannot believe you didn't tell me! You're getting married!?"

Teneil was dumbstruck as an unsettling feeling grew in her stomach. *Oh, no.* Her gaze drifted over several grandmothers who were all talking at once.

"They are arguing whose house will host your wedding!" Esther shouted over the crowd. "Where is your husband to be? I can't wait to meet him!"

Teneil turned and found David right by her side, smiling as if he was the happiest man in the world. He slid his arm easily around her waist and gave her a loving grin before stretching his hand out to Esther.

"Hello, I'm David."

Esther swooned, and Teneil was momentarily blinded by the ease of his introduction and the warmth in his hand where it rested on her hip.

The grandmothers poked Esther, clearly looking for an answer to a question Teneil hadn't heard. Esther shouted in her direction, "How's Friday?"

"Friday?" Teneil shouted back.

"For the wedding!" Esther laughed.

She looked around, eyes and mouth gaping like a stunned carp. David had been ushered away by the older men, who talked to him as if he understood their language. Teneil thought about the five girls and how David said the sale was happening Thursday. By Friday he would be gone.

She let her attention drift over all the people who had come to help her celebrate this charade. They loved her so much and she loved them. She didn't want to lie to them, but she could never live, knowing she could have helped save innocent lives and didn't.

"Friday sounds perfect!" Teneil announced hesitantly, and the crowd went wild. She saw David's shoulders relax and his smile went from forced to genuine. His eyes met hers and sparkled with pride along with. . . something else. What was it? Mischief? They were now officially in a plot together; they shared a secret. But because of the way he was looking at her, a warmth spread through her, burning in her cheeks, and she was the first to break eye contact.

The rest of the day was spent receiving well-wishers, gifts, and prayers for a blessed union. Teneil played her part, smiling and laughing as she thanked everyone for their blessings.

David watched her constantly out of the corner of his eye, witnessing her joy and love, and the way the people gathered around her. She was not as cruel and hard as he initially thought; she was fierce and protective. She was like a shelter in a storm for people, and shelters had to be strong.

She was also playing her role perfectly; she had even sat adoringly close and leaned into him when he instinctively put his arm around her. She laughed at his jokes and ingeniously made up a fantastic story about how they had met, with her being the heroine, of course. By the end of the day, they had fallen into their roles seamlessly.

David waited as the sun began to fade, but the people never stopped coming. He could see her exhaustion, but she carried on, until finally he stepped in. "Please, it has been a long day and we have so much to discuss. Now, let me take my beautiful bride inside to rest."

The women swooned, the men patted him on the back, and they all filed out quickly. "Thank you," Teneil sighed once the house was quiet again.

He looked at the pile of bananas in the corner. "Think we are good on bananas for a while."

She smiled fondly at the fruit. "People don't have much here, but they sure got excited!" She laughed.

"Was that normal?" he asked.

"No idea. Never got hitched in Malawi before." She practically fell onto the couch.

He followed her in, giving her an appreciative smile. "No, I don't suppose you have." He sat on the chair next to her. "Why is that, if you don't mind my asking?"

"Why aren't I married?" She rolled her eyes again.

"Yes." He laughed. "That seems like a reasonable question. You are, well. . .you- well, you know."

"No, husband. I don't know." She shot a playful glance in his direction. "Why don't you tell me."

Okay, he could rise to that bait, "You are beautiful and smart," he answered honestly. "Brave and kind. You would make a fine wife. Why don't you settle down?"

"Now you sound like my mother."

David laughed but said nothing.

"Men don't want a wife like me, David," Teneil said flatly. The nonchalant attitude in her voice faded. "They like the idea of an adventurous, independent, strong woman, but that's not the girl you marry. At the end of the day men want a woman that is theirs. I can't ever be that."

"Why not?" He tried to cover the disappointment in his voice.

"Because I belong to God." She sighed deep in contentment.

"I can see why the people love you."

"Because love begets love begets love." She smiled.

"I think I should move in," David replied flatly.

Teneil sat up quickly, eyes wide. "Six hours ago, I wouldn't even let you in the door!"

"Yes, and twelve hours ago you were an unsuspecting bachelorette. Now look at you!"

"You move fast."

"Life is short." He gave her a grin. "But seriously. . .I'll sleep on the couch. It won't be anything more than a cover." He didn't actually think that staying in her home was necessary, but he also didn't want to leave.

She didn't think that was necessary either, but it had been such a perfect evening. Facade or not, she had enjoyed him. Several times throughout the day she had thought, *He is just what a man ought to be.* The way he had talked about those trafficked girls as if they were his own daughters. Then there was the way he laughed and treated the people she loved so much with kindness and respect. Playing to his affection was too easy.

"Yeah, I think that's a good idea, too," she amended. "For appearances."

"The lodge is a short walk away. I will go check out and get my bags." He left the room without looking back.

David walked in a stupor. He was somewhere far away in his mind, imagining the future of this invented life. He'd almost walked straight into them.

"Friday?" Aleze said coldly.

"Good evening, gentlemen. That's right!" David said proudly. "And you are *all* invited!" He flashed a bright grin. "Don't forget to bring a gift!"

David shouldn't have taunted the men, but he knew that by Friday the stooges would be locked into a life of manual labor on some prison farm. And he was currently moving in with his fierce and beautiful fiancée, so David was having an extra good day.

"Oh, we'll be there." The man laughed as David walked past.

David didn't run back to Teneil's house, but he had to talk himself out of running the whole time. By then it was closer to midnight, and he was looking forward to the couch. The instant he stepped into her small house he was at peace. He noticed the effort she had gone through to make the couch into a bed, and even set up a charging cord, a bottle of water, and a towel with a bar of soap.

"Welcome home." Teneil greeted him kindly from her bedroom door.

He beamed. "Mind if I take a shower?"

"Not at all. Actually, the bar of soap and towel are me insisting." She pointed to the small wooden door that led to the shower.

She did nothing but pace the whole time he was in there, but somehow managed to make it seem that she was overly interested in an apple when he walked out in nothing but a towel. She'd noticed his impressive physique earlier, yes, especially when she leaned into him during their impromptu wedding announcement party, but seeing his bare chest and legs still wet from her shower was. . .something else entirely.

"Ground rules," Teneil announced. "This. . ." she motioned to his attire, "is not okay." She blushed and turned around. "Clothing, actual clothing, at all times."

He chuckled. "But I don't wear clothes to bed."

"Not a problem. You're not going to the bed; you are going to the couch, and the couch requires clothing."

"I don't- I don't even have anything."

She disappeared into her room and rummaged through her drawer. She came back with two options: yoga pants or tiny rainbow shorts with smiley faces and a lacy trim.

"You are joking, right? It's an inferno outside."

"Then I recommend the shorts." She did not waver, steadily placing the clothes in his hands. "I don't know what kind of women you are used to, Mr. James Bond, but I am not some secretary floozy."

"Secretary floozy?"

She walked away, but before she disappeared into her room she turned back, taking one last glance of the hardened warrior wearing nothing but a bemused expression and a towel in her living room. "Good night." And she was gone.

He picked up the shorts and sighed. "Night," he called after her. "Secretary floozy," he chuckled under his breath.

The heat was enough to keep him awake, but this close to the lake the mosquitoes were the real problem. He couldn't stand the blanket, but when he finally kicked it off there was an army of blood suckers ready to drain him. The sun was not quite up when, blessedly, he heard her get up.

She saw he was wearing the rainbow shorts. They were absurdly small; he looked ridiculous. Good. She hated how she'd reacted to him in a towel, but she was human after all. She had allowed the line of their professional relationship to blur yesterday. Teneil had to remind herself that she was not his beloved; this was his job. In four days, he would leave and she would go back to her life alone here. She'd spent the night constructing a wall around her heart, and those shorts were the mortar that would help to hold it together.

David sat up and gave her a bleary look. "Good morning." He was groggy and needed coffee. She didn't even ask; she just handed him a black cup of sludge. He took a sip. "This is perfect!"

"I guessed." Her own coffee was light and sweet. She sat next to him on the chair and he couldn't help but notice the oversized blue basketball shorts she was wearing.

"Seriously?" He looked pointedly at her.

She just shrugged. "What'cha doin' today?"

"Shopping for some new pajamas."

She laughed. "Good answer!"

He drank the rest of his coffee in one large gulp and stood up. He walked toward his bags and got out a set of clothing. "I have two men arriving on the ferry today."

She noticed that while the rainbow smiley faces and ruffle on the hem of the shorts screamed girl, there was no hiding the masculinity that wore them. Teneil realized the towel had been far more modest, so she quickly excused herself to her own room to get ready for the day. She called out from her bedroom, "I think it's really great that you were able to have *family* come in so quickly for the wedding."

He thought about that for a moment. It was perfect. "Yes, my two *brothers*, Ben and Eli, will be very interested to meet you, I'm sure. I was hoping we could give them a tour of the bay?"

She knew that it was stupid, but when he said she would be meeting his "brothers" she put back the yellow dress and pulled out the blue one. She looked excellent in blue and only God knew why she wanted to look excellent; they were most definitely *not* his brothers, but she still wanted to impress them. She piled her hair up in her usual way and added a little pink to her lips and cheeks. "Should we walk to town?" she asked, walking back out into the sitting room.

David looked up and froze. Yesterday she was beautiful straight from the lake. He had swallowed his boiling hot coffee in one gulp when he had seen her in her pajamas, but this blue dress, with her hair piled high?

"What do you think?" Teneil prompted in the awkward silence.

"You look amazing," he replied, and meant it.

"About walking to town." She giggled.

"That too," he said, unwilling to look away from her.

"Stop staring," she insisted, but her face was flushed with color.

He did stop, but only because he had spent most of his life following orders.

They walked side by side, talked a bit, and laughed even more. When they came to the edge of town, he reached down, casually lacing his fingers in hers. "For appearances." He winked at her playfully, but she was smacked with reality: he did not like her. This was his job, and he was very good at it.

"Of course." There was resignation in her voice, and he felt like an idiot. He had wanted to hold her hand all morning, but he needed to respect her space. After all, hadn't he imposed himself on her enough?

Ben and Eli, aka his brothers, arrived at the port on time. They said nothing to Teneil, but the look they shared was clear: they were not happy to meet her. That look wasn't lost on Teneil as she hailed a taxi and ushered them all to her house. The two men asked no questions about her or why David was with her. They wasted no chatter on her at all. Teneil tried hard not to take it personally, but couldn't help thinking, *what a waste of the blue dress!*

After a hushed conversation at her kitchen table, which she was not privy to hearing, but serving coffee seemed to be acceptable, the two men retreated to the lodge which she had thanklessly booked for them. All of this took place without either of them even so much as looking at her.

"You're welcome," she muttered sarcastically under her breath while she watched them walk away.

David came up behind her, resting his hands gently on her shoulders. "Don't take it personally," he said, as if he could read her mind. "They're adopted."

That made her chuckle. "I need to get the charcoal going for dinner."

"Would it be okay if I laid down in your bed for a little while?"

She turned to face him; one eyebrow drastically raised.

"I will still sleep on the couch." He held his hands up in defense. "But to be fair. . .it's more of a loveseat than a couch. Not easy sleeping."

He did look tired. His job was important, and she knew he needed rest. "Sure," she conceded. "I'll wake you up for dinner."

Her bed was softer than anything he had been on for months. It smelled like a woman, sweet and spiced. He wanted to read the titles on her bookshelf and look at the photos on top of her wardrobe, but his eyes were too heavy. The moment his head hit the pillow he was done.

It was about an hour later when Teneil knocked lightly on the door. "David?" she spoke quietly and peeked into the dark room. The sun had set and the moonlight coming through the window only allowed her enough light to make out his form.

She sat on the edge of the bed, fully intending to wake him up. But after several long minutes watching his strong chest rise and fall, listening to his steady breathing, and watching his eyelids flutter in whatever dream he was in, she decided that he could have the bed. He needed it more than she did.

She made her way around the sides to put down the mosquito net. Tucking it in under the mattress as quietly as she could, she leaned across him, finding herself close. . .very close. A brief moment of insanity overtook her, and she leaned even closer to place a soft kiss on his cheek. It wasn't because she wanted him; she just wanted to thank him, just for being who he was.

"Hum, Teneil. . ." he whispered.

"Yes?" she breathed out, both excited and terrified that he was awake, but he said nothing else. Had he been dreaming about her?

She left him there sleeping in her bed. She ate alone, which wasn't unusual for her, and after cleaning up, she settled herself on the couch. It was more of a love-seat, she had to agree.

Morning sun streamed in the window at the foot of the bed. *The bed!* Had he slept in her bed? Had she slept on the couch? David pushed out of the mosquito net and made his way to her small kitchen. Teneil had on headphones and the room was quiet except for the sizzling of whatever was in the pan.

He stood next to her dog in the doorway, watching her. He could only guess what music she was listening to that made her dance as she was. Air drums, guitar, and even a spatula microphone were the highlights of her performance. David was entertained by her obvious lack of musical ability, but also by her wardrobe.

"So that's what those rainbow shorts are meant to look like?" he grinned, and Sanji barked loudly in agreement.

"OH!" Teneil cried out, splattering egg all over the kitchen and consequently throwing the spatula at him. David caught it easily, flipped it artfully in the air, then caught it again behind his back.

"Show off." She laughed, removing the headphones. He winked at her.

There was a knock at the door, and he answered it while Sanji and Teneil cleaned up the mess. His "brothers" walked in without greeting. "We have the 'where'," Ben announced.

"The boat dock," Eli added, and they quickly set to organizing plans. Teneil brought out a plate of food for David and offered some to the others, but they only looked at her until she awkwardly walked out of the room. *Never mind them.* She had a big day to get ready for anyway. There was a dress fitting for a wedding that would never happen.

Teneil put no effort into the planning. The wedding was a sham and she hated lying to the people she cared for, especially when they were being so kind. She did, however, veto the purple and lime dress with the three-foot fabric lime green hat in which they fitted her. Sham wedding or no, that should never happen.

But when the shop owner came out with a vintage Victorian lace dress in a pale champagne color, her breath caught. When she slipped on the garment, she looked classic, timeless. She admired herself in the mirror for a good long while until her joy and excitement shattered. She was not a bride. She was not getting married. This was *not* her moment.

The expressions of awe and pride on the women around her filled Teneil with shame. David would leave tomorrow, and she would be here, alone, with all these wonderful people that she had betrayed. How would they ever forgive her? The thought that David would never see her in this perfect dress broke her even further.

"Why are you crying?" one old woman asked.

She wanted to tell her, to tell them all, but she thought about the five little girls and smiled instead. "It's just so beautiful."

Thursday came. They had hardly said a word to each other. David was dressed in all black, his uniform 100% tactical. Teneil saw him for what he truly was then: a regular GI Joe. He was a warrior. It was not that she didn't believe him before but seeing him like this was an entirely different story. The mood was tense in her little home. She knew he was about to do something dangerous.

When he made his way to the door to meet Ben and Eli, she did not say, "Good luck" or "Be careful". No, when he turned to look back at her, Teneil said, "Go get 'em."

He smiled wickedly and a fresh fire burned in his eyes. "Yes ma'am." The moment he left, her bravado broke, and she fell to the floor in prayer.

David, Ben, and Eli sat motionless in their hiding spot near the dock, quiet as the calm lake. The three "brothers" remained there for hours, diligently watching. The designated time for the arrival came and went without one ripple on the lake's surface.

David grimaced and glanced at his team. Something was wrong. Finally, they decided to make their way back to the lodge where they cursed and questioned every aspect of their plan. Ben said, "I will meet with my guy now and figure out what happened."

David stormed out of the room and headed back home. "Home"? He laughed, disgusted with himself at the idea of using that word. He was starting to think this whole thing was a mistake. Consumed with fury, he marched to Teneil's house.

Teneil heard him slam the gate and was ready with the door open when he came to her. "What? What is it? What happened?"

He was in a rage and didn't want to talk about it anymore, so he brushed past her as if she was no more than a bit of furniture and went straight to the shower. It was a long time before he came back out. She sat, not saying a word, waiting for him. Finally, he came out and leaned against the wall opposite her. He growled curtly, "They weren't there." She didn't bother with all the questions she wanted to ask; surely, they were the same questions he was asking himself?

She did catch his eye and say, "It's not over." It wasn't a question.

He snapped at her, "You have no idea what you are talking about."

That kindled her anger. Teneil stood and walked toward him. "You have been here for, what? Less than a month? I have been here, alone, for years. To you this is a case, but to me this is my whole life. Soon you will leave." It hurt her to say it and it hurt him to hear it, but it was the truth. "And when you do, I will be here in this wrecked fantasy you've had me playing. You have no idea what *you* are talking about, David. You say that when this is over you will have the men responsible 'sent away', but I guarantee they won't serve a week before someone bails them out. You will be gone, they will be here, and I will pay for what *we* have done."

She was toe to toe with him now and seethed, "I put my entire life on the line, not for you, but for those five little girls. I will not lose my life for nothing. That's why I am telling you this is not over. You will not give up. You *will* do your job. Figure it out."

He smiled, not at all shying away from her rage but leaning into it. "Yes ma'am." He put one hand on her burning cheek. She froze at the coolness of his touch. His thumb moved slowly across her cheek bone and that small contact sent a shiver down her spine. His heart was pounding into the palm of her hand resting on his chest, though she could not remember putting it there. "Teneil. . ." He was so close she could feel his whisper on her lips. "I-"

A bang rattled the back door. She quickly took a large step backward, leaving him to kiss her ghost.

"It was moved to tomorrow night," Eli looked straight past Teneil, not seeming to notice or care what he had interrupted. "Same time, same place. The girls are here, but we don't know where they are, or why the delay happened today." Then he turned back into a shadow and slipped into the night.

"Tomorrow night?" Teneil gave David a terrified look. "The wedding is tomorrow night." She was instinctively retreating from him, back stepping to her bedroom door.

"Not getting cold feet, are you?" He laughed and matched her strides, apparently in a much better mood.

"This isn't funny, David." She was clearly upset, her words dripped with sarcasm. "Do *you* want to get married tomorrow?" Tears welled in her eyes, several conflicting emotions running through her.

He wrapped his arms around her, and she melted into his strength. "Marry *you*?" He paused for effect. "Absolutely."

"I'm serious." She stiffened in his embrace.

"So am I." He kissed her on the top of her head. "Better get some sleep. Big day tomorrow."

He left her, angry and sad and burning, in the entry of her room and headed to the couch.

His teasing hurt and she tried to hold onto the anger because she could not handle the pain.

When he woke in the morning, she was already gone. A note read:

I have to spend the morning with the women, it's tradition. I will see you at the beach at 4. You have a suit hanging in my room. I guessed on the size, didn't expect you to actually wear it, so I hope it fits! Don't be late. -T

There was a familiar knock on the back door. "Come in, guys."

"We located the girls," Ben relayed. "They're in a small, locked storage unit, guarded by your three best friends."

Something like a growl escaped David's lips. He'd been thinking about that little problem all night. Teneil was right about the stooges; he would have to do more if he wanted to protect her.

"Eli and I have been talking. . ." Ben hesitated, and the two men looked uneasily between each other. "We want to make the arrest at the wedding."

"No." David's voice was so hard that the other two men stiffened at the challenge. They rarely ever disagreed, but when they did 2/3 ruling was never questioned. As a plea, David added, "I've put her in enough trouble already."

"Look, David," Eli began in a placating tone, "it's clear you care for the woman. Honestly, we are really happy for you." Ben scoffed. "Well, *I'm* really happy for you," Eli corrected. "Ben's just jealous." Then his voice grew harder. "The safety of these five girls and making the arrests are the top priorities. You shouldn't have involved a civilian in the first place, but you did, and if you made her our asset, we are going to use her."

David glared at his team. He began shaking his head, but then Eli asked, "What would she want you to do?"

David thought about telling Teneil the plan. She would probably say something stupid like, "*How can I help?*" David couldn't help the smile that spread on his face. He said, "She would insist we do it."

"Really?" Ben nodded, making up his mind about the girl.

It was true, all of it, and David had no defense. "Fine. At the wedding, but we make this seamless." They all agreed.

While they worked out their plan, the women were pampering the bride to be. Teneil was numb. She had woken up that morning and spent the day like a person facing an execution. She knew that no matter what, she was not walking out of this without a broken heart, but she continued on anyway.

Finally alone, fully dressed and ready, she looked in the long mirror. "For the girls," she told herself. There was a light rapping on the door. She was ready for this to be over. "Come in," she called in a hollow voice.

David entered, closing the door behind him before turning to look at her. She was the loveliest vision he'd ever seen. His heart stopped, his voice caught, as he stared at her.

His reaction was all she could have hoped for. "Bad luck to see the bride before the wedding." But her smile quivered.

"Teneil. . ." He had to shake his head, *focus*, quickly he walked over to her. "We found the girls."

"You did?" She let out a deep breath. "So, this is over?" She sat down with a heavy heart.

"No." He knelt before her. "Because everyone will be here for the ceremony, the Malawian police will be able to get the girls out safely. Ben and Eli want to make the arrest here because everyone is together. It's dangerous, but if they leave the wedding and find the girls missing, they might scatter. We might not have another chance."

"No, you're right. We have to do it." She nodded, biting her lip. "That's the smartest plan."

"That's my girl." He was beaming with pride. "I want you to take this." He took a small .22 pistol from a hidden holster at his ankle.

"Most women get jewelry on their wedding day." She took the small gun.

"I would feel better if you had it."

"And put it where?" She laughed. "Oh, wait!" She lifted up her layers of skirt and showed him the thickly laced garter belt that the older women had made for her.

His mouth went dry. "That's. . . lovely," he choked out.

She rolled her eyes and neatly tucked the .22 into the band of lace and ribbon on her thigh. Then they stood and she took his face in her hands. "I'm so proud of you." She looked deep into his eyes.

"You are the most beautiful bride I have ever seen," he whispered, almost to himself.

The door swung open and several of the grandmothers entered the room. They spat many words Teneil hadn't heard them say before and forced David out.

To anyone else, it was a beautiful wedding. The evening was cool and perfect. The flowers were elegant and everywhere. The natural sound of waves crashing on the beach and the torches lit on every surface gave a dreamy quality to the occasion. The bride and groom looked like a wedding cake topper.

To everyone who knew the truth, it was an elaborately decorated lion's den. Teneil stood behind a curtain and waited for the music that would tell her to enter.

"What are you doing, Teneil?" came a familiar voice behind her.

Her teeth clenched. As she turned, Teneil was grateful for the feeling of David's polished steel on her thigh. "Curly." She smiled at the brute of a man. She'd liked the names David had picked out for the three stooges. "I'm about to get married."

"You don't even know him," Aleze spat.

"I love him." The words came out honest, both shocking and affirming in her heart.

"You think I don't know what this is? What are you doing?" He sneered. Leaning close, he whispered, "I'm the one who moved it to Friday, just to watch what you would do. You don't have to go through with this, Teneil. It's over."

Her blood ran cold. This was a set up, then. He knew everything, but she wasn't going to give him the satisfaction of any of it.

"I'm not sure what you are talking about," she responded coolly. "I love him in a way that I have never loved *anyone*." Her eyes dug into his. "I am going to marry him. And you are going to watch." She turned her back to him, afraid that he would see her cracks.

"If you do this, I won't just kill him," Aleze hissed at her. "I'll kill you, too, for the heartbreak you have caused me."

She turned to face him, but he was gone. The curtain pulled back and she was faced with a room full of people and serene music. She hadn't even heard the tune begin. She saw David and his two "brothers" at the end of the aisle. She walked toward David, wishing that she could tell him everything that had just happened. But she could not jeopardize the plan, so she smiled through all the tradition.

Most of what was said during the ceremony was in a language that David could not understand. Teneil refused to look at him, her head bowed or scanning the room. Something was wrong. When she finally did lock eyes with him, there was a sadness and worry that broke his heart.

It was time for David to say his vows, and she glanced away again. "Teneil. . ." His voice held an ache that brought her full attention. "I have never met anyone like you. You are so kind and brave. You are smart and sexy and strong. I'm fascinated by you in such a way that it's driven me mad. You are all I think about. I think I've loved you from the first moment I met you. There is no one else like you, and I would spend my life in regret if I ever walked away from you. Now, I'm asking you, truly, with all my heart, to be my wife. I promise to protect you with all that I am. Love and cherish you for all that you are. For as long as we have."

She was looking at him now. Truly looking. He did love her. *He was serious.* Could she actually marry this man? The thought of him leaving was simply unacceptable to her, she knew that. But. . .marry him? She cocked her head to the side, weighing the man in front of her.

He was strong, he was capable, he was a true hero. He was also in love with her. There were so many things she didn't know about him, but she knew who he was at his core. He was a man of integrity. The details of who he was would come with time and she wanted to know it all. And if she married him. . .

David cleared his throat. "Teneil?" A few murmurs went through the handful of people present.

She nodded once. "Okay."

David's body relaxed and he let out a shaky sigh. Ben barked a hardy laugh and slapped David on the back hard. Behind David she could see Aleze reach into his jacket, hate in his eyes.

Liquid ice flowed through her veins. It wasn't fear but something else: rage, and an overwhelming desire to finish the torment she and so many others had endured under Aleze. He had threatened her for years, but it did not affect her as it did now that he had threatened David.

David, who would be her future.

She dropped to one knee and attempted to pull up the layers of her skirt to rip the gun from her garter. But there were too many ribbons, and the grip was stuck in the lace. So, she quite literally shot from the hip.

The bullet grazed the outside of David's leg before hitting Aleze in the shoulder. The knife he was holding dropped to the ground at the same time David's knuckles connected with the big man's nose. David, Ben, and Eli acted swiftly and zip-tied the three men in one fluid movement.

"Great shot!" That was the first thing Ben had ever said to her. She couldn't help but smile at his warm praise.

No guests were still in the tent after the gun went off. David helped Teneil off the floor and took the pistol from her shaking hands. "We call that 'going rogue' and it's frowned upon in my line of work." He looked at her gravely.

"Two words, David: 'Thank you'. Those are the words you're looking for." She grinned at him.

He pulled her into his arms and kissed her in the way he had wanted to for a long time. When he finally set her feet back on the ground, she was breathless. "I was thinking more along the lines of 'I do'."

"Do you really?" She beamed at him, knowing the answer she had found in his kiss.

"I do." He held her away from him. "Do you?" He searched her face for the answer.

She smiled and tears filled her eyes. "I do."

The end. Well, kinda. . .

EPILOGUE

Believe me, dear reader, I too wish that this romance were mine, just as much if not more than you do. But here is something you must remember: this book is still my kina-biography. Perhaps more like my diary, but still filled with truths about my life in Africa and America. My real life, which seems like a dream most days, is easy to get lost in.

In no way do I regret my life *alone* in Malawi. I have been blessed to be able to work with thousands of people. Providing immediate assistance and a brighter future for those in my area, all while still maintaining a healthy imagination. I'm not sure what my tomorrow holds, but there is always Jesus and hope.

Hope the funding will be sufficient, faith in the struggle to leave the world a better place than it was when I found it, fight running through my veins to stand up for the oppressed and still more hope. Hope that maybe, just maybe, *he* is out there somewhere dreaming about me too.

TO LEARN MORE ABOUT TENEIL JAYNE AND THE EFFORTS OF LIVING OUT LOUD INC.:

Follow her on her website: www.teneiloutloud.com

Or follow her daily life on Facebook: www.facebook.com/teneil.jayne

Instagram Account: @teneiljayne

And subscribe to her podcast at www.anchor.fm/teneiloutloud

Follow along and help Teneil feel just a little less. . . you know, *alone.*

Made in United States
Troutdale, OR
06/15/2023

10609963R00174